EMMA AND THE SILVERBELL FAERIES

TALES OF WIDOWSWOOD BOOK 3

MATTHEW S. COX

DIVISION ZERO PRESS

Emma and the Silverbell Faeries
Tales of Widowswood Book 3
© 2017 Matthew S. Cox
All Rights Reserved
Cover and interior art by Ricky Gunawan

ISBN (eBook): 978-1-949174-54-0

ISBN (Print): 978-1-949174-55-7

CONTENTS

1. Higgledy–Piggledy   1
2. Making the Rounds   18
3. Sky Dragons   31
4. Cookies and Bread   44
5. Neema   54
6. A Tiny Plea   58
7. The Elder Grove   64
8. Mawr   68
9. Lineage   78
10. Vines   83
11. The Why of Why   92
12. Faerie Magic   96
13. Brynshire   100
14. Homesick   111
15. Darbolg   115
16. Golem   128
17. Child of Linganthas   136
18. Old Enough   142
19. Fire Chickens and Lightning Cats   152
20. The House That Doesn't Belong   156
21. Faerie Tricks   165
22. Trespass   170
23. Parting Ways   179
24. Promises   184
25. Conjurations   193
26. A Burden to Bear   196
27. Faerie Circle   200
28. A Few Minutes   206
29. Of Dragons and Tea Parties   212

The Story Continues   220
Acknowledgments   221
About the Author   222
Other books by Matthew S. Cox   223

CONTENTS

1. Higgledy–Piggledy   1
2. Making the Rounds   18
3. Sky Dragons   31
4. Cookies and Bread   44
5. Neema   54
6. A Tiny Plea   58
7. The Elder Grove   64
8. Mawr   68
9. Lineage   78
10. Vines   83
11. The Why of Why   92
12. Faerie Magic   96
13. Brynshire   100
14. Homesick   111
15. Darbolg   115
16. Golem   128
17. Child of Linganthas   136
18. Old Enough   142
19. Fire Chickens and Lightning Cats   152
20. The House That Doesn't Belong   156
21. Faerie Tricks   165
22. Trespass   170
23. Parting Ways   179
24. Promises   184
25. Conjurations   193
26. A Burden to Bear   196
27. Faerie Circle   200
28. A Few Minutes   206
29. Of Dragons and Tea Parties   212

The Story Continues   220
Acknowledgments   221
About the Author   222
Other books by Matthew S. Cox   223

HIGGLEDY–PIGGLEDY

*C*ontent to stroll along the road in no great hurry, Emma smiled up at a bright blue sky filled with puffy clouds of all shapes and sizes. She basked in the sun on her face and the mush of cool dirt between her toes.

The air would soon take on the chill of winter, but the afternoon still held enough warmth for swimming—at least in her opinion. Tam never seemed to care about cold water. He'd probably leap into the creek with snow on the ground if Mama didn't tell him not to. In another week or two, she wouldn't permit any of them to play in the water until spring. Emma tried not to let the approaching season dampen her mood. With winter came the need for boots, which made it her least favorite time of the year.

The past two weeks had gone by faster than Emma expected, and she had dutifully kept her word to Da and not used a lick of magic until her punishment time ended. No further sign of thieves or danger had shown up in Widowswood since Nan's ritual, and aside from boring, the two weeks had been pleasant. Loud too, as the workmen Da hired to add on to their home had lately been hammering away from soon after sunrise to late in the afternoon. Today, Mama had sent her into the village to bring spices and seasonings to Eoghn's Inn, the first time she'd been permitted out of sight of her, Da, or Nan since she'd run off into the woods to scout the location of the thieves. Of course, Tam's knocking over a bucket of tools and scaring one of the workers had played a large part in Mama sending them off on an errand. Emma grinned, her chest full of warmth at Mama's trust, and remained intent on her mission to watch over her younger siblings.

She carried a parcel of glass bottles wrapped in burlap under her left arm, her right hand kept a firm grip on Tam's. Kimber traipsed along on the boy's right, holding his other hand. Between the two of them, they could hold him back from darting off if he saw something interesting.

Kimber's mood seemed as sunny as Emma's; she smiled at everything and everyone, from villagers to animals to rocks they passed on the way into town. The girl had added white and pink ribbons in her bright red hair to go with her plain white dress, and a little circlet of wildflowers around her left ankle.

Tam insisted on a grey tunic because it made him feel like he wore the armor of a knight. He carried his fancy new practice sword tucked in a belt of rope about his waist. Its maker had crafted it to look as much like a real sword as wood allowed, though the blade had a rounded edge that stood up to being knocked about. Da told him real soldiers trained with similar wooden replicas, only bigger ones.

Mrs. Harrow waved from the small garden in front of her house. Wonderful aromas, a mixture of bread and fruit pie, wafted from the doorway behind her. A little brown remained in her mostly grey hair, matching her well-worn dress. Wrinkles around her eyes deepened with her smile. "Mafindwel, children."

Emma released her brother's hand for a few seconds to return the wave. "Morning, Mrs. Harrow."

The boy waved as well, and made no effort to avoid her grasp when she reached for his hand again. "C'we 'ave pie?"

"It's still baking," whispered Emma. "And I don't think she's making it for us."

He pouted, but disappointment faded in mere seconds.

Kimber stood on tiptoe to fling her arm around in an exuberant greeting while yelling, "Hiiiiii!" at the elderly woman.

The downhill path wound past a few more houses and on to the Village of Widowswood. Near the end of the dirt road where it met the cobbled streets of the town center, a bevy of chickens congregated, casually avoiding an older teenaged boy trying to round them up. Emma stepped around their droppings, and had to give Tam a gentle tug to the side to stop him from walking right into one. The teen paused in his pursuit to let the children pass, offering a warm, if tired, smile of greeting. A nearby white goat chewed on something and appeared to be laughing at the older boy's futile effort.

Emma stepped from dirt onto sun-warmed cobblestones that chased the mid-autumn chill from her toes. Kimber squealed and cringed at a sudden spray of water from a chicken fluttering in a puddle. She spent a moment fretting over a few dirty spots on her dress, but wound up giggling.

The road curved to the left a few minutes later, leading them past a few shops and into a light crowd. Kimber still hadn't gotten used to people smiling at her (instead of shying away to guard their coin purses), and kept grinning and waving at anyone who made eye contact. Five shops later, Emma followed the first right turn, taking the street that connected to the town square.

Mr. Carrow hovered in the door of his bakery shop. He gave Emma a polite nod, though watched the three of them the way a banker might watch men in dark cloaks trying to flank him. He leaned on the doorjamb, blocking it off as though expecting them to try to get past him. The man tolerated children well enough, provided they stayed out of his bakery.

Emma returned his nod, but didn't bother with a false smile or even looking at him for long. Someone who had to force himself to be polite to children wasn't the sort of man she wanted anything to do with. And she most certainly would never spend so much as a single copper bit there.

Other townspeople met them with genuine smiles. More distant people waved, others patted her on the head whenever she came within arm's reach. Since she'd been taken by the thieves and found safe, most everyone had heard about her magic. It seemed as though the whole village expected her to follow in Mama's footsteps, wandering the town and caring for those within. She grinned back at the locals, tolerating all the squeezing and hugging. Though it annoyed her a little, she bore it with aplomb. Nan had told her she shouldn't feel obligated to let anyone touch her if it bothered her, but she always kept quiet since they all seemed so friendly; she didn't want to be rude. Large helpings of affection made her feel happy and welcome, a much better greeting than people running and screaming—something Da had been concerned about should they ever visit a larger city where not everyone would be so open and trusting of 'forest witchery.'

The town square looked empty in the absence of the Feast of Zaravex.

A few wilted flowers and birds pecking at moldy bits of sweetbread here and there proved it hadn't been too long since the holiday, but with all the visitors from outlying villagers having gone home, it seemed as though half the town had vanished.

Guards Arnir and Filner stood by the fountain, chuckling amid conversation. They greeted her with broad smiles before returning to their amusement at what some fool did last night after having too much ale.

Tam got a whiff of baking chicken coming from Eoghn's Inn, and leaned forward; if not for Kimber and Emma holding his hands, he'd have fallen flat on his front. "C'we eat?"

"'Et smell good," said Kimber.

Emma pulled her brother upright. "We've got food at home."

"Aww." Tam made faces at the ground.

The porch creaked as they climbed the three steps and walked into a blanket of warm air laden with the fragrance of wood smoke, spices, and cooking meat. Emma's mouth watered at the mixture of roast chicken, ham, and beef stew on each breath, biting her lip at a touch of guilt. Strixian would allow her to speak to any of those animals... eating them seemed wrong, yet sniffing the air made her stomach growl.

Can wolves talk to rabbits? She scrunched up her nose in thought.

Almost every eye in the room shifted toward them. Except for two well-dressed men, the eleven or so other people seated at tables had all gone into the woods to search when the thieves had abducted her and Kimber. Neither outsider paid them more than a seconds' worth of attention. Emma didn't mind since those men didn't know her, and most adults paid little attention to village children. Between the warmth of the hearth and the sea of smiling faces, the room radiated a tangible feeling of safety.

Tam poked her in the belly. "You're hungry too."

Kimber giggled.

"I didn't say we won't eat." Emma huffed. "Mama's making us food. And we don't have any money."

Tam blinked. "Money? I don't wanna eat money."

Emma smiled at everyone while she walked up to the bar, the counter at the level of her chin. "Mr. Cooper *sells* food. It's not like home where Mama just feeds us."

His jaw dropped open. "You gotta pay money for food?"

"If'n ya donnae 'ave any money, ya donnae eat," whispered Kimber. "S'why I 'ad ta find apples 'afore."

The girl's expression didn't look as sad as she sounded, but Emma still winced inside at reminding her of the past. "Sorry."

Kimber smiled. "I'as okay. I'as happy now."

"Mafindwel, Emma," said Eoghn Cooper, his deep voice raining down on them from above.

Emma peered up at a small giant; reddish cheeks and curly ginger hair left no doubt in her mind the man was Rydh's father, though the boy lacked his father's immense, curved moustache. Fortunately, the elder Cooper had an entirely different temperament from his son, being gentle and reserved, despite his enormous size.

"Good morning, Mr. Cooper." She put the bundle up on the bar. "Mama sent me to bring this for you."

"Ahh, grand!" He plucked the parcel open and appraised eight bottles. Two held liquid, one orange, one dark green, while the rest contained powders or finely chopped herbs. "Most excellent. Wait here a moment, girl. I've something to send back."

Emma nodded and glanced out over the dining area while the big man ambled into the kitchen through a curtained archway, carrying the bottles. The two well-dressed men went on about their meal as though the children didn't exist, while the locals continued to offer the occasional warm smile.

Sharp clicking footsteps approaching from behind made Emma turn.

A girl about her age, though a bit taller, approached with a hesitant step. She seemed familiar, but no name came to mind. Her light brown hair hung to her waist in lush curls, adorned with a half-circlet of flowers around the back of her head. The cream-colored gown she wore, elaborate and puffy, filled Emma with an immediate sense of discomfort at the idea of being trapped in such a garment. Her white leggings and shoes didn't have so much as a tiny smudge of dirt anywhere on them, and the faint scent of lilac clung to her.

It took Emma a second to remember that she'd seen the girl before in a lemon-yellow gown at the Harvest Hunt... the daughter of a wealthy family, the one who hadn't wanted to touch anything on the field. She'd seemed so afraid of dirt, she'd not bothered to pick up a single firefruit, merely walked around observing and trying not to get too close to anyone running around.

"Hello," said Emma.

"Hi," chirped Kimber.

"Is she a princess?" whispered Tam.

"You're Emma?" asked the girl. "Your father is the captain of the Watch?"

"Yes." She nodded.

"I'm Ambril." She regarded the dress Nan had made with a faint cringe.

Emma put her arms around her siblings. "This is my brother Tam, and my sister Kimber."

Ambril cracked a smile at the look on Tam's face. "I'm not a princess. My father sells glassware, windows, and sometimes jewelry."

"Oh. Mr. Starling." Emma bit her lip in thought. "Da talks about him sometimes."

"I'd imagine so." Ambril rolled her eyes. "People always try to steal from us. Father has a jewelry store in Calebrin, so they think he sells expensive things here too, but he doesn't bother with much that's too precious here." She glanced down, a hint of confusion in her eyes.

Sensing the girl staring at her feet, Emma raised and lowered her toes. "What's wrong?"

"You're not poor," whispered Ambril. "Your Da's family has some standing in Calebrin... Why do you run about dressed like a peasant?"

Emma narrowed her eyes. The girl hadn't added any venom to her words, but even in an innocent tone, the question carried contempt. "It makes me happy to feel the grass when I walk, and I adore being close to the forest."

Ambril clasped her hands together in front of her, and bit her lip. "But you're covered in dirt."

"We'as not cover'd 'n dirt. You'as tae clean," muttered Kimber. She pulled her white dress out, studying it. "I'as not dirty."

Tam got a wild glint in his eye as if he intended to show Ambril what 'getting covered in dirt' really looked like. Before he could run off and dive headfirst into a mound of earth, Emma squeezed his hand.

"Fancy dresses and nice things make you happy," said Emma. "The forest makes me happy."

"Oh." Ambril looked her up and down again. "Doesn't it hurt walking around with no shoes?"

Emma smiled. "Doesn't it get exhausting walking around with such a heavy dress on?"

"Da did get Em a nice dress, but she like Nan's more." Tam patted his wooden sword. "You look like a princess. If a dragon comes to take you 'way, I'll p'tect ya."

Ambril grinned. "That's cute, but I don't think dragons are real."

"Emma said a bandy-wee not real an' a bandy-wee got us." Tam puffed up his chest. "I'm not 'fraid of dragons."

"Did that really happen?" Ambril narrowed her eyes at Emma. "Is it true what they say? That you're a little forest witch?"

Emma giggled. "I'm not a witch. I'm a druid."

"Oh." Ambril's suspicion faded; she raised and lowered her head in a slow nod, agreeing but not understanding.

"'Ere ya are, Em." Mr. Cooper set a cloth sack on the bar top. "This is for you an' yours. Oh, would you mind doin' an old man a favor on your way home?"

Ambril offered a quick wave and hurried back to a table where two women sat, both in equally elaborate gowns. One looked enough like her to be her mother.

"What sort of favor?" asked Emma.

Mr. Cooper held up another, somewhat larger, sack. "Would you ferry this over to Widow Poole's place? They're a bit on 'ard times, so I'm 'elpin' them out."

"Of course." Emma reached up.

Kimber carried the bag destined for home, while Emma took Widow Poole's. The fragrance of onions and cheese seeped from the fabric, and the form of a large round bread loaf pressed obvious in the bottom. She slung it over her left shoulder and held Tam's hand as they walked out of the inn and headed across the town square to a road leading north. At first, they passed more shops: a general store, a weaponsmith, a potter, a tanner, and a leatherworker's. After a few cross-streets, they walked among private homes. Those nearest the town center belonged to people with money, but before long, the houses grew smaller and plainer, and once they neared the outskirts, ill-kept and tiny. Alley cats and the occasional lamb, chicken, or goat wandered around in the street. One breath caught the smell of baking bread, the next something foul and sharp, like spoiled wine.

The closer they got to the part of town where the poorest residents lived, the more nervous Kimber became. By the time they'd passed eight cross-streets, the girl hovered so close her breath warmed the back of Emma's neck.

"He's gone," whispered Emma.

"I'as know." Kimber looked around. "I'as 'fraid o' thieves what wan' tae bring me ta' Cal-brin."

Emma glanced over her shoulder at terrified green eyes set in a porcelain face. "They don't have any reason to come after you."

"They'as said I hadda go back wif 'em an' be a proper thief." Kimber jumped at a sudden loud *crack* and a boy's wail of pain.

Two small pigs zoomed across the street a few houses up ahead.

"Those thieves only wanted to scare us. If they wanted you in Calebrin, they'd have taken you away from that awful man." Emma giggled at a third pig racing onto the road so fast its hooves scuffed and skidded. The small animal wiped out and rolled into the door of a hut across the street, squealing in panic.

"Pigs got loose," said Tam. "They's too small ta be Hadrath's."

"Someone's hurt." Emma moved up to a jog. "And Hadrath doesn't live here. His farm is a long walk south of town."

Another small pig wandered onto the road and stopped, staring at them. Emma hurried to the corner where it had come from and hooked a left. Three houses down, a shirtless boy in tattered brown shorts and a thick layer of mud sat on the dirt by a broken gate, cradling his hand to his chest while crying. Most of his face hid behind an unruly mane of black that hung an inch or two past his shoulders. An older woman with steel grey hair stooped over him, attempting to coax his injury into view. Behind them, two piglets remained within a fenced area next to a rickety-looking one-room cabin, while nine or ten larger pigs milled around the field outside, snuffling at the dirt as if searching for buried treasure.

A woman in the house behind them shouted and chased a pig out of her home with a broom.

Emma hurried over to the elder. "Mrs. Poole... What happened?"

The boy, probably a year or so younger than Emma, blushed and bowed his head.

"Aww. Tis nary a thing to worry over, lass." Widow Poole ruffled the boy's hair while smiling at Emma. "M'grandson got ambushed by a pig 'fore he could close the gate."

Emma offered the large bag. "Mr. Cooper sent this for you."

"Oh, that man's so kind." Widow Poole took the bag. "Thank you, Emma."

"Are you hurt?" Emma squatted in front of the boy. "I heard you yell."

He didn't move.

"G'won, Davin." Widow Poole nudged his shoulder.

Emma summoned her most innocent smile.

The boy reluctantly uncovered his hand; his right index finger bent left toward the thumb at an impossible angle, clearly broken.

Kimber whined out her nose and clutched her hand to her chest, squirming with sympathetic pain. Tam's eyes widened in awe.

Emma winced. "Hold still." She cradled his broken hand between hers and closed her eyes, muttering, "Great Uruleth, please lend me the gift of life." She called out with the desire to mend his injury, and the warmth of life energy filled the air in front of her.

"Wow," whispered Davin.

She opened her eyes, and gazed at a fist-sized cloud of green light hovering between her hands. "I'm sorry if this hurts a little."

Davin tensed.

As gingerly as she could, Emma grasped his finger and moved it straight while concentrating on her want to have the life energy go into him. He started to cry out in pain, but the yell faded to a surprised stare of confusion. The glowing mist seeped into his hand and a faint crunch, like stepping on a twig, came from his finger.

Emma wiggled and squeezed at his hand. "Does it still hurt?"

"No," whispered the boy. He kept his head down. "I'm sorry for letting the pigs out, Grandma."

Widow Poole sighed, shaking her head. "Tis not your fault, lad. Those pigs are a might unruly."

Tam nudged Emma. "Tell 'em pigs ta get back inna yard."

"Umm." She looked around at the scattering of relatively small pigs with mixed feelings. On one hand, Widow Poole and her grandson needed them to survive. On the other, that meant the pigs would eventually wind up as ham. "It doesn't feel right asking them to go back inside so they can be killed someday."

Widow Poole lifted the broken gate and re-hung it on its pegs. "Fetch me a few nails and the hammer from the shed, Davin."

"Yes, Grandma." The boy gave Emma a thankful smile before jogging into the muddy yard and disappearing behind their home.

"Em," said Kimber, "wolves eat rabbits. I donnae 'fink they'as feel bad 'bout it. An' Nan say 'at spirts jes go back an' be part of every'fing again." She held her arms out to the sides. "An dem pigs is farm pigs, nae wild. 'Ey not be okay inna wild."

"Oh, if only it were that easy," muttered Widow Poole to herself. "Asking them to come back." She chuckled. "I suppose we'll make do."

Strixian, please grant me the Wildkin Whisper. Emma smiled at the little points of light gliding around her arms and chest. It felt so good to be off punishment and able to use her magic whenever she wanted again. Her smile faded as she thought back to how much she'd worried her family by running off into the woods after thieves.

Seconds later, the random grunts and squeals from the pigs became speech to her.

"Oh wow!" Sniff. Sniff. "What's this?"

"Can I eat it?"

"Mmm. Taste good."

"What'cha got?"

"Can I eat that?"

"I dunno, but taste good."

"Lemme have some."

"I found it. It's mine."

"I want some too."

Emma turned at the pair of pigs butting heads over a rotting squash. "Hi. Will you please go back home?" She pointed at the gate.

Kimber burst into giggles.

Emma moved only her eyes, shifting her gaze to Kimber while continuing to point at the fence. "What?"

"You'as makin' noises like a pig." Kimber giggled again. "Funny."

Tam grinned. "She's animal talking."

Widow Poole smiled at her.

"Too fun here." Pig One shook its head hard. "Not going."

"Eeeee!" yelled Pig Two as it ran off.

Emma walked up to a third pig rutting around some wildflowers one house south. "Hello. You need to go home before you get hurt out here."

"What's that?" The pig leapt up, whirled to face her, and started sniffing at her legs. "Food?"

"I'm not food."

The pig kept sniffing at her. "Not food." It trotted to the right a few steps and sniffed at a giant horse dropping. "Food?"

"Eww!" yelled Emma as she ran up to the animal. "Most certainly not. You should go back into your yard."

"Food?" It sniffed at her again. "Not food."

She sighed at the sky.

A fourth pig ran by cheering.

"Are you tellin' 'em to go back?" asked Tam.

"They're not listening." She set her hands on her hips. "They're just running around yelling or looking for something to eat."

"Like Tam?" asked Kimber.

Emma covered her mouth to stop from laughing as her little brother scowled. His angry look changed to a silly smile after a few seconds of him glowering at Kimber's grin. Davin emerged from behind the house carrying a hammer and a small cloth sack. He ran to the gate and handed the items to Widow Poole.

"We kin 'elp catch 'em," said Kimber.

"They're not listening." Emma folded her arms and turned her attention back to the pig in front of her. "G'won. Get back in the yard."

"I not in the yard," said the pig.

"Yes. I know you're not." Emma patted him on the side. "Go that way."

"I not in the yard." The pig rooted at the ground, digging up a cluster of roots. "Smells like eat."

Tam pulled the wooden sword out of his rope belt and leaned it against the fence. He took off running when another pig trotted by. After a brief chase, he leapt upon its back and wound up riding the animal for a few seconds before it threw him off and he went sliding over the mud. When he skidded to a halt, he emitted an odd moaning noise.

Emma gasped. "Tam?"

The strange sound coming out of him became laughter.

She exhaled a sigh of relief.

Kimber tried to sneak up on a pig, which ignored her until she grabbed it. She, too, got dragged for a little ways, but managed to trip it. After the pair slid to a stop, she grunted and lifted the tiny animal. Hooves flailing, the pig squealed as she carried it back to the gate. She deposited him over the fence and jogged up behind a somewhat larger pig that kept muttering "eat?" repeatedly.

"Come on then," said Emma.

She wrapped her arms around the food-obsessed pig. As soon as she attempted to lift him, he bolted. Emma held on tight, yelling, "Stop!" over and over, but the animal kept running in a frantic side-to-side swerve. Her chin bounced off its head a few times; the street, grass, fence posts, and another few pigs raced by in a blur. She kicked at the ground behind her trying to find traction, but succeeded only in causing sprays of mud.

Emma yelled, "Stop runn—"

The pig jammed to a halt, catapulting her forward. Emma screamed and thrust her arms out as she flew. Her mouth wide open, she landed in a gloopy patch of mud so deep she went under, and gagged at the taste of soupy dirt she nearly swallowed. Frantic for air, she pushed her fingers deeper into spongy muck, trying to right herself. Her head broke the surface of the mud puddle, which came up to her middle when she shifted to kneel. Gagging, she scooped mud off her eyes and face, spitting dirt and pebbles.

"Yay mud!" cheered the food-obsessed pig, right before diving in next to her.

Emma shrieked and covered her face as a brown wave fell over her.

She scraped mud away from her eyes for a second time and stared at the pig.

"Mud mud mud mud mud," said the pig, wiggling its butt as it settled itself deeper. "Mud mud mud mud."

Somewhere behind her, Tam's laughter went by too fast for him to be running. A wooden crash like a stack of broomsticks going down preceded the rattle of a metal bucket and Kimber squealing with glee.

Emma hugged the pig and tried to lift him out of the wallow, but her feet plunged deeper rather than the pig going upward. "This isn't going to work."

"Mud!" cheered the pig. "Wonderful!"

"There's nicer mud in your yard," said Emma, deadpan.

"No. That mud is not same mud. This mud is soft and deep and... ahhhhh." Its eyes half-closed as it shimmied.

She frowned at the puddle, now up to her armpits, the consistency of pudding. "Great Uruleth, please grant me the strength of the Bear Spirit."

Faint green light materialized around her, fading as the roar of a distant bear seemed to come from the forest in the west. Emma grunted and pulled her legs out of the bog while keeping her arms around the pig, which continued to repeat the word "mud" over and over again in varying pitch, singing a song where every word was "mud."

Emma grunted and heaved, lifting the pig out of the mire. It went from singing about mud to waving its legs and screaming.

"I'm falling up! Aaaah! Help!"

She didn't think much of carrying a pig almost as long as her height until Widow Poole gawked at her. Mama had said the spell she'd used, the one she gave to Da in potions, wouldn't make her stronger than a grown man, but she might've been *as* strong as a man. Either way, not until the old woman's reaction did she realize a slight girl her age should not have been able to carry a pig of that size.

The Widow, jaw hanging open, pulled the gate aside.

Emma slipped into the yard and set the pig down. "Your mud is over there." She pointed.

"Oh boy!" The food-obsessed pig pranced over to a wallow at the corner where another three pigs relaxed.

"My, my, Emma…" Widow Poole fanned herself. "You're quite full of surprises."

Davin carried one of the piglets back, as did Kimber—who had gotten her nice white dress filthy. Of course, neither of them came close to Emma's level of dirty. She felt like a candied apple that had been dipped in mud, completely covered except for her eyes.

Kimber blinked at her, then giggled.

For the better part of the next hour, Emma, Kimber, and Tam chased errant pigs, while cheering and laughing. It turned into a game, and they spent more time sliding into mud and rolling around after missing grabs than actually catching pigs. Tam wound up on his back laughing too hard to move for a good ten minutes after a pig threw Kimber headfirst into the soupy mud like an arrow, her feet sticking straight up. Emma didn't bother keeping the Wildkin Whisper going, since the pigs' silly rambling only made it frustrating. By the time they'd gathered the last pig, all three of them looked like child statues made from mud.

"That's the last one." Emma lowered a little pig to its feet within the yard, and walked out as Widow Poole secured the gate.

At the sight of her siblings, Emma couldn't help but laugh, and held them in a squidgy hug while they tried to catch their breath.

"Why thank you, children." Widow Poole shed a tear of joy. "That was very kind of you."

Tam, out of breath, managed a grin before leaning forward with his hands on his knees to breathe.

Emma curtseyed at the old woman. "You're welcome."

"Uh oh." Kimber held her arms out and looked down at herself. "I'as got ae smudge on me dress."

Emma stared at her sister for a few seconds. Her fluffy red hair had matted against her head and back, the formerly colorful pink ribbons had the same shade of mud brown as everything else. The only bit of her not covered in dirt consisted of small spots around her eyes and mouth. "That's a bit more than a smudge."

Kimber stuck out her tongue. "I'as know. I'as bein' silly."

"We gonna get in bads?" asked Tam.

Emma bit her lip, regretted it, and spat dirt. "I don't think so. We were helping Widow Poole. We didn't just jump in mud for no reason."

Tam collected his wooden sword, but didn't try to put it in his belt.

After picking up the bag Eoghn had given her to take home with a two-fingered pinch, Emma led the way back along the dirt road until it became cobblestones again, and followed it for another few cross-streets to the town square. Tam and Kimber giggled while talking about the pig chase and how fun it had been. People stared at them with a mixture of confusion and amusement. Evidently, the layer of mud made them unrecognizable, as no one said hello or waved.

Near the western exit of the town square, Ambril yelled, "Emma? Is that you?"

She stopped and looked to her left. "Yes?"

The wealthy girl emerged from behind a merchant cart and approached, her dress gathered in both hands. "By the gods, what has happened to you?"

"Widow Poole's pigs got loose. We helped catch them."

Ambril covered her mouth and gasped. "You're... *covered* in dirt." She writhed. "Oh, that's horrible! How are you not screaming?"

"It's earth. It's not bad." Emma grinned. Chasing those pigs around, while tiring, had been a lot of fun. Fun this rich girl would never know. Ambril couldn't bear to wander Hadrath's field picking up Firefruit; she'd never chase pigs. "It only means we need to have a bath. It's a lot more fun than having to stay clean and perfect all the time."

"Aren't your parents going to be furious at you for getting so dirty?" Ambril took a step back as if afraid the mud might spray on her.

Tam shrugged.

Kimber shook her head. Emma giggled. Her younger sister looked so strange without her fluffy hair swooshing around.

"No. But your family's different," said Emma. "You've got to worry about what people think of you. About being proper and pretty and everything. What people think of me doesn't matter to me."

"Oh." Ambril glanced down, looking thoughtful. "So you... had fun getting so dirty? That sounds like a book I read where this man is all alone in the forest, hiding, swimming, and hunting fish."

Emma grinned. "Yes. It was tiring, but a lot of fun."

A genteel man in a fine black suit cleared his throat, frowning at Emma, Kimber, and Tam.

Ambril looked over her shoulder for a second and back to Emma. "I'm sorry. I must go."

"Bye." Emma waved.

While Ambril scurried back to the well-dressed man, Emma headed toward home. Curious looks and a few laughs followed them out the western edge of the village proper, thinning to the sunny quiet of a late afternoon on the long trail between town and home. A little while later, their house came into view as the road curved up and over a small hill. Mama stood on the porch with the broom, whistling to herself as she swept.

Oh, no. Why is she sweeping? I'm supposed to do that. Emma walked faster, almost at a jog.

Mama looked up for a second, pushed the broom once, and snapped her head up to stare. "Children? By Ralithir's feathers... what's happened to you?"

Since she seemed more surprised than angry, Emma held up the bag. "Mr. Cooper sent this to you. He says thank you for the spices."

Mama took the bag, folded her arms, and tapped her foot.

"He asked me to take some food to Widow Poole. We went there and all her pigs had gotten out. We helped her catch them."

"Oh." Mama's lips twitched as if fighting hard not to smile. "I don't think you could've gotten filthier if you'd jumped into the mud on purpose." She leaned the broom against the railing. "Go around back. The three of you aren't setting foot inside the house until you're no longer head to toe in mud. Wait by the pump. I'll be right there."

"Yes, Mama," said Emma.

Mama went in the front door with Eoghn's bag while Emma wandered around the house to the backyard and headed for the water pump. Tam left his sword on the porch before running to catch up. Assuming what Mama would soon instruct, Emma grabbed the handle and started filling the bucket.

A bare wood scaffold formed a rough outline of the space Da had decided to add to the house to the left of the back porch. The small hallway that led from the main room to Nan's bedroom would be extended past the kids' new room to end at the door to a new bedchamber for Mama and Da. The workmen were nowhere to be seen, likely off having lunch.

The back door opened, and Mama carried the bathtub outside, setting it on the ground a short distance from the porch steps. Tam peeled off his tunic and shoved his breeches to the ground, his middle stark pale against the dark mud covering most of his arms, legs, and head. He stuck his face into the pump flow, prompting Emma to pick up the bucket and dump it over him.

Tam shrieked with glee and shivered where he stood.

Mama approached and took over pumping. Emma pulled her dress off and held it out to examine. Mud everywhere. She sighed and swatted at it. Mud, both wet and dried parts, fell off in patches, leaving it clean underneath.

What? She blinked. On sudden inspiration, she snapped the dress like a towel, and an explosion of dirt filled the air. When the dust cloud fell to the grass, Emma gasped.

The dress looked spotless.

"Wow," said Kimber.

"Mama?" Emma looked back at her mother, who carried two buckets of water to the tub. "Did Nan put magic in this dress?"

"What do you think?" Mama winked.

Emma grinned.

"You still need a bath, Em. Your dress might be clean, but you are still quite the opposite."

Emma showed off her dirt-covered body; she may as well not have even had the dress on since mud got all over her.

Kimber took her dress off and snapped it as well, but the garment remained a damp, muddy mess. She frowned.

"Nan will make you one too." Emma put an arm around Kimber.

"Oh, will I now?" Nan walked onto the porch with a cauldron of steaming water, which she tipped into the tub.

Clutching her hands together at her chin, Kimber widened her eyes.

"Well, I suppose I could." Nan winked.

Kimber grinned and bounced on her toes.

The children stood in place, swatting dirt from their bodies for a few minutes. Soon, Mama had added enough well water to cool the bath, and the kids climbed in. Kimber attended Tam with a soapy cloth, while Emma washed Kimber's hair. One by one, she extracted the ribbons, rinsed them off, and dropped them in the grass to dry. Mama sat behind Emma outside the tub, working a lathered-up cloth around her ears.

The bathwater turned brown in under a minute.

"My word, Em. You've got mud *inside* your ears." Mama chuckled. "Did you go swimming in it?"

Emma adored her mother's careful touch. "The pigs didn't want to go back into the yard. I tried to talk to them, but they didn't listen. It's like having to look after twelve Tams."

Her brother grabbed her foot and tickled.

"Aah!" Emma squealed and tried to pull her leg back. "Stop!"

"Be still," muttered Kimber. "We'as got more dirt in' our hair, 'an ol' Widow Poole's 'ole yard."

"'Ere's more dirt in your hair an' mine." Tam stuck out his tongue and raspberried. "You got more hair."

Mama poured water over Emma's head. "That was very sweet of you to help Mrs. Poole like that. I'm proud of you all."

Kimber leaned back, beaming. Tam dunked his head, shook it for a few seconds, and sat up.

Eventually, once she could find no traces of mud on anyone, Mama urged them out of the bath. Kimber and Tam ran inside in search of clean clothes while Emma picked up her blue dress.

"Em, that was just covered in mud. Go put something clean on."

"It *is* clean." Emma held it up, turned it to show the back, and turned it again.

Mama chuckled. "Seems Mother rather expected you to be a fast learner. All right, Em."

"Learner?" asked Emma.

"Well, if she's enchanting such little dresses for you, she's obviously convinced you're going to need it."

Grinning, Emma wriggled into her favorite blue dress, knelt, and set to the task of washing Kimber and Tam's clothes.

"Come inside when you're finished and we'll eat." Mama stood.

"Yes, Mama."

Emma smiled as she worked. Despite the day not yet being half over, she found herself tired enough to look forward to bedtime.

2

MAKING THE ROUNDS

The next day after breakfast, Emma and Kimber sat in the meadow behind the house, watching a group of ten men working to build up the floor for the new section. Tam hovered around them, edging closer and closer until someone asked him to move away. He'd fade back a couple steps, and repeat creeping up on a worker until the man again told him to back up.

Emma liked that her new bedroom would be closer to Nan, but not being in the same bed with her parents anymore felt scary too. Whenever she used to wake from a bad dream, they'd be right there for her to hold on to. Da's plan for the new room had three separate beds for the kids.

I won't be dreaming of spiders anymore. She swished her feet side to side, tapping her big toes together while trying to figure out if she'd be lonely with her own bed, or if she'd prefer not being squeezed against the wall all night long. *I'll not dream of thieves either.* Emma eyed the privy shack. The Banderwigh might haunt her nightmares still. She had told Kimber she found the thieves scarier, but thieves didn't have strange powers or curses. Those men also didn't seem too happy that they had to mistreat children due to their fear of the wizard. The Banderwigh, however... that creature had been evil. If she awoke from a nightmare in her new room, what would she do? She'd be the eldest, so it would be her job to protect Kimber and Tam from bad dreams.

I could go to Nan's room. Emma glanced left at fast motion, smiling at a bird skimming low over the wavering green. *I beat the monster for real; I can best a foul dream.*

Kimber stuck a dandelion in her hair. "Wha's got ya lookin' sad?"

"Bah, darn it boy!" yelled a workman. "Watch yourself."

Tam scooted back from a man carrying an armload of lumber. The worker seemed angry, but Tam fought not to laugh.

"I don't know if I'll like the new bed." She looked away from the workmen, her attention drawn by the flutter of a white butterfly weaving over the meadow.

"I'as share the bed wi' you, so's you'as not 'lone." Kimber smiled.

Emma laughed. "Okay."

Kimber scooted close behind her and rested her chin on Emma's right shoulder. "'Fink 'a faeries be watchin' us?"

"Maybe." Emma stared into the woods. The echoes of hammers made it sound like another group of workers had gone off into the forest. She spotted a few birds and one deer, but no faeries. Something *did* feel strange, but not as dark or frightening as when the Banderwigh had been watching her—almost as if the forest had the sniffles. For a moment, she felt tempted to beckon Greyfang and go exploring to find what made the forest feel 'sick,' but she decided against it. The sense of something not being right didn't strike her as strong, and she wasn't supposed to go running off. "I don't see any."

A man let out a yell of surprise. Emma spun toward the sound as a worker carrying two metal pails stumbled over a board jutting out from the incomplete floor. Tam scrambled to get out of his way, his being too close the evident reason the man hadn't been watching where he was going. The worker waved his arms upward, trying to keep his balance, but stepped on a plank that shifted under him. Two buckets of carpenter's nails went flying as the man waved his arms, trying not to fall. They crashed down; nails scattered everywhere on the floor, bouncing, rolling, and dropping between gaps in boards as well as littering the grass. The worker flew into a pair of sawhorses and sent a few long pieces of wood tumbling into the air on his way to the ground.

Tam started to laugh, but as soon as the man turned red in the face and roared, he went wide-eyed with panic and sprinted over to hide behind Emma.

The worker lunged upright and came stomping after him, seeming intent on giving the boy a whack. Emma pulled her feet in close, ready to jump up when the man towered over them. Kimber clamped on to her side and stared fearfully up at the man. Emma kept her expression guarded, trying to seem unafraid without being insolent.

"Dammit boy," yelled the worker. He pointed at Tam, shook his hand, and let out a great sigh of exasperation. "You need to stay out of our way."

"Sorry," whispered Tam, into Emma's back.

"He's only curious," said Emma. "I'll keep him out of your way."

The man shuddered with anger, but the red in his cheeks lessened. "Aye." He tromped over to the house, went to the back door, and knocked.

"I didn't do anything," said Tam. "He tripped onna board."

Emma shifted around to look at him. "He was trying not to step on you. Watch them from back here."

"Aww." He hung his head.

"I'as 'fought he'as gonna hit us," said Kimber in a small voice.

Emma pulled her into a hug. "He wouldn't if he knows what's good for him. Mama and Nan are both home."

Kimber's fledgling tears switched to a smile. "Yeah."

Mama answered the door, and the workman grumbled at her while gesturing back at the kids a few times before pointing at one of the buckets lying in the grass. Mama nodded.

"I don't think he would have hit Tam." Emma squeezed Kimber tight for a second. "He was angry, not mean."

The worker headed back to the area where he'd tripped while Mama glided off the porch and walked over to the children.

"Tam..." Mama folded her arms. "Go collect those nails you made that man drop. When you're done, you're to stay out of their way."

"Yes, Mama," muttered Tam.

Tam trudged over to the worker, who murmured at him and pointed to the half-built floor. The boy crawled under the boards into the narrow space between the floor and the ground. Emma started to get up, but Mama shook her head.

"That's for him to do, Em. He's only going to get the ones that fell where the men can't reach. There's no need for all three of you to get in their way." She smiled. "When he's done, bring him inside. The three of you may as well come with me into town, give these men a bit of peace."

Kimber nodded.

"Yes, Mama," said Emma, smiling.

A small arm came out of the hole in the floor, set a fistful of nails on the wood, and disappeared below. The workman grumbled, crawling around the grass, gathering nails back into his bucket. Emma peered into the woods once more, as that sense of strange unease returned.

"Mama?" asked Emma.

"Yes?" She stopped three steps into her walk to the house and returned to stand by Emma.

"Do you feel anything in the forest?" Emma pointed. "Something is different."

Her mother stood tall, gazing amid the trees for a little while. "There is something unusual, but I wouldn't worry about it. Whatever it is, it doesn't feel dangerous."

Kimber looked back and forth between the tree line and Emma. "Faeries?"

"Not everything is faeries." Emma smirked and tickled her.

Kimber laughed, squirmed, and tickled back.

"I don't think it's anything worth worry just yet." Mama squinted. "Nevertheless, I'll have a look later on."

"Yes, Mama." Emma grinned, trying to defend her sensitive sides from Kimber's fingers while hunting for an opening to tickle the girl to the point of squealing.

Her mother went back inside. It didn't take too long for their battle of searching fingers to fade to the two of them lying in the grass, out of breath and laughing. Eventually, Tam stopped putting handfuls of nails up through the hole. Once it became clear he had gone from searching for nails to playing under the floorboards, the workman shooed him out, and the boy came running over to Emma, grinning. She rolled to her feet, and escorted the two of them to the house.

Mama gathered some bottled potions and a few bundles into her satchel, then wrapped both Emma and Kimber with child-sized shawls before draping a little hooded cloak over Tam.

As soon as Mama let go of him, he raced across the room to claim his wooden sword and struck a dramatic cloak-swooshing pose. Kimber fidgeted with her green shawl, eyeing the old black one around Emma's shoulders with a hint of guilt.

Mama held out her hand for Tam, and he ran over to take it. She walked outside, the girls following two steps behind.

"What's wrong?" whispered Emma.

Kimber held up her shawl. "It's new. You'as got a old worn 'un."

"She wants you to be warm and knows I like this one because it used to be hers from when she was little."

"Oh." Kimber smiled with relief.

Mama approached the third house they passed on the way to the town, handing one of the potions to Mr. Knolwick via an open window. They exchanged brief pleasantries before Mama departed and walked straight south off the road.

Tam swatted at tall grass with his wooden sword, though he still vanished up to the shoulders in the sea of loam green. Emma kept her arms out in front of her to part the way until they made it across to another dirt trail a little while later.

They stopped at the Heath's farm, where Mama checked on a few horses. Emma hovered close, listening in with the Wildkin Whisper as her mother made sure the animals were in good health and spirits. Tam and Kimber remained quiet, though the boy kept an eye out for imaginary goblins trying to steal livestock.

The Heaths and their three grown sons chatted with Mama for a bit before expressing their relief that Emma had been recovered safe from the thieves. Emma curtseyed and thanked them for their concern, enduring head pats and shoulder squeezes.

Mama returned to the road and led the way into town proper, stopping a few minutes later at the blacksmith's shop. Mr. Burland stood by an outdoor forge under an awning attached to a store where he sold finished goods, mostly farm tools, horseshoes, and such.

"Oy, Arn," said Mama. "Mafindwel."

Mr. Burland hurried over. "Mrs. Dalen… Thank you for coming."

Mama smiled. "You know I always stop by."

"The boy didn't find you then?" Mr. Burland shook his head, sending his long black hair and beard waving back and forth. "No matter. Eric has burned himself."

Emma gasped. "Is he hurt badly?"

"His hand," said Mr. Burland. "Uhh." He stared at Emma, hesitance clear in dark blue eyes. "Perhaps you should watch the little'uns while your mama attends to Eric."

Emma looked up at Mama, eager to observe her work, but also understanding the blacksmith's son had probably suffered an injury bad enough to where he didn't want a girl her age to see it. "Can we wait in the shop?"

Mama nodded. "Let us waste no further time then."

Mr. Burland led the way through a side door. Emma took Kimber and

Tam by the hand and turned left out of the storeroom toward the main shop floor while Mama followed the blacksmith to the right and up a flight of stairs. Faint moans of pain in the voice of a teenaged boy came from above.

The elder daughter, Lilliana, stooped over a counter, fiddling with a quill pen and parchment. She'd be seventeen in a few weeks, but had not settled on a boy to marry yet. A simple white dress with a brown vest covered her to the ankles, soft brown shoes poked out from under the hem. She had blonde hair like her younger sister Julianna, who made her way around the shelves of tools with a duster.

"Hello," said Emma, looking up at the thirteen-year-old.

Julianna peered back over her shoulder and smiled. "Mafindwel, Emma. Hello Tam… and?"

"Hello," said Lilianna without looking away from her writing. "Please don't let him touch anything sharp."

"This is my sister, Kimber." Emma adjusted her grip on Tam's hand. At the sight of Julianna's slender arm reaching to dust a metal-banded shield, her mind returned to that awful, awful dream the Banderwigh made her have… where she'd stepped on the poor girl. Again, she felt the cold sponginess of a dead girl's arm underfoot. *Julianna did not die when this place burned down. The Banderwigh lied in my dream.*

"Are you all right?" Julianna walked over. "All the color faded from your cheeks."

Emma swallowed, forcing a smile. "Yes. I'm fine. Thank you."

Tam gravitated to the one small rack holding swords, three items out of almost a hundred. He pulled at her, trying to get closer, forcing Emma to set her heels.

"Are you sure?" Julianna tilted her head. "You looked like you'd seen a ghost."

"I had a bad dream where the whole town burned," said Emma in a half-whisper.

"Aww." Julianna hugged her. "Did you really get taken by some monstrous creature?"

Tam nodded. "Yeah. And she thumped it! Like she thumped Rydh."

Lilianna chuckled. "Don't pick on her suitor."

"He isn't!" Julianna blushed. "I think he likes me, but he won't even talk to me."

Emma scrunched up her nose. "Bleh. He's not nice."

"He's big and tough, so everyone's afraid of him… but he's nice inside."

Julianna twirled the feather duster around in her hands. "Why don't you like him?"

"He stepped on Stick Knight's horse!" yelled Tam. "Killed him. An' he laughed at me. Pushed me over. 'Ey were gonna put me inna barrel, but Em thumped him."

Emma narrowed her eyes. "He broke my brother's toy and made fun of him for getting upset over it."

"Oh. That's not nice." Julianna frowned. "Is that why I hear he's afraid of you?"

Emma shrugged.

"He's probably afraid of her mother." Lilianna at last looked up from her writing. "But Emma's a forest witch too, so maybe he doesn't want to be turned into a pig."

The older girl hadn't said 'forest witch' in a way that sounded bad, so Emma let it go. "I don't think we can do that… turn someone into a pig. It's just a legend."

Kimber leaned up on tiptoe, her lips an inch from Emma's ear, and whispered, "Banderwigh's a legend tae."

Emma grinned. Maybe Nan *could* turn people into pigs.

"Thank you!" bellowed Mr. Burland, loud enough to hear from upstairs.

"Well…" Julianna returned to her dusting. "If Rydh ever finds the courage to speak to me, I shall ask him about your brother. I do hope he has a suitable answer as I'll not waste my time with someone who finds joy in tormenting small children."

Mama walked in with the blacksmith right behind her. "Is all else well?"

"Aye," said Mr. Burland. "Much obliged to your ministrations. I hope that boy is more careful with the forge."

"His hand will be sore for a few days. Best not to make him work too hard." Mama shook her head when the man attempted to hand her coins. "I'll take a few for the elixirs to offset the cost of bottles, but Mythandriel's favor is freely given."

The blacksmith bowed at her.

"Hello, Mrs. Dalen," said the daughters at once.

"Mafindwel, girls." Mama smiled at each of them.

Emma waved farewell and followed her outside and down the street, dragging Tam away from the shiny blades. They stopped in the town square where Mama bought three small sweet breads for the children before heading to the eastern edge of Widowswood Town. Beyond a scattering of a few homesteads, the vast rolling plains continued to the Sparkling Run. Da had described the great river once, which flowed down from Calebrin City and continued all the way south into the land of Sondaren. She nibbled on the apple-cinnamon-flavored bread and tried to picture what it would be like to ride a boat like Da had along such a mighty waterway.

The dirt trail Mama followed away from the cobblestone street grew familiar, and set Emma on guard. She knew they headed to the Cooper farm, which meant an encounter with Rydh. With both Mama and Emma there, the boy wouldn't dare tease Tam, but her little brother would probably run at the mere sight of him.

A thick grassy aroma pervaded the air, laced with a hint of flowers. Buzzing announced the presence of a handful of mouseaters a short distance away. At the arrival of the egg-sized bees, Kimber gasped and clung to Emma.

"Tell 'em nae sting us," whispered Kimber.

Emma patted the hand clinging to her arm. "They won't sting unless you get too close to their nest or try to hit them." Her anxiety built the closer they got to the place, worse since Tam didn't seem to realize where they'd gone.

Soon, they reached the gate in the wooden fence around the Cooper farm.

"Mama," asked Emma. "Should I take Tam somewhere else?"

Tam looked at her, confused.

"Why?" Mama raised an eyebrow.

Emma nodded toward the house. "Rydh…"

"I'm not 'fraid of him." Tam patted the handle of his wooden sword. "Imma knight."

Mama held back her grin. "Oh, I doubt that boy will be a bother to you."

Emma squeezed his hand. "All right."

A winding path led between two fields planted high with corn and wheat. The end opened onto a longer, wider path that curved off eastward to larger fields out in the plains. Tiny figures, farmhands, milled about, looking like bugs from so far away. Straight ahead past a grove of aspen trees stood the Cooper's two-story farmhouse. To the left of the house, Rydh Cooper and two smaller boys lobbed rocks at a stream.

Despite being thirteen, Rydh had the size of a much older boy, nearly as tall as Da. Fluffy reddish hair made him seem even taller. His friends, both on the skinny side, looked like little children next to him even though they had to be at least twelve.

Kimber drifted to the right amid the aspen grove, drawn to a swing hanging from a thick branch. Emma followed her while Mama kept going on toward the house. No doubt, she wanted to check up on the new calf and its mother, since the birth two weeks prior had been difficult. Again, Emma resisted her curiosity for the sake of allowing Tam some distance from the Cooper home. If Mama had thought she needed to learn anything here, she would've said so.

Kimber pulled herself up on the swing, smiled, and got it moving.

Rydh had gone statue still since he'd spotted them, gaze locked on Emma. The expression on his face said he'd likely run off screaming if she so much as glared at him.

Tam grumbled.

"What?" she whispered.

"Rydh's 'fraid of you." He scrunched up his nose. "He's not 'fraid of me."

An older man answered the door, spoke to Mama for a few seconds, and walked with her around to a fenced-in area where cows grazed.

Emma turned her head to the left, meeting Rydh's gaze. He flinched. *Does he think I'm going to hurt him?* She tried to ask 'what?' with her eyes, but the huge boy didn't react. The sight of him cowed at her mere presence bothered her. It's not like she'd flown in on him like Nan had come after the thieves. Seeing the look on Nan's face when the cellar door opened both frightened her and brought comfort. She'd never seen the old one so angry, neither before nor since, and that she had become so because Emma's life had been threatened filled her with tingles and warmth whenever she thought about it.

Still, having Rydh Cooper ready to run away from her didn't sit well in her stomach. While she remained cross with him for breaking Tam's toy, his continued dread of her brought guilt. With all the townspeople learning she had 'the gift' as well, perhaps the boy thought Emma was too much 'forest witch' and not enough Mama.

"Tam. Stay here with Kimber. I'll be right back."

"'Kay," muttered Tam, squeezing the handle of his wooden sword. "If he's mean, I'ma thump him."

"Protect Kimber in case there's goblins hiding in the grove." Emma winked.

Kimber put a hand over her grin to muffle a giggle.

Tam nodded.

Emma pivoted on her heel and walked up a shallow hill toward the side of the house, straight at the three older boys. Rydh leaned away, causing the other two to snicker at him. She stopped a few paces distant and put her hands on her hips.

"Rydh… why are you afraid of me?"

She almost smiled at watching this near-adult-sized boy's cheeks wobble with fear. He stood at least a foot and a half taller than her and had to weigh three times as much, yet he looked ready to flee. When he'd crushed Stick Knight's horse, she hadn't even believed in magic. She'd gone into a frenzy, punching at his face, but couldn't possibly have hurt a boy that big. The other two had Emma by about five inches in height.

"Hullo, Emma," muttered Rydh. "Here to see the cows?"

"Hey Rydh," said the boy on the right. He had light brown hair and large eyes that would've made him appear innocent if not for his malevolent smile. "*This* is the girl you're afraid of? She's smaller than a faerie."

"Umm." Rydh fidgeted.

Emma tilted her head. "I'm not going to hurt you unless you tease my brother again. You don't have to be scared of me."

The brown-haired boy laughed, pointing at Rydh. "You are! You're really afraid of this little twig."

"She's a witch, Alan," muttered the black-haired boy.

Alan walked up to Emma, a cocky grin on his lips. "She's a little tiny thing. You ought'a toss 'er in the pig wallow. Show her not to threaten you."

Rydh's bushy red eyebrows crept together. "I don't hit girls… An' she killed that bander-thing, an' a wizard, an' like a hundred thieves."

Emma rolled her eyes. "I didn't—"

"Yeah, right," said Alan. He leaned at her, glowering. "I smell horse apples."

She folded her arms, shifting her weight onto one leg. "A cursed grown man chased me through the woods with an axe bigger than you are. I'm not at all afraid of you."

"Oh, really?" Alan grabbed two fistfuls of her dress and swung her to his left, pressing her into the wall of the house, holding her up off her feet. "What are you gonna do, huh? Maybe I should knock some respect into you?"

The black-haired boy got paler. "Maybe you shouldn't do—"

"Shut up, Conall," barked Alan.

"Stop," said Rydh, putting a bear-paw hand on the smaller boy's shoulder. "Don't hurt girls."

Tam let out a war cry and charged up the grove. Alan ignored him, pushing Emma into the house until his knuckles dug painfully into her chest. Rydh tugged on him but not with enough motivation to move him. Conall took a step back as if expecting something bad to happen.

"Yaaaaah!" screamed Tam. He sprinted up and walloped Alan in the back with his sword.

The older boy grunted but didn't move. "Grab that little turd. He hits me again, I'm going to break that stick over his head."

"Mama!" yelled Kimber. "Mama!"

"Aww, little girl crying for her mommy," muttered Alan, his sinister grin baring teeth. "Come on, little forest witch." He lifted her a few inches higher.

Tam smacked Alan in the back of the leg. The strike made a sharp *snap*, but only caused the boy's face to redden in anger.

"Rydh!" said Alan. "Grab that little snot, *now.*"

"Put her down." Rydh stepped between Tam and Alan, but didn't attempt to grab him.

Emma scowled at Alan and muttered, "Great Uruleth, please lend me your strength."

The boy let off a gasp as faint green light swam over Emma's body and a mild, sudden breeze kicked her hair about. She grabbed Alan's wrists and pulled his grip away from her dress, sliding down the wall to her feet. Once her toes had purchase on solid dirt, she leaned forward and shoved him with both hands. The growl of an annoyed bear came out of her, much deeper than any noise that ought to have come from her small body.

Alan flew as if a grown man had thrown him. He landed hard on his back a few paces away, barking like a kicked goose. Tam raised his sword and started to charge, but Emma clamped a hand on his shoulder, holding him back.

"Stop, Tam."

Her brother twisted around, blinking at her in confusion.

"Knights don't hit their opponents when they're down."

Tam nodded and pointed his sword at Alan. "Unhand my si—the maiden."

Alan flapped his arms and wheezed, gawping at the air like a landed fish.

Conall rushed over and pulled Alan up into a sitting position. Alan coughed and got wind in his lungs again a few seconds later. Both of the smaller boys gawked at her in fear while Rydh looked ashamed of himself.

"She *is* a forest witch," whispered Conall.

"What's going on here?" asked Mama after jogging over.

"Alan was hittin' Em, but she thumped him!" Tam held up his sword. "I thumped him too."

Mama looked at Emma, raising a questioning eyebrow.

"It's fine, Mama. Alan pushed me into the wall 'cause he said I was too small to frighten Rydh. He thought I was going to be afraid of him."

"I'm sorry, Mrs. Dalen." Rydh stared at the dirt, kicking it. "Alan's makin' fun of me for bein' feared o' Emma."

Emma brushed the rumples out of her dress where Alan had grabbed her. "I didn't kill the wizard. Spiders as big as horses did, because he hurt Mama. I didn't kill any thieves either. Mama and Nan scared them out of the forest because they kidnapped me." She walked up to Rydh. "I don't have any quarrel with you as long as you leave my brother alone."

Alan wheezed, still struggling to breathe.

"Uh huh, Emma." Rydh nodded. "I won' bother 'im."

"I still think you're nasty for stepping on his toy. That was mean."

Rydh scratched his head behind his right ear. "I stepped on a pile of sticks… didn't mean to. When he cried, I, uhh, thought it was kinda silly he cried over sticks is all."

Emma frowned. "It's not what it was… it's what Tam thought it to be. To him, those sticks were a knight's warhorse. Besides… you're thirteen and huge. Picking on a boy half your age doesn't prove you're strong. It proves you're afraid of anyone who can fight back. You're even afraid of Alan… you wanted to pull him away from me but didn't."

Rydh fidgeted. "I didn't wanna hurt him. Pa says I'm too strong for my own good."

Emma's angry glare softened a touch.

"Alan Miller," said Mama. "What's gotten into you? I mean to have a talk with your mother about what you did."

He bowed his head. "Yes, ma'am. I'm sorry."

He's only sorry because he got caught. Emma decided against doing anything more, since the two other boys already appeared frightened of her. She looked up at Mama. "Are the cows healthy?"

Mama smiled. "Yes, Em. They're both doing well. Come along then… I've another elixir to drop off, and the Holsteads are expecting me."

"Baby!" cheered Kimber. "He's so adorable! Do you think Anna will let me hold him?"

"Maybe." Mama winked. "But you'll have to ask politely."

Kimber jumped up and down, clapping.

Alan wandered off toward the stream, grumbling and kicking dirt. Conall followed, glancing back over his shoulder at Emma.

"Sorry, Emma," said Rydh. "I shouldn't 'ave let 'im push you into the wall. Want me to hit him?"

Emma shook her head. "No. You're right. You'll probably hurt him."

"If you'as like Julianna, you'as ought'a talk tae her," said Kimber.

Rydh's cheeks went as red as his hair.

Tam made a gagging face.

"All right, children. Come along." Mama took Tam and Kimber by the hand and started in the direction of town.

Emma followed, walking slow for a few steps while grinning back over her shoulder at Rydh. It seemed maybe he wasn't quite the nasty sort of person she'd assumed. *He's like a big bear afraid of its own strength.* She'd have to talk to Julianna again since she hadn't spoken kindly of the boy to her. Perhaps if she went with Mama on her errands again tomorrow, though she'd likely be sent into town soon enough. Stopping by the blacksmith's for a moment shouldn't be a problem.

She smiled at Mama and followed her back toward town. All the while, Kimber rambled happily about getting to hold Anna's infant son.

3

SKY DRAGONS

ith no errands begging her attention the next day, Mama spent some time after breakfast teaching Emma about Linganthas, the spirit who looked over plants in all forms. Everything from the great trees to creeping ivy, flowers, and even weeds. He could make plants grow faster, make them grow backwards and become smaller, create bramble patches or giant roots. To demonstrate, Mama called a tendril of vine as thick as Da's arm, which made a whipping motion in the air a few times like Tam 'fighting goblins.'

Kimber and Tam ran about the meadow, a little farther from the house than where Emma sat with her mother in the grass.

"When you get a little older and you've had more time to let magic flow through you, you can try to ask Linganthas for aid."

Emma nodded.

"You can also ask the roots for help." Mama smiled and raised her hand. The root coiled around Emma as gentle as could be, and lifted her up to the height of the house's roof. "If you needed to climb over a wall." The root lowered her and set her on her feet. A second later, it coiled around her, pinning her arms at her sides. "And if you want to stop a fight without hurting someone…"

Emma squirmed, emitting a playful growl. The root unwound and sank back into the earth. Mama took a seed from a pouch on her belt and poked it into the ground.

"Ask Linganthas to help make that melon grow," said Mama.

Emma scooted to kneel next to her.

"Nan asked him to make the cherry tree big, didn't she?" Emma grinned and held her hands over the tiny hole in the soil.

"Perhaps a bit more than that." Mama winked. "That tree's got a spirit."

"She trapped a ghost in it?" Emma blinked.

Mama laughed. "No, Em. She channeled so much energy into the sapling that the tree's spirit grew stronger than most."

"I sensed it when I picked cherries. The tree knew I was there." Emma smiled again and focused on the spot of ground beneath her hands. "Linganthas, please hurry this little seed along. Grant it a whisper of your breath." She tried to picture the little black dot, and as she did with her healing spell, desired energy to flow into the seed. A slight phantom tug pulled at her, and three inches of stem popped up. "He listened!"

Mama beamed with pride.

Emma sat back on her heels and looked up. "That little sprout won't stop a wizard."

"Em." Her mother's smile faded. She put a hand on Emma's shoulder. "Almost all of the spirits can be called upon for protection. The more you talk to Linganthas, the more you will be able to ask him for. You pictured that melon seed growing. What your magic does will change depending on what you envision, and what you ask. Linganthas knew how much I wanted to protect you, and how I needed to stop that man from using his magic."

"I'm sorry." Emma bowed her head. After a second or two of sniffling, she leaned over and hugged her mother. "You got hurt because I was foolish."

Mama stroked her hair for a few silent minutes until she calmed. "Everything we do is a chance to learn. I'm sure you learned quite a lot from the choices you made that day."

Emma nodded. "Yes."

Attempting to evade the 'princess' trying to kiss him, Sir Tam ran while looking back over his shoulder at Kimber, and careened into one of the workmen. He bounced off and landed on his bum, while the man flailed his arms after dropping the board he had been attempting to hammer in place. Kimber went from giggling to frozen still, staring in fear at the worker.

"Em, why don't you take them to the stream for a bit? It's warm today, and there won't be too many more warm days left this year. I'll see if I can give the men a little something to speed them along."

"Sorry!" yelled Tam. He rolled onto all fours and sprinted for Mama, as wide-eyed as if he fled from an enraged troll.

The workman shook his head and stooped to pick up the board.

"Yes, Mama." Emma stood. "I'll keep him away from the workers."

Mama held back the laugh, but couldn't stop from smiling.

"I didn't mean to," whined Tam, as he ran around to hide behind Mama. When it became clear the man would not give chase, he relaxed.

Kimber trotted over, still with an uneasy expression.

"Let's go swim." Emma pointed at the woods. "It's warm."

He grinned ear-to-ear.

"All right." Kimber nibbled on her lip with an expression like she contemplated doing something she'd get in trouble for, but wanted to do anyway.

Mama patted Emma's back and kissed her atop the head. "Keep an ear out. I'll call for you in a bit when it's time to eat."

Emma headed off toward the creek while Mama went into the house. She held her hands out to the side, caressing tall yellow flowers poking above the meadow grass. White butterflies zipped and corkscrewed, flitting in and out of view amid the green. After crossing the remainder of the meadow, she led the way into the Widowswood Forest. The trees wrapped around her like a welcoming embrace, and she found herself smiling at them.

A few minutes later, Emma halted at the side of the stream and tested with a toe. She cringed, but she'd gone into colder water before and the season didn't have many days left in it that would allow them to swim.

Tam flung off his tunic and breeches before diving in without the slightest bit of hesitation. He stayed under for a five-count before bursting up from the surface and cheering.

Kimber also stuck her toes in the creek. "Eee! Is 'a cold!"

"A little." Emma pulled her blue dress off, wadded it up, and dropped it next to Tam's clothes. She leaned close to Kimber and whispered, "Mama wanted me to keep Tam away from the workers… you don't have to go in if you don't want to."

Kimber giggled. "Aye. He makin' ae mess."

"Emma, come on," yelled Tam.

She crept into the water until it came up to her thighs, and froze. "Oh… it's a little cold."

"Don't do it slow." Tam slapped his hands down on the water. "Do it fast an' it's not bad."

"You're right." Emma took a couple breaths to get ready, and jumped forward.

Icy water wrapped her in a blanket of needlepoints. She curled into a ball, holding her breath until the shock of the plunge faded. Feeling energized and alive, Emma kicked off the bottom and surfaced with a shriek of glee. At a bright flash from the creek's edge, she whirled, expecting something strange and magical, but the harsh glare turned out to be Kimber's paleness catching the sunlight as she pulled her dress off.

Tam stared at her for a second before covering his eyes and screaming, "Aah! I can't see!"

After folding the dress in a neat square, Kimber set it down and waded knee-deep into the water. Emma offered a reassuring smile. They'd been to the creek a bunch of times, and more and more, she seemed to relax around the water. Emma put her feet down, finding herself shoulder-deep near the middle of the creek.

Kimber trembled, though she seemed more cold than frightened. Her green eyes narrowed with determination, and a second later, she jumped forward. A great cloud of red hair spread out around her as she glided along underwater. Emma watched her, poised to help if she sensed panic. Kimber rolled over, facing up, and made a silly face. Bubbles leaked out of her nose.

Emma laughed, which caused Kimber to attempt to laugh. Sputtering and coughing, Kimber stood, the water lapping at her chin. Emitting an uneasy whine, she hurried a few steps back toward the bank until the water only came up to her armpits.

"You're doing great," said Emma. "Jumping in like that makes the cold not so bad. It's awful when you try to go in slow."

"I'as w-w-want a b-b-bath." Kimber folded her arms, teeth chattering. "B-b-b-aths are warm."

"Here..." Emma swam over to her and stood, her feet sinking in clammy muck. She held her arms out underwater. "Go like you're swimming. I won't let you dip under."

Kimber stared into her eyes for two seconds before giving a hesitant nod. "'Kay."

She pushed off the creek bottom and stretched out. Emma let Kimber lay across her outstretched arms, keeping her face above water. The girl shivered something fierce, but seemed comforted by the close contact.

Before Kimber had been part of the family, her only experience at 'swimming' had been when her cruel father had held her underwater in a horse trough as punishment for not bringing home enough copper. The man had only cared about his Faeberry wine. Emma beamed from ear to ear watching Kimber dive underwater on her own. A few weeks with a *real* family had made a big change in her.

"Move your arms like Tam's doing, and kick," said Emma.

Kimber watched the boy swim around for a moment before mimicking his motions. Emma turned about in a circle, letting Kimber feel as if she swam through the water. Soon, she seemed to get the hang of it, and Emma started to lower her arms.

"Don't let go!" yelled Kimber.

Emma braced her again. "I'm here. You were doing it. You were swimming."

Kimber grinned as she paddled.

"You don't need to be afraid here. This is just a little creek. We can stand in the deepest part and still keep our faces out of the water. If you get scared, just put your feet down."

Kimber scowled in concentration. "'Kay."

A few minutes later, Emma walked sideways, still holding her up. "My arms are getting tired. Can I let go?"

"I'm scared."

"If you're scared, just put your legs down and stand. The water isn't deep."

Kimber whined a little, but nodded. "'Kay."

Emma let her weary arms dangle in the slight current. Kimber swam around in a lazy circle, smiling… until Tam splashed at her. She screamed. Water foamed around her as she flailed in a panic.

"Tam!" said Emma in a loud voice, not quite yelling. "Don't splash her. Please. She's not ready, and doesn't like water hitting her face." She hurried over and took hold of the girl's arm. "He's only playing."

Kimber clung for a moment until she calmed enough to get her feet under her. She gasped, out of breath, standing shoulder deep, her face hidden behind a wall of red. Emma poked her in the forehead with two fingers, then pulled them apart, opening a heavy curtain of hair, which she tucked behind the girl's ears.

Tam dove under, his feet flicking out of the creek like a sea-dragon's tail. His blurry form glided down to the bottom and pawed at the stones. Kimber relaxed, but seemed content to stand while waving her hand side to side right under the surface. Emma swept her arm across as well, and they got to seeing who could get the most silver air bubbles clinging to the back of their arm without breaking the surface. Tam popped up for a breath and went back down.

Kimber shrieked and jumped on Emma, wrapping her arms around. "Something bit me!"

A small hand grabbed Emma's left ankle. She sighed.

"It's Tam being dumb. He grabbed your leg, didn't he?"

"Umm." Kimber sniffled, and went from frightened to annoyed.

When the boy came up again, she splashed him. He splashed her back, then gave Emma an 'oops' look. Since Kimber laughed and splashed him again, Emma nodded. A three-way water-flinging war eventually gave way to quiet floating once everyone ran out of energy.

A soft hum grew into loud buzzing from the left; a trio of longflies glided over the creek, zipping closer. As the eight-inch insects neared, Kimber let out a yelp and ducked under. Emma waved at them, not that the bugs reacted. One passed close enough for the breeze from its wings to brush her face.

Kimber stared up at her with an expectant look.

After the longflies went by, Emma took her hand and pulled her upright. "They don't bite people. They bite other bugs."

"They'as scary lookin'." Kimber shivered. "Big as daggers!"

Emma grasped the girl's chin. "Oh. Your lips are blue. Time to get out." She turned to find Tam, but didn't see him. An instant before worry set in, she caught sight of a boy-shaped blur gliding along the creek bed.

"Aye." Kimber held Emma's hand while walking toward the bank. "Yours a' well blue."

Emma stuck her face in the water and yelled, "Tam!"

He bobbed up to the surface.

She pointed at the bank. "'Mon out. We're goin' ta catch cold."

Tam rolled around in the water and swam toward her.

His lack of pleading or protesting to stay in longer worried her a little. If *Tam* was cold enough to not argue at being told to get out of the water, maybe they had stayed in too long. She reached out her free hand to take his, and guided her siblings up onto the grass beside the creek. Kimber found a nice patch of sun and flopped flat on her back to dry. Emma lay down next to her, adoring the unexpected warmth.

"Why's the water so cold but it's warm out?" Tam sat cross-legged beside her.

"'Cause the water spirit's feeling cold." Emma gazed up at puffy white clouds. "The water's always colder than everything else."

"Oh." He shivered.

"Cat!" said Kimber, pointing at a cloud.

Emma leaned left, touching heads with her, and stared up the length of her arm at the sky. With a little imagination, the cloud she indicated could be a cat. "Yes. That's a cat all right."

Tam lay flat, hands behind his head.

Water droplets tickled here and here, making Emma look for bugs every few seconds. A slight hint of pumpkin pie invaded the fragrance of the woods. She scratched at her belly, eager for Mama to call them back for the midday meal.

"Wolf." Tam pointed up.

Emma hoped he'd spotted Greyfang or one of the others, but he too, gazed at the clouds. That one did look like a wolf. Though disappointed she hadn't seen her 'other family' for a while, she didn't let it show on her face.

"Yeah," said Kimber. "An' 'at one's a horse."

Emma picked out a few cloud shapes as well, a chicken and a bull, and one that reminded her of a house. After a while, they had dried off except for the girls' long hair. Kimber sat up and leaned to one side, head tilted, pulling her fingers through her hair to squeeze water out. Emma did the same, though Tam remained sprawled on his back searching the clouds.

Her brother had gotten so upset over Stick Knight's steed because of the rarity of finding a bit of a branch that had broken off in such a way as to resemble a horse… in the way Kimber's first cloud resembled a cat. Someone lacking imagination (like Rydh) would only have seen a hunk of wood.

I wonder if Linganthas would let me grow a root in the shape of a horse.

"A dragon," said Tam, pointing at another cloud.

Emma looked up at a huge billowy mass of white. Evidently, Tam's imagination had hers beat. It didn't look like much of anything at all.

"It is!" he said, a touch of whine in his voice. "You got that face on. The head's on the right side. That bit wif the sun glowin' on it is a wing."

"Umm." She squinted, trying to see it. The boy had spent so much time with Shrub Dragon, perhaps a giant bush looked like a dragon to him. "I can almost see it."

A moving dark spot overhead caught her eye.

"Wha's 'at?" asked Kimber, pointing. "Ae bird?"

Emma stared. Whatever it was, it disappeared for a second *above* a cloud. It emerged from the far end of the shapeless cloud after a second. Narrow at the front end, it widened to an oval middle, and tapered again in the shape of a tail. Wings stretched out to a span twice the length of the shadow. They flapped once and went straight and still again.

"That's too high for a bird. It's over top of the clouds." Emma's jaw hung open. "I… think that's…"

The shadow flapped again, gliding overhead from west to east.

"A dragon!" shouted Tam.

He leapt to his feet and ran, screaming, in the direction of the house, forgetting his clothes.

Emma stared, awestruck, until the shadow tracked too far to the right to see past the trees.

"We'as ought'a go home." Kimber stood and hurried into her dress.

"Yes." Emma leapt up and pulled the dress Nan had made her back on before gathering Tam's tunic and breeches.

Kimber fell in step at her side as they jogged out of the woods to the meadow. Tam jumped up and down on the porch, pulling at Nan and pointing at the sky. The old one cackled with amusement. Emma's fear diminished, and she slowed to a purposeful walk. Soon, the boy's fervent insistence that they'd seen a real dragon drowned out the workers' hammers. By the time Emma reached the porch, her hair had soaked a damp spot into the back of her dress.

"It's true!" Tam spun to stare at Emma. "Tell her you saw it too!"

Emma handed him his clothes. "Yes, Nan. We saw something in the air… it did look a bit like a dragon, but it was so high up it's just a shadow with wings."

"Is a dragon!" Tam sat on the steps to get his legs in his breeches.

Kimber scooted under the porch roof, as if trying to hide from the sky. "Is 'ere such ae 'fing a' dragons, Nan?"

Tam stared at her as if she'd said sweetbreads were bad.

Nan sent a quick glance up. "There are dragons out there, but they don't bother with people much. When they fly, they go very high so no one notices them." Wrinkles around her eyes deepened with a smile. "Not many people have time to watch the clouds, so almost no one ever spots one."

"Is it gonna burn the town?" Tam jumped up and wriggled into his tunic, grabbing at his belt area like a knight who'd misplaced his sword.

"'Er they mean?" asked Kimber.

"Oh, Tam." Nan chuckled. "No. I doubt any dragon would object to our little town being here. And yes, Kimber… sometimes they are mean, but people can be mean too. Dragons are quite smart." She tapped a finger to the side of her head. "And they're also rather arrogant. Some can be nice and some can be mean."

"Ar'gant?" asked Kimber.

Nan smiled. "It means they think they are better than us, and they take great pride in feeling better than us."

"It's bad for people to be arrogant," said Emma.

"Dragons *are* better than us." Tam waved his arms. "They're huge. They spit fire. They can step on houses. Only knights can stop them. Soldiers and guards can't."

Emma grinned, as did Nan.

"Shoul' we tell Da 'bout seein' ae dragon?" asked Kimber.

Nan shook her head. "If you spotted one that high, whatever business it's got has nothing to do with Widowswood. I'd not bother the man about it."

Mama's face appeared in the window. "Well. You've got a sense of time, Em. I don't need to yell for you. Come in and help me set the table?"

"Yes, Mama." Emma smiled and darted inside.

AFTER LUNCH, EMMA SAT ON THE EDGE OF THE BACK PORCH. KIMBER KNELT nearby, setting up a bunch of small stones in a circle around a large, flat rock. Tam tolerated sitting quiet for less than two minutes before he stood, drew his wooden sword, and held it up.

"I have to guard. There's goblins."

Emma pointed to the right (away from the workers) and gasped. "Something moved in the grass. I think it might be a goblin!"

Kimber looked up, mouth open. When Emma winked, she went from worried to grinning.

Tam pointed his blade in that direction. "Fear not, fair maidens. I will p'tect you."

He marched off a short distance into the meadow, adopting a spot-on impression of Guard Kavan's walk. Emma leaned forward and held her hands out over the dirt between her feet. Soft clicks and scrapes of Kimber rearranging stones filled in the relative quiet between periods of hammering going on.

Emma pictured a woody vine growing up from the ground and arranging itself into the general shape of a tiny horse. "Linganthas, please send forth some of your roots."

"Wha's ya' doin?" asked Kimber.

A sprout of brown root emerged from the ground beneath Emma's hands, twisting and growing. She stared at it, trying to feel its presence and control how it moved. Kimber glanced over, but seemed to notice her concentration and didn't press for an answer. Inch by inch, the root crept up from the ground and bent into the shape of a legless horse. The main part swelled, stopping a little fatter than the handle of her broom, then sprouted 'legs' as big around as Emma's fingers.

She picked it up and closed her eyes. "Thank you, Linganthas." After a moment of silent reverence, she smiled at Kimber. "Practicing. I asked the spirit of trees and vines to make this for Tam."

"Is 'at what Rydh broke?"

Emma nodded and set the 'horse' on the porch behind her. "This one looks more like a horse than his old one."

"You'as maked it 'at way." Kimber handed her a little wooden cup. "Tea."

She giggled and took the cup. "What kind?"

Kimber sniffed a similar empty cup. "Faerie tea." She indicated the table and seats she'd made from the rocks. "Is ae faeries' tea party. Donnae be tae loud 'er 'ey'll run off."

"Yes," whispered Emma. "They don't like loud noises."

Kimber raised her nose like a tiny noblewoman. "Me faerie friends, 'ey don min' 'a hammrin'."

"Oh." Emma pretended to sip faerie tea.

"'Ey not same as 'a ones what come tae eat 'em treats ya made." Kimber pretended to pour tea into tiny cups made from acorn caps. "These faeries 'er braver."

"Do they live in cities like Neema?"

Kimber stooped and whispered over the rocks. "'Ey live inna woods. Sleepin' on big mushrooms." She stared at Emma, eyes wide with eagerness, but trying to act calm. "Neema's friends, 'ey live inna city?"

"Nan said the Silverbells live like little elves. Da said the elves have cities, but even the big ones aren't like ours. Theirs are part of the forest... he said you can sometimes walk right past an elf's house and not even notice it. The big cities are s'posed to be beautiful." Emma daydreamed about an elven city, full of delicate carvings, bridges, little waterfalls right in the middle of town, trees everywhere.

"I'as wish 'em faeries would visit again." Kimber seemed sad for a little while, but cheered up and got to whisper-talking to her pretend faeries while refilling their tea.

Emma played along as Kimber introduced her to the king of the Mushroom Meadow Faeries and his court. From there, they talked about how these faeries spent their days having fun, playing tricks on humans, and *not* having to do chores.

"Care for some more Faeberry tea?" Emma mimed picking up a teapot.

"No!" snapped Kimber. "'Ey no'a drink 'at." She shook her head hard. "'Tis 'gainst the law in 'a Meadow Mushroom Faerie Kingdom. Anyone caught wif Faeberry is magicked ta sleep, an' ne'er wake up." Her expression hardened; she looked like a small queen prepared to punish someone severely.

Emma froze, holding the make-believe teapot over the table. *Does she know what Mama did? She doesn't look sad.* She pretended to open the lid of the teapot and sniff. "Oh, my mistake. It's not Faeberry tea."

"'Es bad." Kimber's glare softened to a look of urgency. "Et make people mean."

She's afraid of it... like it'll make us all want to hit her. Emma scooted closer and put an arm around the girl's shoulders. "No Faeberry for me. Nan said it's poison to us."

Kimber clung to her, nodding and whispering, "Poison."

Emma hugged her back. Her tone made it seem as though she blamed the Faeberry wine for her father's death, and not what Mama added to it… though maybe she *did* mean 'poison' in the literal sense and accepted it. Even Kimber had to know that man would've eventually hit her too hard one day and hurt her badly, or worse.

At that horrible thought, Emma squeezed her and sniffled.

"Wha's wrong?" asked Kimber.

"Nothing." Emma leaned back, wiped her tears, and smiled. "I'm just happy you're my sister."

Kimber grinned. After a short, contented silence, she resumed rambling with the imaginary faeries. Their conversation took much of the remaining daylight hours, and as the sun weakened overhead, Kimber announced that the king evidently had two daughters: one young with red hair, the other a little older with black hair. Emma grinned.

"King say 'is li'l daughter is a scared o' e'rryfing, but the older daughter kep her safe. He'as nae knowin' what tae do wif the older 'un 'cause she always scare 'im. She tries to do 'fings she nae growed 'nuff for, an' almost gets hurt alla time."

Emma leaned her weight back on her hands and raised one eyebrow. "Oh? What's he going to do about that? You know, I bet the older daughter's really sorry for scaring them both."

Kimber covered her mouth to stifle a giggle. "He a'say he' lock 'em boaf inna house if she do et 'gain."

"Ooh. That sounds bad."

Kimber nodded. "'E don' wan' 'er runnin' off an' gettin' 'urt."

Emma sat up and fussed at Kimber's hair. "I don't think she'll do that."

"Brush?" Kimber's eyes lit up.

"All right." Emma grinned.

The workmen had gotten most of the outer walls built, and some of the roof framing up as well. Actual work had given way to standing around and talking for some time. Amid the fading sun, they gathered their tools and packed up for the day. Tam came wandering back from the meadow as soon as he noticed them preparing to leave.

"No goblins." He saluted her.

She smiled. "O brave knight, you deserve a reward for your courage."

Tam's eyes got wide for a second before narrowing. "Knights don't kiss princesses."

Emma held back the urge to laugh. Grinning, she reached behind her and pulled out the little horse she'd made. "A knight needs a warhorse."

He took it in both hands, stared at it for a little while, and clutched it to his chest while sniffling with watery eyes. "You healed him."

"Yes. Stick Knight's horse is a horse, and a horse is an animal, and I'm a druid."

Tam grinned. "Thank you." He hugged her tight, and jumped to his feet. "I think I hear a dragon."

The boy raced inside. Kimber returned with a brush, handed it over, and took a seat at the edge of the porch. Emma scooted up behind her. After a moment or two organizing hair with her fingers, she ran the brush down Kimber's dense, red hair with slow and gentle strokes.

"'Fink the faeries are watchin' us?"

Emma continued brushing while eyeing the woods. "Maybe. We could ask Nan if she'll help us make more treats for them."

"Why donnae Faeberry make 'a faeries mean?"

"Because," said Emma with confidence. "They're *Fae*berries. Humanberries would make faeries mean."

Kimber laughed.

Emma brushed for a while longer. Eventually, Kimber switched places and got to brushing Emma's hair while attempting to sing one of Mama's songs she didn't know the words to. A sudden tickling sensation on her foot made Emma glance down at a glimmering green beetle crawling over her toes. She smiled at it and let it be, continuing to brush her sister's hair while they still had a few minutes of daylight left.

She wished the sun would stay up a little longer before Mama called them in.

4

COOKIES AND BREAD

*E*mma lay on her side upon the thick fur rug, head propped up on her left hand, studying a wooden board full of glass beads. Warmth from the waning fireplace washed over her as she contemplated her next move of a blue 'gem.' Kimber had nine left, two more than her, but Emma didn't want to make it look obvious she didn't care who won. Either way, she adored the time with her family.

The rat wandered over from his box and curled up beside her, rolling belly up once she started skritching him.

Kimber sprawled on her stomach, chin resting on both hands while swinging her feet back and forth in the air. Her stare fixed on one of her gems and she nibbled at her lip, looking worried. The gem in question had made it three squares away from Emma's side of the board and would take away one of her 'life stones' if it got all the way across. As much as it seemed like Kimber longed to get that piece to the edge, Emma had a gem in position to 'kill' it. Not doing so would be obviously letting her win. With a twinge of guilt, Emma grasped her gem and captured Kimber's piece, taking it from the board.

She braced for a bad reaction, but Kimber's eyes gleamed like the emeralds of a dragon's hoard. Grinning, she slid her one remaining purple gem (pieces that could move any number of spaces in diagonals, but could not steal life stones) and captured one of Emma's soldiers. The move left three of Kimber's soldier gems in position to reach Emma's side of the board without any way to stop them.

She tricked me! Emma narrowed her eyes. "Sneaky."

Kimber stuck her tongue out, but broke up in giggles.

A tiny squeak came from the rat as he stretched his paws out over his head and yawned.

Tam flopped near the bear rug's head, trotting Stick Knight around on his new warhorse. Mama and Da sat together on one of the large, cushioned chairs by the fireplace, discussing the work on the house, the Watch, and the town. No one mentioned thieves, banderwighs, spiders, or goblins.

"How much longer until they're finished, Liam?" asked Mama.

Da chuckled. "You're quite eager, then. Perhaps we should have them add a third bedroom while they're here."

Mama whispered something at his ear that made him grin.

"Oh, it shouldn't be too much longer. The roof will start in the morning, and they'll have the inner walls done in a few days. Perhaps next week they'll cut the doorway into the old wall. Assuming the boy doesn't make them quit."

"Your son was good today. He stayed out of their way." Mama winked at Tam.

"Why not have your mother help with her magic?" Da flashed a rogue's grin. "That'd hasten things along."

"We can't alter dead wood," said Mama. "That's wizard's work."

Nan ambled in from the back hallway, clutching a book. "Oh, I could open the wall up if you like."

Emma's mind filled with the memory of the great roots tearing the cellar door apart. She moved another piece forward one square. Kimber would probably win no matter what she did, so she raced for the back row.

"All right then..." Nan came to a stop between the girls, peering down at the board. "Almost time for bed."

"'Tis nae over," said Kimber.

Emma sat up. "It is. You won."

"You'as quittin'?" Kimber gave her an apologetic look.

"No. You outmaneuvered me." Emma reached forward and tickled her. "You've got three warriors that'll get to the back row no matter what I do. I've only got two life stones left. I'll play to the end if you want, but you beat me when you made that capture."

Kimber grinned.

The rat grunted, reaching for Emma's hand with both of his paws, until she laughed and resumed scratching his belly.

Tam sprang up and ran to the shelf at the foot of the family bed. He traded his tunic and breeches for a nightshirt before crawling up onto the mattress. As neither of them needed to think much about strategy, their game finished in a few minutes, Kimber winning. Emma gathered all the beads into their storage box while Kimber changed into her nightdress. After putting the game on a shelf, Emma carried the rat back to his nest box and got ready for bed.

With her brother and sister tucked close at her side, Emma propped herself up with her back against the wall. Nan pulled a small chair close and opened the book that likely contained anything but a story. Emma suspected that Princess Isabelle from the story was really Queen Isabella, but the queen hadn't been a fifteen-year-old in a long time. The way Nan had told of the forest witch and her little daughter didn't seem right. If the little girl in the story was Mama, the queen shouldn't be that old.

Maybe Nan's making things up and mixing real stuff with story stuff.

Nan opened the book and flipped a few pages. "Having freed Sir Aemon from the ice demon's curse, Princess Isabelle journeyed to visit the forest witch, who brewed up a potion that could cure her father, the king. The old woman held up a bottle, fat at the bottom and narrow at the top. A glow like moonlight shone from the potion, making shadows dance about the room. Princess Isabelle took the bottle with both hands, and gasped. 'It's warm,' she whispered, eyes wide like huge sapphires."

"What's a sapphire?" asked Tam.

"It's a precious gem of bright blue," said Nan in her usual tone before clearing her throat and talking like a scary forest witch. "The forest witch laughed. 'You were expecting it to be cold? You're trying to thaw him out.' Princess Isabelle stared deep into the ghostly brew. 'It looks like it should be cold, but it's warm.'"

"Wow," whispered Kimber. "It sounds pretty."

Nan held the book to her chest as she leaned in. "It was. So rare a thing to see, a bottle of moonlight."

Emma grinned. "Could you make that kind of potion like the forest witch made?"

"Hmm." Nan wiggled an eyebrow, giving her a sly wink. "I suppose it might be possible, but that particular concoction had only one purpose...

removing a powerful necromantic curse from the king. The components to make it are quite difficult to find."

"Who made up a potion only one man can drink?" Emma blinked.

Nan chuckled. "Well… we can imbue potions that remove curses. The particular curse that had befallen the king was strong, and quite specific. The forest witch had to fiddle with the recipe a bit. A strand of Isabelle's hair went into it to lend it power. I believe her innocence is why it glowed white."

"'Nuff potions," said Tam. "Story."

Emma wiggled a finger into his armpit, making him squeal.

"Quiet," whispered Kimber. "Donnae make Nan stop."

"Princess Isabelle thanked the forest witch, but she seemed afraid. After putting the potion in her satchel, she looked the old woman in the eye and asked, 'What is your price for this potion?' To that, the forest witch smiled. 'I will not ask of you a price, for what you do serves our kingdom. The wizard must be stopped. I have only ruin to gain by not helping you.' The witch patted her on the shoulder and guided the princess to sit at her table. 'Now, the two of you should eat before you go. You will need your strength.' Sir Aemon still did not trust her food, nor did he trust that no price would be asked. To his protests, the witch said that she would not ask anything of the girl, but if the inclination to be thankful struck the king, she would not turn away a boon. Princess Isabelle did, however, trust the forest witch, and at her urging, they took a hearty meal."

Emma's head started to nod back, the bed too warm and comfortable. She caught herself and opened her eyes wide.

"Princess Isabelle and Sir Aemon rode through the forest night and day, racing back to the castle. In the early evening of the third day, they arrived in the capital city. Isabelle's heart thumped in her chest"—Nan held the book tight and hit it with her fist like a heartbeat—"as she feared they may have taken too long. When they reached the castle, her fear grew, for half of the building gleamed with a coating of ice."

"The king was breathin' ice," muttered Tam. "Magic ice like a dragon."

Kimber pulled the blanket up to her nose, looking frightened.

"Isabelle rode her horse straight over the drawbridge and into the castle keep, stopping in the grand hall by the stairs. The air inside was so cold, her breath made fog. She leapt from the saddle and ran as fast as she could."

"She can't run in a dress," said Tam.

"Princess Isabelle's not wearing a dress." Emma yawned. "She's got breeches on, like a soldier... so she can ride and fight."

"Oh." Tam shrugged.

Nan turned a page. "The whole upstairs hallway had filled with ice. Princess Isabelle slid and stumbled, snow spraying from her boots. Two men in chain mail guarded the king's bedchamber door, looking stern. When she got to them, they refused to let her in."

"What? Why?" asked Kimber.

"Shh," whispered Tam. "Nan's tellin' it."

Emma's head sagged to the left, leaning against Kimber's. She blinked slow, resisting a yawn.

"The princess ordered them to clear the way, but they refused, claiming Advisor Gerath warned them that the king's situation was most dire, and he should not be disturbed by anyone. Isabelle shouted, 'Gerath's the one who did this! I am the princess, now stand aside!' Still, the men refused to move. Isabelle tried to push past them, but they shoved her away."

"No," whispered Kimber.

Nan turned a page. "Sir Aemon put his hand on his broadsword and raised his commanding voice. 'You two men,' he said, 'have come free of your senses. Gerath's word does not outrank that of the princess herself. Stand aside or answer to me as traitors.'"

"Fight!" whisper-yelled Tam. He made a *psssht* sound and mimed drawing a sword.

"The guards stared at Sir Aemon, their faces blank of emotion. It didn't take Aemon long to realize the men had been ensorcelled. The knight gave Princess Isabelle a pointed stare. She knew he meant to distract them. Sir Aemon backed up two steps and ran at the guardsmen. They tried to draw their swords, but he jumped on the guards and took them both to the floor, all three men sliding off on the ice. Princess Isabelle rushed for the door, but found it locked."

Emma gasped.

"Kinnae princess pick 'a lock?" asked Kimber.

Nan chuckled. "She doesn't know how... nor does she have the tools to do so."

"Oh." Kimber nodded.

"The key swung from the belt of one of the guards as they rolled about on the floor." Nan raised her hands, pantomiming a fistfight. "Sir Aemon did not want to hurt them, since he felt sure that dark magic had touched their minds. Isabelle ran in, heedless of the fists flying about, and seized the key. The man bellowed and punched her, knocking Princess Isabelle to the ground."

Tam's jaw fell open. "That's bad! Why's he hittin' a girl?"

"Dark magic," whispered Emma.

"Isabelle did not lose her grip on the key, and tore it away when he knocked her down. She scrambled to crawl off, but he grabbed her leg." Nan seized Kimber's ankle, making her squeal and kick at the blanket. "She kicked at him until her boot came off, and ran slipping and sliding back to her father's bedchamber."

"She's walkin' on ice wif a bare foot?" asked Tam.

Nan nodded. "Yes, Tam. The princess was so worried about her father, she didn't even feel the cold. She unlocked the door and shoved it open. Wind howled in the window, turning the royal bedchamber into a wintry nightmare. Inches of snow gathered on the floor, and a great cloud of unnatural gloom blotted out everything except the king upon his bed. A man only a little older than your father lay still and grey, looking like an ancient warrior laid to rest."

"No!" said Emma, louder than she'd intended, but not quite a yell. "He can't be dead! He just can't!" She sniffled as a heavy feeling fell over her heart. "All she did to get that potion… she can't not save him."

Kimber chewed on the blanket while Tam glared at both of them and made a 'shh' gesture.

"It's all right, Emma." Nan smiled. "The king remained alive… but just barely."

Emma exhaled with relief.

Nan's eyes gleamed with mischief. "His skin had gone pale and grey, covered in wrinkles. Every breath he drew creaked like the bones of an old house in the wind. 'Father?' whispered Isabelle as she hurried to his side. 'I've brought you something that will help.' Still, the king did not move, staring at the ceiling. She took the potion from her satchel and stooped over him to pour it into his mouth."

Emma clenched two fistfuls of blanket and held her breath.

"The potion bottle neared the king's lips and the glowing liquid gleamed in his eyes. At last the king moved, shifting his gaze not at Isabelle, but past her as he summoned the strength to give a faint wheeze."

Emma and Kimber squeaked out their noses at the same time.

"Did Sir Aemon beat up the evil guards?" asked Tam.

"Princess Isabelle spun around"—Nan flung her arms into the air—"as Advisor Gerath leapt from the shadows with a knife!"

Kimber screamed. Emma gulped.

Tam growled. "She's gonna thump him!"

"Princess Isabelle let out a shout of surprise and jumped to the side. Gerath lunged past her, and stabbed his dagger down into the mattress. Her bare foot slid out from under her on the ice and she landed on her backside, but Sir Aemon ran in before Gerath could attack her. The Advisor pointed at Sir Aemon, and with a great *crack*, a bolt of lightning flew from his outstretched finger, striking the knight in the chest." Nan poked Tam over the heart.

Emma shivered and burst into tears at the memory of the wizard almost killing her mother. "Mama…"

Nan drew a breath to say something, but Mama ran over and sat on the edge of the bed. Emma dove into a hug.

"Mother, what are you telling them?" Mama patted Emma on the back.

She sniffled into her mother's dress, wracked with guilt. "I'm sorry, Mama."

"Ahh…" Nan nodded with realization. "The part of the story where Gerath gives Aemon a zap."

Kimber patted Emma's back as well, kneeling close. Tam held her hand.

"I suppose that's a good place to stop then," muttered Nan.

"Aww," said Tam.

"You'as cannae leave 'et off 'ere." Kimber kneaded the blanket in her lap. "Wha' happen'd?"

Emma wiped her nose on the back of her arm. "It's all right, Nan. I'm fine."

"Don't carry around so much guilt," whispered Mama. "It's a stone you'll never be able to lift."

Emma cuddled up in her mother's lap.

Nan and Mama exchanged a quick look and the old one nodded. "Very well." She settled in her chair before clearing her throat. "Now where was I? Oh… yes. The room flashed with a bright stroke of lightning, but even that did not pierce the darkness lurking in the corners. Sir Aemon grunted and fell to one knee. Princess Isabelle leapt to her feet and drew her shortsword, but a chainmail-clad man grabbed her from behind, pinning her arms to her sides."

"Oh no," whispered Kimber.

Emma shivered, clutching her hands together at her chin and whispered, "Advisor Gerath…"

Mama kept stroking her hair.

Tam raspberried. "He's mean. He made Em cry."

Nan nodded. "Yes… he is mean. The wicked Advisor Gerath waved his knife at Princess Isabelle, walking closer. 'You couldn't just be a nice, sweet princess, could you?' Strong light from the potion in her hands cast his face in deep shadows that made him seem older. The closer he got, the deeper his lips curled into a sneer. 'You had to go and make everything difficult. Do you not wish to be queen? You could have been a docile little puppet, comfortable on the throne… but I'm afraid you've gone and made yourself an obstacle.'" Nan reached out and put a finger to Kimber's throat, making her lean back, eyes wide. "Gerath touched his cold knife to her chin. She froze, no longer struggling with the guard lest it cut her. 'And obstacles need to be removed.'"

Emma sniveled. Kimber climbed into Mama's lap with her.

Nan leaned forward, looming. "A *scrape* of metal to the left broke the silence as the second guard approached Aemon, drawing his blade."

Tam's eyes widened, but he didn't make a sound.

Emma snuggled into Mama's arms.

Nan gestured as if pulling a broadsword from her belt. "Sir Aemon roared and jumped to his feet. He drew his blade and stalled the ensorcelled guardsman's strike. Advisor Gerath scowled, and whispered a magical incantation. Princess Isabelle couldn't move her arm enough to swing her sword, but as soon as the advisor's attention shifted to Aemon, she dropped it and yanked a dagger from her belt—the dagger Sir Aemon told her never to be without."

"Yes!" whispered Tam.

Kimber squealed out her nose with anticipation.

Emma smiled.

The old one brought her fist down. "Princess Isabelle drove the blade into the leg of the man holding her. Magical darkness formed around Gerath's arm, collecting into a mass of netherworld power. The guard screamed and released Isabelle, falling to the side. She flipped her dagger about and hurled it as hard as she could"—Nan made a throwing gesture—"piercing Gerath's heart."

Emma bounced in Mama's lap, grinning.

"The magic around his arm dissipated before it could fly to Sir Aemon. Advisor Gerath let out a harsh wheeze and collapsed dead on the floor.

Both guardsmen fell asleep once the spell released their minds. Princess Isabelle rushed to the bed. She forced her father's mouth open and poured the glowing liquid past his teeth, as fast as she could without spilling it all over him."

All three children stared at Nan in rapt silence.

Nan smiled. "After she fed him the whole potion, she stepped back, clutching the bottle to her heart. At first, nothing happened"—The children drooped with disappointment—"but after a little while, the king's lips returned to their normal color. Warmth radiated outward from his face, spreading over his body until the grey, and the wrinkles, had vanished. A sound like a thousand windows breaking filled the air, and all the ice turned to fog."

"Yay!" Kimber clapped.

Emma beamed up at Mama, thrilled the king survived.

"But the necromancer wasn't done." Nan raised an eyebrow. "Advisor Gerath flew to his feet, Princess Isabelle's knife still in his breast. He raised a lifeless arm to point at the king and spoke in a voice that came from everywhere at once, too deep to belong to a simple man. 'This vessel was but a mere tool. I shall return, and my wrath will be most dire!' Sir Aemon leapt forward with a cry of 'foul wretch!' He took off the demon's head with one swing, and the Advisor fell, dead once more.' The king sat up, his strength returned, and embraced his daughter."

Tam tilted his head. "Is Sir Aemon and Isabelle gonna married?" He stuck his tongue out.

"No, silly," said Emma. "Sir Aemon is too old to marry her."

Tam looked at her. "She's fifteen; that's old."

Nan chuckled. "No, Tam... Sir Aemon doesn't marry the princess. He's only a knight, not a royal. Besides, Isabelle thinks of him more as an older brother... the way Emma looks after you. You wouldn't want to marry Emma, would you?"

Tam shook his head furiously. "No."

Emma laughed, as did Mama and Nan.

"'Cause all she knows how ta cook is bread an' cookies." The earnest seriousness on his face got Nan cackling.

Emma scowled and poked him. "There's more to getting married than knowing how to make food."

"Food's most important." Tam folded his arms.

"The boy's got a point," said Da from over by the fireplace.

Mama scoffed, fighting not to smile. "Oh, does he now?"

Emma laughed.

"All right, you three." Mama lifted Emma and set her on the bed. "Time to go to sleep."

"Yes, Mama." Emma crawled back into her spot by the wall and snuggled into the blankets.

Kimber huddled up next to her while Tam sprawled out where Mama and Da would eventually be.

Thrilled that Princess Isabelle had saved the king's life, Emma closed her eyes and drifted off to sleep.

5

NEEMA

*E*mma held her breakfast, a long piece of toasted bread slathered in berry jam, in both hands and munched. Mama had cut Tam's piece into little bite-sized bits, which he popped in his mouth as fast as he could chew. Kimber had asked to have hers cut only in half. Over the past few days, she had at last slowed down, no longer eating as if she expected someone to take her food away before she could finish it. Mama and Da picked at an assortment of apple slices, cheese, and cold sausage, while Nan enjoyed jammed bread.

Eww. Emma made a face at the idea of tasting apples and cheese at the same time.

"I'll be making a stew today for dinner," said Nan.

Da grinned. "The sun will take forever to recede then."

"Hah." Nan chuckled.

"Liam always did fancy your stew, Mother." Mama studied a bit of cheese.

"Bah, yours is just as good." Nan winked. "Em, you'll be helping. We'll start soon."

Emma blinked. "We're eating now…"

"Aye, but it takes all day to cook." Nan finished the last of her bread and dusted her hands off.

"Pity I won't be home to enjoy the wonderful smell all day," said Da. "I'm sure you'll drive the workers to frenzy."

"You may as well invite them to stay for dinner." Nan stood. "There'll be more than enough for everyone."

"A grand idea." Da put a piece of cheese atop a piece of apple, and ate it.

Emma looked away. Nan retrieved the large cauldron from the fireplace hook and lugged it out back to rinse. Tam finished his breakfast and flopped on the floor by the bed, Stick Knight and Shrub Dragon once again locked in their endless battle. A few minutes later, Nan brought the cauldron back in and set it upon the hook, swung out into the room.

Soon, Da left to attend to his duties with the Watch. Mama decided to keep Tam out of the workers' way by bringing him with her on her daily rounds while Emma and Kimber stayed behind to help Nan cook.

"Kimber, be a dear and count out ten potatoes, five onions, a dozen carrots, five turnips, and ten mushrooms," said Nan.

"Aye." Kimber darted over to the cabinets.

Nan shuffled over to the table and readied a cutting board. "Em, fetch two buckets of water. We'll likely need more, but two will get us started."

"Yes, Nan." Emma grinned and ran out the back door.

She plucked a pail from the porch and hurried over to the water pump. After setting it under the spigot, she grasped the lever with both hands and worked it up and down, grunting. Water gushed into the bucket, a bit spraying her legs.

"Emma!" cried a faint voice. A trail of white glow shot out of the grass and zipped up to hover in front of her face. "Emma!"

She blinked at a tiny woman floating before her, wearing a short-skirted dress of leaf-shaped pieces of light that made her dark tan skin seem even darker. Silver butterfly wings fluttered, dripping flecks of energy. Melodic tones like muted bells filled the air around her. Long, straight silver-white hair hung down to the little woman's knees, and her eyes resembled glimmering sapphires. Emma blinked, realizing she stared at the faerie she'd freed from the lantern.

"Neema?"

"Is Neema, yes!" she chirped and pointed into the woods. "Helps we need you from."

Emma pulled the pump handle down again, sending a surge of water into the bucket and all over her feet. "What's wrong?"

"Faeries help needing you. Trouble finding us. Queen talk to please."

"Neema…" Emma bit her lip, worry growing heavy in her gut. "I promised my parents I wouldn't run off alone again. I shouldn't go without telling them."

The faerie zipped closer, grabbed her left thumb, and pulled. "Please going with. You not alone be with Neema. Neema adult. Few minutes back in be."

Emma blinked. "Umm. What?"

"Dying and danger. Faeries pain having. Protect can Emma the faeries. Not alone." Neema patted herself on the chest. "Adult. Protecting Emma. Return minutes in few."

She let the pump handle go up. "You're saying that something is hurting the faeries, but you think it will only take a few minutes?"

Neema nodded. "Yes!"

"How can I fix something that's hurting faeries in only a few minutes?" Emma took a step toward the house. "Nan will know what to do."

"Wait." Neema tugged on her shoulder until she made eye contact. "Emma druid is bigger much than faerie. Magic we have like different. Emma danger the stop. Faerie queen happy be." Neema's pleading expression picked at her heart. "Minutes, a few. Promise. Saving the lives."

Concern crashed headlong into guilt. The little woman's gemstone eyes seemed to grow enormous with a look of pleading. Emma couldn't bear the thought of anything wanting to hurt someone so cute. The idea that maybe she didn't need to bother Nan with this became stronger. *It'll only take a few minutes.* "I..." She looked back at the house. "Let me tell Nan that—"

"Time there no is. Death and dying." Neema burst into tears, and her wings rained specks of glimmering energy. "Return minutes few. Walk from house far is not. Minutes few. Promise."

All of a sudden, Emma's heart grew heavy with sorrow. If she waited too long, faeries could die. Her desire to run to Nan faded. She could help them herself. Hands on her hips, she whispered, "You promise? I'm going to count. If we go too far away for me to see the house, I'm going to go back to get Nan."

Neema nodded. "Helping, please."

Not telling Nan made her uneasy, but concern for the little faerie overpowered her hesitation. She might only be seven inches tall, but Neema had the shape of a grown woman. She had to be an adult. *I'm not running off alone. I'll stay with her. It's probably nothing, but if it's serious, I'm going to get Nan.* Emma walked in the direction the small woman tried to pull her. With each step, her worry about getting in trouble lessened as a building need to protect the faeries took over. She tried to figure out if going would be 'foolish,' but her mind could only seem to settle on worry over the adorable faeries.

Neema rolled over in midair, flying forward while continuing to tug her along by one finger. Energy streaming from her wings sent tingles up Emma's left arm, causing an involuntary shiver. The faerie led her across the meadow to the nearer grove that held the giant cherry tree. Neema continued past it, heading deeper into the forest.

Emma glanced over her shoulder at the house, a little too small for comfort. "I'm going too far from home. I should get Nan."

"Being here is." Neema pointed at a huge pine.

"You live in that?" Emma followed her, approaching the massive tree.

Rather than stopping, Neema went around to the left toward a circular arrangement of bright colors. A rainbow of shin-high flowers formed a ring large enough for Da to lay down inside. Most of them had metallic-looking silver teardrop beads hanging from bundles of white petals. Various smaller flowers of pink, blue, and yellow weaved among them, creating a quite obvious ring.

Neema closed her eyes and emitted a puff of yellow energy that burst outward from her tiny body in a sparkling cloud. The glimmering dust blew like smoke upon the wind, settling on the flowers, which wavered as if in response.

Emma stepped over the ring, and let out a gasp of surprise when the air went from autumn chill to a warm summer breeze in an instant. A wash of strong floral fragrance mixed with a trace of mint fell over her—and the woods changed.

She blinked in awe at the forest ahead: lichen-covered trees with ropey roots towered into the sky, making her feel as if she'd shrank to the size of a faerie. The distant roar of a waterfall came from the left, and all around her, the trill of musical birds echoed. Soft emerald moss covered almost every inch of ground except for the dirt within the circle at her feet. Emma had to squint at the overwhelming *green* of this forest, so bright it hurt her eyes. It looked nothing like Widowswood.

She turned to peer back over her shoulder.

Where her home had been, miles and miles of verdant woodland continued without end. The strange feeling that she didn't need to bother Nan weakened. It seemed as though she'd done something she shouldn't have. Fear and guilt got her legs quivering.

Oh, no... What did I do?

6

A TINY PLEA

*E*mma spun around, gazing in awe at the strange forest. The smallest tree in sight could've had a peasant's hovel carved into its trunk and still had enough width left over that it wouldn't have died. Rather than sit upon the ground like normal oaks or pines, they split apart into bundles of round roots about six feet above the forest floor, all the trees woven together in a dense carpet. Some of the root domes had enough space beneath the trucks for a person to live in, others bundled too dense to find entry. Roots ranged from as thin as her wrist to six- or seven-feet thick. Without being able to fly, travelling any distance from the circle would require quite a bit of climbing and crawling.

"Where are we?" whispered Emma. "I have to go home. I promised my parents…"

"Worrying not." Neema tugged on her hand. "Knowing you are gone they won't. Return minutes few you will." A puff of white-silver light burst from her wings with a trio of melodic bell-tones.

The faerie seemed so sure that whatever she needed to do would only take minutes… Emma cast a worried glance about at the strange forest, but nothing about Neema's demeanor suggested she lied. As Emma stared back in the direction they'd come, it seemed all of a sudden like a good idea to go. She glanced again at Neema, who flashed a pleading smile with huge, teary eyes. *Of course* Mama and Nan would want her to help the faeries. Her worry about leaving home shrank to near nothing. Though she knew it *should* bother her, it didn't at all. A growing need to protect Neema and her people took its place.

That's what she would—no, *must*—do… as a druid. She had to protect the forest and everything in it, even if this place wasn't quite *her* forest. Mama wouldn't be upset with her. She didn't run off *alone.* She had an adult with her, even if that adult happened to be seven inches tall.

"All right…" Emma balled her fists at her sides. "But we have to hurry up. I don't want to make my family scared."

Neema glided ahead. Emma hurried for a few steps before reaching a root so thick it came up to her chest. She jumped up onto pale green lichen that felt like velvet, and scrambled over the top. On the other side, a hollow formed where three huge roots touched held a pool. The faerie glided over the water, which looked only waist-deep to Emma, the bottom crisscrossed with much smaller roots coated in dark-green algae.

She lowered herself into the water, not caring if her dress got wet. Warm, slippery, slime mushed under her steps and oozed between her toes as she crossed the pool. Emma pulled herself up on the opposite side and jumped to the dry forest floor. The dress Nan had made her dried in seconds, the water dripping off the hem. She gawked down at the blue fabric, amazed at Nan's magic. When she looked up, the faerie had vanished.

"Where are you?" asked Emma.

Neema popped up from behind a dense root cluster a short distance ahead.

I don't think I'm going to be back in a few minutes. She swallowed a lump of guilt and trudged over, peering up at the rounded underside of a root as big as a normal tree trunk. Having no way to climb it, she got down and belly crawled under it.

"Ugh." Emma dragged herself past a tight spot, shimmied on her hands and knees for a few feet, then stood. "What is putting the faeries in danger?"

Neema flitted over and sat on her left shoulder. "Attacking are animals. Having rage not natural. Eating try they do. Have to, but killing want we don't. Being not their fault."

While climbing and ducking roots, Emma's brain ground on the faerie's words like a millstone. She found a long, straight root that ran in the same direction, so she climbed up on top of it and held her arms out to the sides while walking heel-to-toe along a soft carpet of velvety moss flecked with tiny flowers. The elevated path made travel easier for a little while, skipping over other roots. Eventually, Neema pointed off to the side, so Emma jumped down.

The faerie's wings fluttered during the brief fall, tickling Emma's neck and cheek, and making her laugh.

"Being funny is not." Neema pouted.

"You tickled me…" Emma offered an apologetic smile. "Sorry. So… animals are attacking you? What kind?"

"Wolves. Foxes. Bears. Cats."

Emma held her hands about housecat size apart. "Cats?"

"Bigger," said Neema.

"Lions?"

Neema shrugged. "Riding for big enough you."

Emma stopped walking. "I really should tell Nan. This sounds dangerous."

"Please!" Neema's eyes seemed to grow huge again. "Being here is already you. Asking dangerous do you not. Talking animals druid."

"What if they don't listen to me?" Emma shivered at the idea of a lion finding her annoying. The wolves, at least, she hoped would sense her kinship with Ylithir.

"Protect will Neema you. Faerie small but not weak." The tiny woman hugged the side of her head. "Letting not harm find you. Talking Nymira Queen you to, and know the everything."

"All right. I will talk to your queen, but if it is too much for me, I have to go home. I'm sure Mama or Nan will help you."

Neema pointed. "There. Wanting we not do to kill, so Neema remember to animals you talk. Ask stop to them not attack faeries so they do."

"You want me to ask the animals why they're attacking you and get them to stop?"

"Yes!" Neema grinned. "Want go to war, Silverbells some do. Want queen animals to killing not but." She twirled a finger around her little pointed ear. "Being not in the senses are they. Belongs them not to the blame, queen says."

Kimber is going to be jealous. "I'll help if I can. Do faeries like tea?"

Neema grinned. "Faeberry tea!"

"Umm." Emma cringed. "Any other kind?"

"Too being mint good is."

"I like mint tea." Emma hauled herself over another large root.

After what felt like an hour of traversing the frustrating terrain, Emma got a sense that the roots formed walls on either side of a sort of pathway. It required a lot of weaving and turning, but if she stayed at about the midway point between trees, the larger roots formed a corridor she could follow with a minimum of heavy climbing.

Purple and blue seeped into the bright green up ahead, and soon, Emma found herself walking among a forest of mushrooms the size of huts.

"Did you shrink me?" asked Emma.

"No." Neema tapped her chest. "Being this tall to me would you be if shrinking you I did."

"Wait, you *can* shrink me?"

Neema nodded. "Good not doing so done haven't it, but doing it I can. Want you only if. Don't can I do if not you want. Neema making tired it will."

Emma stared at the faerie for a few seconds, having no idea whatsoever what she just said.

A vast lake of glowing deep-blue water spread off to the left where a fallen mushroom formed a natural bridge over the river feeding it. Glowing-eyed creatures that resembled brown and white woodchucks the size of housecats peered out of the thick grass on the far side. All of them ducked out of sight as she got closer, and scrambled into the undergrowth. Emma climbed up onto the spongy trunk, which felt like walking on her bed. Arms raised for balance, she crossed. Aside from emitting dark-blue light, the clear water offered a perfect view of the riverbed. It looked too deep for her to stand in, but the glass-like surface suggested a slow current. Round fish, like apples with fins, glided about in no particular hurry. Brilliant yellow, striped with green, some even seemed to be looking at her as if wondering how a human got here.

Where am I? Oh... I've been gone for more than a few minutes. Nan is going to be worried and angry. Why didn't I go inside to get her? She was only a few steps away... She furrowed her brow at not being able to remember walking from her porch to the circle.

"Being sad don't. Helping are you the Faerie. Lives are you saving."

"I'm breaking my promise."

Neema shook her head. "Minutes. Taking the troubles Neema promise if you get."

Emma lowered herself to sit on the squishy mushroom once the bridge reached the far bank. She hesitated for a second before letting herself slide to land on soft dirt. This side of the river had different trees, without the chaotic roots. The dense, gnarled forest remained green and verdant, but offered much easier passage to those who lacked the ability to fly.

Hardened roots broke the ground here and there, anchoring trees so twisty they looked like one of Nan's towels in the middle of being wrung out. Long, wide branches started low to the ground and clustered dense, offering easy paths to climb up to their topmost heights.

Brilliant red birds glided by. Each had twin tails twice the length of their bodies that rippled like ribbons in the air behind them, the tips aglow with the light of embers. When one squawked at another, a small puff of flame spat from its beak.

Emma gasped.

"Arriving are almost we." Neema glided off her shoulder, leaving a sparkling trail of silvery-white energy hanging in the air.

Emma jogged after the trail. Within a few minutes, a strange ring of close-packed trees became apparent, as if magic had grown them as a wall around something. Yellow and green light with dashes of pink glowed from between the gaps, and the area rang with hundreds of soft bell tones.

The faerie zipped over to a space in the tree-wall, where a thick tangle of vines had grown into the shape of a gate full of intricate whorls and spirals. At the little woman's approach, the vines un-grew, crackling and creaking as they retreated to either side. Strands of brown curled back on themselves, clearing the passage. Emma slowed to a walk and crept closer to the wall that encircled an area a little larger than Eoghn's Inn. Neema smiled and sat once more on her shoulder.

"Welcome to home Silverbell Faeries of."

Emma grasped the tree on the left, and peered in. The sight beyond stole her breath away.

From where she stood, a faint dirt path led forward, becoming a circular walkway around a crystalline fountain. Dozens of Silverbell Faeries, glowing spots of colored light, glided around or rested within a tiny city on the scale of dollhouses. Their hair varied in color from black to white, pastel blue, teal, silver, and cherry red. Each faerie's wing color matched their hair, and left trails of magical energy in midair behind them. Flower-bearing vines covered the inner face of the wall-trees, so thick with lichen Emma felt like she stood at the bottom of a massive well.

Individual buildings nestled among the forest, both freestanding as well as hollowed out from their trunks. Windows and doors spotted most of the trees around the edge, with steps made from shelf mushrooms. Acorn-shaped flowers dangled from thin stems, glowing like miniature streetlamps. Rivulets of water ran from leaves in tiered waterfalls that collected in pools held by cup-shaped purple mushrooms, some large enough that she could bathe within them.

Beyond the fountain stood a massive tree with a hollowed space at its trunk. Tiny doors and windows corkscrewed around it, going up as high as she could see. Within the gap at the base, a platform of round stones lined the floor of a throne room that appeared made for dolls. Grape-sized flowers hung from the walls inside, emitting pale green light like tiny lamps. A faerie, her bright red hair so long it would drag upon the ground if she walked, sat upon a chair of amethyst, regarding Emma with a mixture of surprise and curiosity.

Emma's jaw hung open.

"Welcoming you to the Elder Grove," said Neema.

Wow. She stared, speechless.

Neema tugged on Emma's hand for a few seconds before zipping around behind her and flying bodily into Emma's back over and over, trying to shove her. "Forward going. Queen talking to."

"It's so beautiful." Emma stared at all the faeries circling about, the great trees and delicate spires of miniature buildings.

About a quarter of the faeries flew; some hovered, while the rest lounged on leaves, mushrooms, or the edges of various natural pools.

Neema darted into Emma's face and slapped at her cheeks. "Waking up."

Emma went to grab her, but the faerie zipped to the left with a burst of faerie dust that made her sneeze.

All the bell chimes stopped at once. Dozens of Silverbells all froze in their tracks, staring at Emma in horror as if she were a ravenous lion who'd found a coop full of chickens. A group with spears hurried forward after a momentary hesitation.

She raised a hand and offered a wave. "Umm. Hello. I'm Emma." She curtseyed. "May I please talk to your queen?"

A pink-haired woman bearing a spear tipped with a sharpened chip of amethyst floated up to her face and gave Neema a disappointed look.

Neema chattered rapidly in a high-pitched language Emma couldn't understand. After a tiny sigh, the guard-faerie shifted her spear to her left hand and gestured at Emma to move forward.

7

THE ELDER GROVE

*E*mma offered a polite smile to the guard-faerie, not entirely sure how much of a threat a six-inch spear might be. She crept forward into the tiny city, placing her feet with care to avoid stepping on anything that would break.

Two of the other faeries with spears zipped up into Emma's face, brandishing their weapons, their wings glowing with sparking energy. They appeared to disagree with the first guard who waved her in.

Neema chattered at them in the faerie tongue, too fast and indecipherable to tell where one word stopped and the next began. The faerie guards snapped back at her, gesturing at Emma. While she couldn't tell what they said, she got the feeling they didn't want her here. Unsure if she should leave or go inside, she stood still, glancing around at the group of tiny, shouting people encircling her head. Neema flailed her arms rapidly, gestured at Emma, and rambled in a pleading tone.

A deeper voice, more akin to that of a small human woman, emanated from the base of the giant hollow tree at the innermost part of the city. All the armed faeries glided back from Emma, and no longer held their spears in a threatening way. After speaking a few words in the faerie's tongue, the voice switched to the language of Emma's home. "Come forward, human. I am Queen Nymira of the Silverbell Faeries, and I grant your request to have an audience."

Emma gazed at the fountain covered in curious faeries. There appeared to be an even mix of men and women, but not one appeared to be a child or old. Every one of them looked about Mama's age. Were they human, she'd have thought them all between eighteen and twenty. People often commented her mother looked much younger than her twenty-seven years.

She tiptoed around the fountain to a lush patch of blue-green grass on the other side, peering at a regal faerie woman sitting upon a throne within the hollowed tree. Aside from extremely long flame red hair and a delicate crown with three emeralds as big as peas, the faerie queen didn't appear much different from the others: no taller, no older, her wings the same size, and she didn't wear a massive gown as she'd imagined a faerie queen would.

The guard-faeries hovered close, as if expecting her to be dangerous. Six more faeries, four female and two male, stood in a row between Emma and the queen, clutching spears, as if they'd be able to stop a human from attacking. All had similar dark tan skin, and seemed distrustful of her.

"Thank you for allowing me to see your home." Emma stepped from the grass onto a patch of soft green moss, and knelt with her knees inches away from the edge where the living carpet met the throne chamber's floor of flat stones. She bowed forward like the characters did in Nan's stories when meeting royalty.

More faeries collected around her and behind. One or two seemed familiar, perhaps from the group that had come to enjoy the treats. Some risked touching her. She straightened from her bow, but remained kneeling, and smiled her most earnest smile around at the group.

One male faerie gawked at her. "Huge."

"Human," whispered a woman next to him.

The faerie on the throne spoke in a slow, confident tone, her voice deeper than the others. "I am Queen Nymira, and this is my realm. I would know why you have come here."

"I've been told you are in danger. Animals are attacking and they're not in their right senses. Neema visited me and asked for help."

"Larger should humans I thought be," said a male guard with black hair in front of her knee.

The pink-haired female faerie with the spear landed next to him and tapped him on the arm. When he looked at her, she indicated her own shapely chest, then pointed at Emma. "Child she is, Rin. A young child."

She floated up to hover in front of Neema. "Bringing a human child here for why? Time wasting you are."

"Helping she can!" yelled Neema. "Pimlin, please!"

Pimlin shook her head. "Not should you have her here brought. Too young."

"An adult human wouldn't have come here," said another male with long snow-white hair.

Neema stared at him. "Imril, she can help!"

"What do you believe you can do here, child?" asked Nymira.

Neema zipped in front of Emma's face. "My Queen, lantern released me this child did from."

"This is the one you spoke of?" asked Nymira.

Neema glided down, alighting on her feet in front of the throne. She sank to kneel, and bowed her head. "Yes. My wings she saved."

The mood among the faeries shifted in an instant. Suspicion and distrust exploded into glee. In seconds, Emma wore a coat of adoring, hugging faeries, except for Nymira and her guards.

It took all of Emma's concentration not to giggle from the sensation of fifty or sixty sets of faerie wings flitting against her. "Neema told me that animals are trying to hurt your people. She thinks I can talk to them and learn why, maybe stop them."

A female faerie with pastel-blue hair and wings glided up to Emma, staring into her left eye as if it were a mirror. "Blue pretty. Saving Neema life, thanking." The woman hugged her face.

Emma raised her hands cupped, and the tiny woman accepted the seat. A sense of excitement filled her at getting to hold such a creature; she stiffened, not wanting to accidentally hurt the faerie. "Hello."

"There is a dark energy driving the denizens of the woods to become mad with rage." Nymira bowed her head. "We have had to do things I regret to protect ourselves. My people have lived in harmony with the forest for thousands of years. This imbalance cannot be tolerated. Pimlin is correct. You are a child, and despite your being human, I question if you would even be capable of assisting us."

"Yes! Helping Emma can. Talking so know why attack. Change mind even?" Neema gasped and shrank to kneel again. She muttered something in the faerie language that sounded distinctly like an apology.

Nymira waved at Neema with a slight smile. "I regret that our sister's enthusiasm for your assistance has brought you here. While you are many times our size, you remain a child. We will not fault you if you wish to return to your home right away."

Faeries continued to flit over to touch her hair or whisper thanks for freeing Neema from the lantern. A few of them appeared disappointed at the idea she may leave without helping them, but none more than Neema herself who teetered on the verge of tears.

I'm already going to get in trouble... what's a few more minutes? Emma sighed to herself. "I'm already here. I may as well try to help."

Neema perked up. After a brief adoring look, she zoomed up from the ground and hugged the side of Emma's head. "Oh! You thank!"

"You're..." Emma scrunched her left eye closed, unsure how to react to having a faerie adhered to her face. "Welcome."

Neema zipped around to stand on Emma's right shoulder, beaming.

"Very well," said the Faerie Queen. "Our warriors will protect you, but if, as I suspect, this threat eludes the abilities of a child, I will insist you be brought back to your home."

Emma bowed. "I understand."

8

MAWR

*D*ismissed from Queen Nymira's audience, Emma wandered along a path of purple glimmering stones around the crystalline fountain. Neema perched on her shoulder while a number of other Silverbell Faeries came and went as curiosity or whim took them.

The miniature city fascinated her. She marveled at doors high up the sides of trees with no stairs, patios with giant leaves for roofs, and elevated porches furnished with mushroom chairs. Some of their dwellings weren't even as tall as she. The miniature buildings did not have solid walls like human houses, rather grown from branches and vines woven together, forming intricate patterns. From one angle, the gaps between branches let her peer right inside, but three steps away, the walls appeared solid.

Emma forced herself to stop sightseeing. She had come here to help the faeries, and roaming around gawking wouldn't get her home any faster, nor would it help Neema. She circled once more, hunting for signs of what might be causing animals to attack. Finding nothing, she headed to the gate and outside the ring of trees that encircled the grove. No tiny homes existed beyond the barrier, though several faeries lounged or played on branches. As far as she could see, the too-green forest stretched in all directions, unlike any woodland she had ever heard of.

Standing there watching the faeries, Emma found herself a touch disoriented and overwhelmed, doubting her eyes that such a massive, beautiful forest could exist. Her situation didn't make much sense. Why would faeries need a human's help, especially that of a child? With all Kimber's talk of faeries, she wondered if she'd fallen asleep at the water pump and simply dreamed all of this. The familiar sense of kinship she'd known with Widowswood had ceased as soon as she'd stepped over the circle of flowers. These woods radiated another kind of energy, noticeably stronger. The trees pulsed with potent magic that sent waves of tingles over her skin from toes to forehead.

"I'm not dreaming."

"Dreaming not," said Neema. "Help us Emma know I can you."

She continued exploring, hunting around for something—anything that looked important, but didn't have the first idea of where to look. Her instinct sent her on a spiraling path, drifting gradually farther away from the grove as she went around in circles. Soon after she passed the gate for the fourth time, she stopped short at the sight of a burn mark on the side of one of the great trees. If she put her hand on the trunk and walked around it, she could likely count to thirty before she reached where she started. Emma crept up to the spot, a patch at her chest level where something had scorched the coating of emerald lichen black and cored a pit in the wood deep enough to hold her fist.

"What did this?"

Neema bowed her head. "Attacked by bear. Faerie magic to protect. Hurt animal." She scrunched up her face in thought for a few seconds before she raised her arms and wiggled her fingers. "Fighting magic. Like wizard. Why is Emma we helping need. Silverbells arcane magic. Meadow Faeries magic have like Emma, but far away live, and games play more than help. Act like child do more than Emma they."

"A… faerie did this?" Emma stared at the damage to the tree. For all their cuteness, perhaps these small people *were* dangerous—or able to protect her.

"Yes. Pimlin maybe or Imril. Oldest being they are. Magic hit angry bear, out other side go it and burn tree."

Emma's heart sank. "They killed the bear?"

"No," said Neema in a half-whisper while shaking her head. "Angrier it get. Chased into woods, hill down it fell. Take long to climb out, fled so we."

"A faerie threw magic at this bear, and the magic went in one side and out the other." Emma gestured as if a bolt struck her back and emerged from her front. "Came out and hit the tree… and the bear was still alive?"

Neema nodded.

A hint of fear made Emma shiver. She squatted and looked around for signs of blood, but aside from the burn mark and a few more like it, found nothing. *Maybe it's like the way a ghost walks through walls.* The image in her mind changed from a bloody mess to a streak of light that didn't leave a mark on the bear.

What am I doing? She walked a little more, stepping around roots and bright red flowers she didn't recognize, and didn't trust to touch. *Nymira is right. I'm a little girl. What can I do?* Emma folded her arms and tried not to think about the disappointed look that would take over Mama's face when she found out Emma had gone off on her own again. The last time, she'd almost gotten her mother killed. She let out a silent sigh. *The faeries don't want to bring Mama here. Is she too big for this place? Oh, what would Mama do if she were here?*

She crouched again, looking for tracks of any kind. "Do the animals always attack from the same direction?"

Neema pointed into the distance, past the grove. "From there."

"How do they attack?" Emma stood and walked where the faerie pointed, keeping her gaze on the ground and trees, searching for clues.

"Claws or biting," said Neema.

Emma stopped, and hung her head. "No… I mean… do they hide and jump out at you? Do they rush out in the open? Many at once?"

"Oh. Being I sorry am. Changes for animal. Runs in roaring the bear. Sneaking foxes from the dark. Dropping from trees the snakes."

Snakes? Emma froze statue still. After a second, she edged her head backward until she could peer up into the branches above. "There's snakes?"

"Yes. Were three. Pimlin, Raa, and Fila…" Neema hesitated, and whispered, "killed them."

"Oh." Emma frowned.

"Scared so much, too much magic used." Neema shook her head. "Burst to itty bitties the snakes."

Emma shivered. A few steps later, she spotted a track. She squatted and studied what appeared to be a wolf print about the size of her palm. A series of burn marks on the ground nearby made her think the faeries tried to scare it off rather than hurt it. *This is too much for me.* She glanced off to her right at the Elder Grove, too far away for comfort. *I should've listened to Mama.*

"Eated Glyn this wolf." Neema sniffled, sparkling luminous tears rolled from her sapphire eyes.

"What?" whispered Emma. "I'm sorry if I don't understand you."

"Faerie. Glyn. He was Neema friend." She reached up and grasped her right wing. "Bite on wing, rip. Glyn magic go back to forest magic." The little woman bowed her head and sobbed into her hands.

Emma scooped Neema off her shoulder and cradled her like a beloved doll. "I'm so sorry." She tried to pat her on the back soft enough not to hurt. *I want to help, but... what can I do?*

"Chased away the wolf." Neema wiped her eyes, but couldn't stop crying. "Wanted not to kill did Glyn, so did what he wanted the others."

Her throat tight with a lump, Emma found herself on the verge of tears as well. How full of love for animals must these faeries be that they would try not to kill a wolf who had just murdered one of their own? Neema's sadness radiated from her, as contagious as a yawn. She wandered forward, lost in a swirl of sorrow, worry, and fear.

Snap.

Emma stopped and spun around, sweeping her gaze over the forest. "What was that?"

Neema glided out of her hands, floating up to hover at the level of a man's head. She scanned the woods in a slow turn for a few seconds before leaning forward to squint. Another loud *snap* came from the direction Neema faced. Emma stared into the trees. In seconds, she spotted a moving shadow.

"There's something over there." Emma edged to her left, taking cover behind a tree.

She peered around the side, watching the forest where the darkness had moved. A sudden chill ran down her back, numbing her fingers. She shivered, clinging tighter to the tree. For no reason she could understand, she knew something bad approached. A similar kind of malice to the Banderwigh's presence drew near, but it didn't have the same *evil* feeling. More an unnatural power... like magic.

"Something's com—"

An immense reddish-brown bear trundled into view, emerging from a dense wall of branches that cracked and snapped out of his way. On all fours, he would've been eye to glowing red eye with a warhorse had there been one nearby. The size of his head, Emma could've crawled into his mouth and been swallowed whole. She sucked in a gasp, but forced herself not to make a sound.

The bear, evidently hearing her sharp intake of breath, stared straight at her.

Emma screamed.

Red light within his eyes grew brighter. He faced her and let off a roar that shook leaves from the trees and echoed far into the woods. Tendrils of drool waved from fangs bigger than daggers, fluttering in the windblast of his bellow. Emma dove onto the nearest branch, pulling herself up as fast as she could move her arms and legs. Branch after branch, she climbed, refusing to look down.

After an eternity, the tree shuddered from the force of an impact. Emma's feet slipped off the next branch she stepped on, and for a second, she dangled by her hands. Two pastel-blue squirrel-like creatures fell past her, tumbling from higher up. They thrust their arms and legs out and glided on membranes, sailing to another nearby tree where they clung, chittering angrily at the bear. Wailing in fright, she kicked out and got her foot on another branch, shifted her weight, and pulled herself up.

The bear roared again.

Emma wrapped her arms and legs around a branch and held on, not a second before the monstrous creature slammed himself into the tree again. After screaming her lungs empty for the second time, she risked a peek toward the ground. The bear stood on his hind legs, claws falling short of reaching her by a good ways. From her perch, Emma had a great view straight down a terrifyingly large throat.

Neema floated a few inches above her head. Though she seemed to be speaking, only a faint high-pitched warble reached Emma's ability to think and understand.

The bear raked his claws into the wood, growling. He leaned up tall, then let his weight crash against the tree, trying to knock Emma from her perch. Far weaker than the creature's initial charge, the effort merely caused the great tree to sway a little. Given it had a trunk half again as big around as an outhouse, that the bear had moved it at all terrified her. Enraged, the creature gouged his shortsword-sized claws down the wood, peeling curly strands of bark away and lofting the strong smell of sap.

Mama! Nan! Da!

Emma screamed for help in her mind, too terrified to open her mouth.

"Emma!" yelled the faerie. She tugged on Emma's ear. "Try to talk to him!"

She wailed in terror. The bear continued assaulting the tree, but the great plant stood firm. A moment later, she stopped crying. Another moment later, she managed to get her breathing under control. Her first attempt to speak came out as a squeak.

Neema landed on her back. A strange tingle swept over her from head to toe. "There. Falling won't for you a little. Nothing weigh, but Neema touching have to stay."

Emma gradually relaxed her death grip on the branch. A light push upward caused her to float like a bubble. The utter oddity of that stole away the last of her fear. After a few rapid breaths, she found her voice. "Strixian, please grant me the Wildkin Whisper."

The orbs of light appeared as always, but larger and brighter than she'd grown accustomed to. They swirled around and sank into her body. She pushed herself upright and sat on the branch, watching the bear continue to attack the tree. With her magic cast, she understood him to be muttering, "kill" over and over.

"Mr. Bear?" asked Emma. "Why are you angry?"

"Hurt… need to kill… need to hurt." The bear shredded more wood from the trunk.

"Bear?" yelled Emma.

He stopped ravaging the tree, and raised his massive head to stare at her. "Want. Hurt. Yummy." He roared at her in anger.

"Bear, why are you so angry?"

The bear swatted at the tree with somewhat less energy, but continued to snarl and growl at her.

Nymira said something is making them angry… and they shouldn't be. Emma held her hands to her mouth so she could yell louder. "Bear, what is making you angry? Why do you want to hurt everything?"

He continued snarling and clawing at the tree.

"Slowed the bear. Speaking are you to him?" Neema smiled.

"I think so… he's confused. Really angry and doesn't know why." Emma rubbed her chin before raising her voice. "Bear. Stop being angry. Stop trying to hurt me."

He again gazed up at her, drooling. "Can not reach. Mmm. Tasty morsel. I must claw and bite and feed."

"You don't have to," said Emma.

The bear grunted and resumed raking at the wood.

Emma tapped her foot on air. *He's angry but doesn't understand…* She blinked. "Oh, I hope this works."

"What?" asked Neema.

"Nan says that a druid's magic is mostly asking the spirits for help…

not like wizards who learn patterns and have to say the exact right words. Please don't let me fall."

"Won't." Neema grabbed the back of her dress behind her neck.

Emma leaned forward enough to extend both arms toward the ravening bear. "Great Strixian, please grant this bear some of your wisdom. Allow him to understand that he does not need to be angry for no reason." She stared into the bear's eyes, focusing on her desire for him to break free from whatever magic drove him to anger.

Three thin wisps of green threaded away from each of her outstretched hands, creeping vines made of light rushing downward. They twined around each other, elongating toward the bear below. The animal paused to stare at them as if mesmerized. Her glowing vines spread wider when they reached him, cradling his head like a mother's hands caressing an infant's cheeks.

Something tugged at her from within, and a modest sense of tiredness came over her. The crimson glow flickered and faded, the bear's eyes returning to the normal black orbs a bear of enormous proportions ought to have.

"Worked did it?" asked Neema at a whisper.

Emma braced her left hand on the trunk for balance, feeling lightheaded. "I don't know... Strixian did *something*. It made me tired."

The bear dropped down to all fours and shook his head as dizzy as if he'd just sneezed a dozen times.

"Bear?" asked Emma. "Can you hear me?"

"What?" He lifted his head to peer at her. "I am not 'Bear.' I am Mawr."

Emma whispered past the back of her hand to Neema, "He sounds smarter."

The faerie nodded with a big grin.

"Why are you up there?" asked Mawr.

"Because I don't want to be eaten," said Emma.

Mawr tilted his great head to the side. "What would eat you?"

Emma blinked. "Umm. You were just trying to eat me."

"Oh, I think not." Mawr scoffed.

"Look at the tree." She held her right hand out in a claw-like pose. "I didn't do that."

Mawr sniffed at the damaged bark. "Oh... perhaps I..." He looked left and right before standing again on his hind legs and scratching his head. "How did I get here?"

"From over there." Emma pointed. "You saw me and wanted to eat me."

"I…"—Mawr let his weight pull him down; he landed on his forelegs with a heavy *thud* that startled birds from their branches—"remember being so angry."

Emma swung her feet back and forth. "Are you still angry?"

"I am confused," said Mawr, sounding tired. "Something affected my thoughts. Twisted them."

"Saying what is he?" asked Neema. "Hear I all growling is."

Emma eyed the forest floor. Being more than three stories off the ground would've frightened her if not for still feeling weightless. "Do you still want to hurt me?"

Mawr's large eyes widened with regret. "No… little one. Please forgive me. The rage within my heart was not my own. The faeries…"

"The faeries made you angry?" Emma squinted. "But they're so… innocent."

"No." Mawr swung his head side to side. "I wanted to hurt the faeries, but I do not know why. I… believe I did hurt them. Memories of falling."

Emma glanced at Neema, whispering, "Is that the same bear Pimlin zapped?"

The faerie shrugged. "Same the looks, but bears are bears."

"Are *all* the bears here that big?" Emma blinked.

Neema shook her head.

"If I climb down, will you promise not to hurt me?"

Mawr stood on two legs, and bowed. "I will not hurt you, tiny human. Forgive me for frightening you. I will"—he glanced toward the Elder Grove—"I must… help. Atone."

Emma stared at the bear. The strange aura that had surrounded him before no longer radiated. Aside from the enormity of his presence, he didn't feel like anything more unusual than a bear. *The Wildkin Whisper wears off after a time, but I don't think Strixian gave Mawr a gift like that… I think he got rid of something bad. The bear isn't gonna get mean again when my magic stops.* She likened what Strixian did for Mawr to healing an injury instead of bestowing a temporary enchantment.

After a few quick breaths to prepare herself, Emma tried to climb down. She stuck her leg out and stared past her stretching toes at the branch not getting any closer. With Neema's magic making her weigh nothing, she hung in place. *This is so strange.* She grabbed the branch she'd been perching on and shoved herself down, sinking like a soap bubble. As soon as her toes made contact with the branch nearest the forest floor, Neema drifted off her shoulder. The instant the faerie no longer touched her, Emma's weight returned to normal. The branch bowed and wobbled.

Emma let out a cry of surprise and lost her balance. She landed draped over the branch like a towel for a second before it bobbed up, tossing her into the air. She fell a few feet and landed flat on her back in a cushion of forest mulch. Somewhere overhead, Neema giggled.

"Funny." Emma sat up out of the pile of leaves and moss, then huffed a scrap of leaf from her lip. Sprawled on her butt only a short distance in front of Mawr, he seemed the size of a house. Her breath caught in her throat.

Mawr leaned close and sniffed her with a nose wider than her face, making her hair blow back. "You are smaller than I thought. Human, yes? Not faerie."

Emma managed a cheesy smile. "Yes. I'm Emma."

"What is an Emma? I have never heard of such creatures."

"*I* am Emma. That is my name like yours is Mawr. I am a human, but a child... uhh, cub."

"Are you trapped here too?"

She pulled her legs in and shifted her weight onto her feet, standing in a gradual motion she hoped wouldn't spook him. "Trapped? No, I came to help the faeries. Why would you think I was trapped?"

"I..." Mawr leaned back to sit. His rear end hit the ground with the force of a tiny earthquake. Emma waved her arms to keep from falling. "Something about humans and trapped. I do not remember."

She peered at the faerie. "Mawr asked if I am trapped here? Am I?"

Neema landed on Emma's left shoulder. "Trap Faerie Realm can humans if careless are. Neema making sure stuck are you not. Being afraid no need."

Emma peered at the little woman on her shoulder. "Can I do something wrong and wind up trapped here?"

The faerie nodded.

"What shouldn't I do?"

Neema smiled. "Would you nothing anyway. Being nice too much."

"That makes no sense," muttered Emma. "Please, don't play games. I have to go home when the faeries are safe. I don't think this will take a few minutes... it's already been hours."

"Worries have you shouldn't." Neema grinned. "Stuck becoming you if killing me you do... angry making Queen Nymira or."

Emma gasped. "I wouldn't hurt you!"

"Yes. Stuck becoming here why not you will." Neema hugged her.

"She is a child," said Mawr.

Neema peered at the bear, head tilted.

"He said I'm a child."

"Yes." Neema nodded.

Mawr offered Emma a paw almost the size of the table back home. "You have banished the strange urges from my thoughts. I will protect you while you remain here. So I vow."

She grasped one claw, and they shook, hand to paw.

"Do you know where the other animals are coming from?" asked Emma.

Mawr bowed his head. "I do not remember much but being angry. This place does not feel familiar."

"Maybe we can find tracks."

Mawr flattened himself to the forest floor. "Climb upon my back, little one. Your legs are so small… I can travel much faster."

"Thank you."

Emma grinned at him before hauling herself up to sit on his back. His enormous neck wouldn't let her ride him like a horse, she'd wind up in a full splits. Instead, she sat between his shoulder blades, feet tucked to one side. Fur tickled her legs, but guilt at making her family worry mixed with her fear at what may await her in this place kept her from laughing. She fidgeted, scratching here and there when the shaggy fur made her think bugs walked on her skin.

"Go in a circle around the grove, spiraling out, please."

The forest raced by faster than she could run, despite Mawr moving at an even walk. At his size, each stride covered great swaths of ground. She held two handfuls of fur, leaning from side to side to peer at the ground.

"What are you searching for?" asked Mawr.

"Tracks on the ground, marks on the trees, or"—she gulped—"anything dead."

9

LINEAGE

Thirty or so faeries emerged from the Elder Grove at the sight of Mawr's approach, several glowing with a gathering of eldritch magic. Emma waved from atop his back and their hostility changed to bewilderment. Pimlin, ankle-long pink hair trailing behind her, zoomed over and hovered before Emma's face. Her amethyst eyes gleamed with fear, but a little hope crept in as well.

"Harmed this bear has us... but calmed you it?" Pimlin lowered her spear at Neema's nod.

Emma yawned. "His name is Mawr, and he had bad magic on him that made him angry. It's gone now."

"Removed you it?" asked Pimlin.

"I asked Strixian for his help and he listened." Emma glanced up at the darkening sky. "It's almost night."

Pimlin glided around Mawr's face, seeming afraid to get *too* close. "Different seems. Into the Elder Grove he should not go, but tolerate close we will. Too large. Will destroy by being."

Emma nodded.

"Sleep for you now." Pimlin pointed at a spot a short distance from the round wall of trees encircling the grove, where a dense hang of branches formed a roof of leaves.

Mawr meandered over to the shrouded area of thick, mossy carpet. A scattering of orange, pink, and white flower clusters decorated the trees, tulip-like cups surrounded by long, wispy petals that floated in the breeze.

Marsten's shop doesn't have these. Would Nan know what they are?

She let out an uneasy whine, nearly tumbling off as the bear lurched forward and lowered himself to the ground.

Once he settled, Emma slid down from her perch upon his back, landing into a stumble that dumped her on her knees. Perching for hours on his back left her legs sore, and they didn't want to hold her weight. Wincing, Emma rolled around to sit and leaned against the soft, warm fur behind her.

"Moment," chirped Neema, before gliding off.

I'm sorry, Mama. Emma curled on her side and cuddled into the huge bear, half the world obscured by a face full of brown fur. The stars had come out, and the air filled with an odd clicking symphony. She assumed insects made the noise, as it had the rhythmic, repetitive nature of crickets but lacked a 'tweeting' quality—more like an army of Tams continuously breaking handfuls of twigs.

Mawr would provide warmth and comfort for her to sleep, but she longed to be home with her family. She wondered if Nan and Kimber had finished the stew without her. Would Da be racing around Widowswood desperate to find her? Kimber had to be in tears. She imagined Mama holding Tam tight to keep him from running off in search of her too.

Emma curled up against Mawr's side and wept.

"Return," said Neema. "Here… eat."

"I'm not hungry," mumbled Emma.

Something brushed her shin. A moving silver-white glow glided around in front of her face. "Crying why?" Neema landed sitting in fur and reached over to wipe tears.

Emma sniffled. "I miss my family. They're going to be scared and worried about me. You promised I would only be gone for a few minutes."

"Yes." Neema grinned, nodding. "Minutes few. Worry not you do." She zipped out of sight and back in a blink, holding a cake the size of a huge grape. "Food."

"Umm." Emma sat up and took the cake between two fingers. "Is this going to do something bad to me? Trap me here forever? Can you please tell my family where I am?"

"As long to tell as you to help. Not they sad are." Neema shook her head, making her gossamer silver-white hair dance about. "To wicked things only. Steal from who us hurt or." She put a hand over her heart. "Word my give. No tricks."

A strong scent of fruit wafted from the cake, mixed with cardamom and ginger. Emma's stomach growled, but her mind echoed with Nan's advice not to eat faerie food. She opened her mouth, overcome by hunger, but at the thought of never being able to go home again, she bowed her head and cried.

Neema pouted. "Trusting can me you."

"I'm sorry." Emma cradled the little cake in both hands. "The worst thing I can think of happening is never seeing my family again... I'm just scared. Nan told me eating faerie food is going to curse me."

The faerie's hurt look shifted to determination. She zipped away, a comet of white light zigzagging among the trees. Emma glanced at what had brushed her leg. A large leaf folded into a bowl sat nearby, filled with similar cakes. She sniffed at the grape-sized pastry, and her stomach growled in response. *It smells* so *good, but...*

Twin trails of light, one white and one flame red, shot out from between two of the grove wall trees and came toward her. Emma bit her lip, staring at the miniscule comets. Neema, with Queen Nymira at her side, floated over and hovered nearby.

"Emma..." The queen spoke in a soothing, motherly tone. "It is true that consuming faerie food can have... interesting effects on humans. It can curse them such that they must remain in our realm and can never leave. It can make them see things that aren't there... lose years in the blink of an eye, or make someone quite sick indeed." She shook her head. "All the magic weaved by faeries in this grove is subject to my will. As Queen of the Silverbell Faeries, I give you my word that no curse shall befall you from our hospitality."

"I'm sorry, Queen Nymira." Emma bowed her head. "It was rude of me to doubt."

"Be at ease. You are still a child, and I shall not think less of you for such minor lapses in etiquette." Nymira started to smile, but leaned closer, squinting at Emma. "Hmm. Well, how about that?"

Emma stuffed the little cake in her mouth and chewed. The strength of its fruity-ginger-spiced flavor startled her; she eyed the leaf-bowl, intent on devouring all of them. She shifted the half-chewed cake to the side of her mouth so she could speak. "Hmm? About what?"

Nymira drifted closer and put a hand on Emma's forehead. "Yes... I do think so." She smiled. "You needn't worry. There is a little elven blood in you... or something similar. Old spirit."

"I'm not a half-elf." Emma felt her rather rounded ear.

"No..." Nymira chuckled. "You are not. Not that much elf, but I bet you had an Astari—or perhaps an alderswood dryad—somewhere in your lineage. Do people in your family seem to live for a long time?"

"Umm." Emma picked another cake from the bowl and popped it in her mouth. Nan's story about Princess Isabelle did make her wonder. If Mama had been Emma's age when Isabelle was fifteen, Mama should be a lot older than she is. Queen Isabella had to be almost fifty, which... if Mama was nine when the story happened, she'd be halfway through her forties, but as far as Emma knew, her mother was twenty-seven. She'd given birth to Emma soon after she married Da, and she'd married at seventeen. "I think, maybe... but I don't know if it's just a story."

Emma's eyes widened. *What if Nan is like really, really old? Those stories about the forest witch stealing children who don't grow up... could people have been seeing Mama growing up reeeeeally slow and mistaking her for different kids?* She rubbed her forehead, already tired from thinking about such things. If that were true, then she'd have taken a lot longer than ten years to become a ten-year-old.

I don't understand. She yawned. "If I was part elf, wouldn't I still be little while all the other children from Widowswood grew up?"

"Perhaps... but you are not an elf. As children, they age perhaps one year for every twenty that pass... in human terms. When they reach adulthood, they do not age as humans do, but remain youthful for many thousands of years. Humans appear older"—Nymira traced her hand in a curve—"in a gradual march from infant to crone. Elves grow up"—she traced a diagonal line upward to a long flat stretch, then a gradual upward slant—"and stay the same for a long time. When they become *very* old, they start to show some signs of age, but not like humans." She winked. "No wrinkles."

"What about faeries?" The next cake Emma ate blasted her with a strong, sharp sweetness that reminded her of eating an entire lemon at once if it had been magicked to be sweet instead of sour. She coughed. "There's no children in your grove."

"Faeries rarely have babies. A group like ours may see one birth every four hundred years. They grow up about as fast as an elf, and we stay the same forever."

"Wow," whispered Emma. "You don't grow old and uhh, die?" She blushed. "Sorry."

"No matter, you are curious." Nymira smiled. "We can die from any cause that might kill a human, but old age is not one of them."

"Eight thousand years Queen Nymira is." Neema grinned.

The queen scoffed. "I'm 7,612, thank you very much." She fluffed at her hair and muttered, "Eight thousand indeed."

Emma blinked, unable to imagine that many years. "Wow."

"As I was saying." Nymira leaned in to study Emma's face. "Perhaps since the fey ancestor is so removed, you may be hurtling to adulthood as fast as any normal human might, but once you get there, it may take a while for you to grow old." She winked.

Emma ate a few more treats and licked sticky off her hands. Despite the cakes' small size, she felt as full as if she'd eaten a proper meal. *I should ask Nan if they're supposed to do that.* "Thank you for teaching me about elves, and for these cakes. They are lovely!"

Nymira nodded once, slow. "You have broken whatever curse affected this bear. Perhaps you may be able to save us after all. For that, you have *my* thanks. May you sleep well."

Emma yawned. She wanted to sleep, but a pang of homesickness promised to keep her staring at stars for a long time. She stood and curtseyed at the queen. "Thank you."

Smiling, Nymira flew off, back inside the grove.

"Sleepy." Neema curled up in Mawr's fur.

The great bear already seemed to be snoring.

Emma snuggled into his side. Her mind ran off with guilt, imagining her family in a furor over being unable to find her. For minutes, she stared into the vast, night-darkened forest, listening to the clicking of insects and bell-tones of the faeries who glided about like will-o-wisps in the shadows.

"Not sleepy?" asked Neema.

"I'm too worried about my family. I miss them," whispered Emma.

Neema crawled up to her face. "Wasting time worrying. Fine is Emma family." She put a tiny hand on the tip of Emma's nose. "Sleeping now."

Before Emma could think a single word, she plunged into a quiet, restful sleep.

10

VINES

*E*mma awoke to the warmth of the sun caressing her cheek. She yawned and tried to sit up, but her body didn't want to move. With great effort, she forced her leaden muscles to cooperate, and stretched her arms and legs while sitting. After a powerful yawn, she collapsed against Mawr's side, unable to lift even one finger.

"What's wrong with me?"

Neema pushed herself up out of the dense brown fur, peering at Emma from beneath a twisty cobweb of white hair. Mama sometimes complained about what sleep did to her hair, but she had *never* looked even a quarter as messy as the faerie. Neema swayed, her eyes half open. She looked so disoriented, she might not have even remembered her own name.

Emma giggled.

Neema gazed into space for a few seconds before she sneezed, and her hair whirled back to a perfect, straight cascade. "Mornings!"

"Was that a spell?" asked Emma?

"The sleepy?" Neema flashed a cheesy grin.

Emma narrowed her eyes. "That too, but I meant your hair."

"That's faerie." Neema winked. "Was spell sleepy too."

She stared down at limp arms draped across her lap. "Why can't I move?"

"Still sleepy. Much tired you were. Gone be it soon." Neema stood, arms out over her head, and stretched.

Emma yawned.

Mawr emitted a series of low rumbling noises. As he stood out from behind her, Emma flopped flat on her back like a dead fish. No amount of wanting could coax even one finger to twitch.

She yawned again. "Strixian, please grant me the Wildkin Whisper."

"…rning Emma," muttered Mawr.

"Mafindwel," said Emma.

"Hmm?" Mawr twisted around to peer at her. "I do not understand."

She grinned. "It's something humans say where I am from. It means 'may the day find thee well.'"

He bowed his head in a slow nod. "I hear."

Emma propped herself up on her elbows. "Don't you mean 'I see?'"

"Humans are strange creatures," said Mawr. "How do they see words?"

"No…" Emma grinned. "I see means I understand."

"Then why not say I understand?" Mawr scratched his head. "Or do humans think with their eyes?"

Emma sputtered. "Forget it."

"Why should I forget what you have just explained to me?" Mawr blinked.

Argh! "Sometimes humans use words that mean something other than what they sound like they mean. I said 'forget it,' but what I meant was I don't know how to explain seeing and understanding to you, and I am still too tired to think about such difficult things. I can't even move my fingers right now, *please* don't make me think."

"Ahh. I understand, or see." Mawr shook his head, chuckling.

A female faerie with cherry-red hair and a male with black hair glided over, each holding the end of a huge leaf burdened with nuts, berries, and cakes. Behind them, another female with pastel-blue hair and wings carried a smaller leaf-bowl of cakes. She set it down by Emma while the other two offered the rest of the food to Mawr.

The woman who'd carried Emma's food landed seated on her leg. "Morning good. I am Raa." A burst of pastel-blue sparkles flew from her wings. "Happy meeting you I am."

"Pleased to meet you as well." Emma concentrated, and managed to lift her arm, offering one finger to shake the tiny woman's hand. "Thank you for bringing me food."

Raa had tan skin like the rest of the Silverbell Faeries, a shade deeper than walnuts, closer to the wood of Nan's table, stark in contrast to Emma's lily-white leg.

Kimber would burst if she saw this place. I wonder if I could ask them to visit her.

Soon, the odd heaviness left her body and Emma sat up. She nibbled on the tiny cakes, which filled her mouth with flavors of plum, berries, gingerbread, and pumpkin. Mawr devoured his offering in two bites, causing Rin and Fila to exchange looks and chatter in faerie. Whatever they said made Neema giggle.

They're feeding him, and he was trying to hurt them... She scowled. *No... whatever made him angry did it.*

Raa watched Emma eat for a few minutes before grinning. "Like do cakes you?"

Emma nodded. "They are wonderful. How do they make the flavors so strong?"

"Made I!" Raa stood on Emma's knee and waved her arms about.

"Thank you. They're *so* delicious." She gently picked the faerie up and hugged her as if cradling a delicate crystal statuette.

Raa laughed. "Dear friend Neema. Gone for years many. Grateful Raa to you is."

Emma put a hand on her chest at a sudden upwelling of warmth. "I'm glad I found her." *I was foolish, but I did do some good.*

Rin and Fila returned with another burdened leaf, which Mawr took his time with—three bites.

Emma finished the last of her cakes while Raa watched, grinning. *I still don't know what I should do. Where do I start looking for what's making—?*

A chorus of tiny screams rang out from the central grove. All the faeries around her raced off in that direction. Emma leapt to her feet and sprinted after them, grateful that the ground here had no massive roots to climb. Spongy, mossy undergrowth added a bounce to her stride.

Inside the grove, a small army of Silverbell Faeries hovered about six feet from the ground, tossing yellow-white energy bolts at a pack of medium-sized canine creatures with silvery-grey fur. Their tails seemed a bit longer and fluffier, and their ears pointier, but they looked like foxes. In the same way Mawr's had, their eyes glowed bright red.

Some flung themselves into the air, attempting to snap their jaws on flying faeries, but could not leap to the height the tiny guards hovered. One or two foxes got the idea to jump to the roofs of the spires or bound onto tree trunks and jump again. Two came close to getting their teeth on a faerie. Most of the screaming came from a lemon-haired male who had both of his legs trapped in the mouth of another fox.

That fox locked stares with Emma as if bragging about what it had done. A second later, it trotted off.

"No!" yelled Emma, focusing on the Wildkin Whisper. "Stop trying to hurt the faeries!"

All seven remaining foxes jumped at her shout and snarled at her.

Two energy bolts sparked the ground near one's forepaw, and it bolted. Panic seemed to spread over the animals, and they trailed off after the one who'd gotten a meal.

Emma ran after them, painfully aware that she'd never catch up. A vision of her mother racing across the town square shrouded in a ghostly panther came to mind. *Oh... which spirit did Nan say that was?* She leapt a cluster of roots and kept chasing.

Neema zipped overhead, stopped about twenty feet later, and held both arms out in front of her. A crackling orb of yellowish lightning wreathed her hands before streaking off and striking the fox carrying the howling faerie.

The animal leapt straight up, as if it had stepped on some manner of spring trap, and flew sidelong into a tree. On impact, the faerie popped free of its mouth and limped airborne.

Naraja! Emma growled under her breath, trying to force as much speed as she could out of her legs. "Naraja, spirit of cats, please let me run faster than these foxes."

Emma didn't expect much, since she hadn't tried to talk to her before... but within a second, the faint roar of a cougar echoed in the back of her mind. The forest became a blur in varying shades of green. Hair whipping out behind her, Emma pumped her arms and legs, goosebumps rising from a tingly energy wrapping around her from behind.

She gained ground on the foxes, which sensed her coming and ran harder. The bewitched animals flowed like liquid fur between the trees, drawing together in a tight group. Since Neema's spell had freed the faerie, Emma's intention changed from catching a single fox to save one life to following the pack to save all the Silverbells. If she could find out where these enraged animals came from, perhaps she *could* do something. Emma would not make the same mistake as she had with the thieves. If whatever these foxes ran to looked dangerous, she'd leave right away and fetch help.

Low-lying branches made her duck a few times, but she kept right on the foxes' tails. They yipped and snarled at each other, noises the spell didn't translate. The group of foxes flowed over a fallen tree. Emma hurdled it and landed in ankle-deep green muck on the other side, which reeked of pungent moss.

The foxes raced across a small clearing covered in the same mossy-mud mixture, leaving shallow footprints. Emma struggled to chase them, but only four strides later, her foot found nothing solid under the muck. She screamed as she plunged chest deep and bobbed to a halt in a spongy, sticky mess neither warm nor cold. The foxes vanished into the shadows ahead, not bothering to even look back.

"Neema," yelled Emma.

She grabbed at the ground, raking up handfuls of frothy mess but getting no traction. Any damage she inflicted to the surface smoothed out in seconds. Grunting, she tried to get her right leg to move, but couldn't budge it. The foamy mud adhered to her skin wherever it made contact, but didn't cling to her dress. A moment of love and gratitude for Nan bottomed out to heartsick worry that she'd never be able to go home.

The more she struggled to grab on to anything, the more she thought she'd be stuck in this bog forever. Her breaths came rapid, trying to outdo her pounding heartbeat.

Neema rushed over and grabbed her arm. She concentrated for an instant, and a tingly feeling spread over Emma. A focused blast of silver-white energy sprayed downward from Neema's wings as she seemed to be attempting to fly in reverse as hard as she could. The little woman grunted and strained, pulling on Emma's arm, but couldn't dislodge her.

"Can't..." Neema panted. "Can't I... Too are stuck you."

Emma grunted and struggled to free her right hand from the surface. The goblin's snare traps had been far stickier than this muck. She took some small comfort in that she didn't seem to be sinking. As much as the bog wouldn't let her up, it prevented her from going deeper. If she had only stepped one foot in, she could've pulled away with ease. Up to her ribs in it, she couldn't move.

"What is this?" Emma tried not to throw up at the feeling of spongy snot clinging to her body. "Is it going to hurt me if I stay in it too long?"

Neema shook her head. "Moss and tree blood, dirt and water."

"So I shouldn't be too scared?"

"Eat you may something for while flee you can't." Neema bit her lip, as if regretting saying that. "Heavy not foxes sink enough to."

A nervous whimper leaked from Emma's nose. She eyed the forest around her, shaking at the idea of some awful creature happening upon an easy meal. Her feet could move around, but she couldn't push herself upward, more like stepping on a sponge than swimming in goopy mud.

She searched for a stick or vine to grab. Behind her, a giant tree stood at the edge of the bog, split open and leaking dark emerald sap into the froth, the likely cause of it being so sticky. The dying tree appeared ancient, but had no roots or branches anywhere she could reach. The fox tracks had all vanished, the foamy morass in front of her again appearing like flat, safe ground.

"I'm going to try something." Emma didn't like the waver of fear in her voice, and fought to push worry aside.

"What?" asked Neema.

She gestured at the closest tree. "Something Mama did." Emma closed her eyes for a few seconds, trying to convince herself she did not need to be scared. Again and again, she envisioned the way her mother had thrown a thorny root at that horrible wizard. She didn't need it to move so fast, or be so full of sharp points… but she did need a bigger vine than what she'd made Tam's horse from. "Linganthas, I need your aid. Please bend the roots to your will and send your strength to help me."

Eyes open, Emma thrust her arm at the tree, focusing on her desire. Something brushed the outside of her right leg, rising upward from below. A second later, a dark brown root as thick as her arm shot from the bog nearby and stretched over fifteen or so feet to the tree, where it coiled around and tightened.

"Goodness," said Neema. "Growing so fast a child the roots does?"

Thank you! Emma spent a second radiating gratitude toward the spirit of the woods. She grasped the wooden tendril with both hands and struggled. Her body rose a little up from the sticky, elastic muck, but she couldn't pull hard enough to break its grip on her. As soon as she stopped straining, she snapped back into the bog exactly as she had been before, bobbing up and down for a moment.

"No," she whispered. After an angry three seconds, she sighed. "At least I'm not going deeper."

Neema rotated to face back the way they'd come from. "I get—"

Six snarling, growling foxes rushed out of the undergrowth all at once, padding over the pale green muck without sinking in.

Emma screamed, "Go away!"

The animals slunk closer, growling, not responding.

"Why are you angry? Please… we don't want to hurt you, and I don't want you to hurt me. Go back to your den."

The foxes in front of her snarled louder. She forced a smile and reached out as if to scratch under the chin of one, but yanked her hand back with a squeal when it snapped at her.

The Wildkin Whisper didn't do anything; the noises coming from the glow-eyed foxes did not translate into any sort of speech. The unexpected loss of her ability to talk her way out of a dangerous situation shattered her confidence.

"Mama!" screamed Emma. "Da!"

Neema shot a bolt of energy into the bog in front of the advancing fox, which exploded in a bubble of green smoke. That fox stopped short, but the other five leapt at Emma. One went for her face, but she grabbed it by two handfuls of its cheek fur. Another bit her on the left forearm, a third sank its small teeth into her right shoulder. A fourth tried to bite her left ear, but she twisted so it bit her on top of the head. More tiny teeth pierced her left side.

"Help!" screamed Emma. "They're biting me!" She wrestled with the one snapping its teeth at her face and yelled, "Mama!"

The faerie chattered in her native language, her tone dark. A crackling sizzle built up in the air before a yellow eldritch bolt struck the fox trying to bite her ear. The animal let out a wounded yelp and darted back. Emma threw the fox she had a grip on to the right, bashed her elbow into the head of the one gnawing on her side, and grabbed the ear of the one chewing on her left arm, squeezing until it cried out in pain and let go.

Causing an animal to yowl like that filled her with guilt, but she knew something had gone quite wrong with them. Another bolt from Neema sizzled in the air somewhere behind her. A puff of warm dog-breath washed over her hair; the one biting on her skull let out a wounded yelp. It let go of her and backpedaled, whimpering, smoke peeling from its back.

The fox she'd thrown rolled onto its feet and charged at her, murder in its glowing crimson eyes.

"Linganthas, lend me your wrath!" Emma yelled the same phrase her mother had, and flung her arm forward as if throwing a knife. The image of Mama trying to kill that wizard had burned itself so deep in her memories, she pictured it as clear as if it had happened mere seconds before.

A cracking like trampled underbrush surrounded her as a streamer of thin, wooden vine covered in sharp thorns sprang forward from her palm. The whip-like length of root sliced the leaping fox in half and zipped away into the trees, making an eerie scratching *whoosh*. Before Emma could scream at watching a live animal torn in two pieces, the fox exploded into a cloud of pink energy.

No blood.

Not even one hair remained.

She stared at the dissipating mist, mouth agape until a flash of searing yellow light going across from left to right dragged her attention to another fox, which also burst into a pink cloud when Neema's spell hit it. Three foxes continuously lunged at Neema, leaping into the air and snapping their teeth within inches of her feet.

The fourth fox sprang at Emma from the right, trying to bite her on the face again. She managed to catch it, and held it down on the bog in front of her chest, right hand gripping the scruff of its neck while she clamped her left around its muzzle.

"Stop!" yelled Emma. "Why are you doing this?"

It made no attempt to talk, merely thrashing and snarling in effort to continue attacking her.

"Great Strixian, please grant this poor animal freedom from whatever curse it has; give him the wisdom to realize he should not be angry." Emma desired what she had done for Mawr, but no magical energy surged forth from her. "What's wrong?"

"Silly beasts," yelled Neema, a split second before a loud eldritch *bang* shattered the air.

Emma cringed and glanced up to her left. The foxes that had been attacking the faerie remained only as fading clouds of pink mist, and the air had taken on the taste of a thunderstorm. She glared at the one she continued to hold down. "Stop trying to bite me. I don't want to hurt you."

It growled, but ceased trying to wriggle free.

"I'm going to let go now. Go to your home."

It growled.

"Not trusting the fox," said Neema. "Biting you when you do the letting go."

Emma pouted. "I can't kill it."

"Hold it forever can you not either."

Grumbling, she examined the exhausted-looking animal. Aside from eyes made of bright red light, oversized pointy ears, and an abnormally fluffy tail, it looked like an ordinary fox. "What's wrong with you? Why are you so angry?"

It snarled.

"Fox throw. Will I magic so hurt you cannot it do."

"You're going to kill it," said Emma. "I don't—"

The fox burst into a cloud of pink mist.

"Aaah!" Emma screamed in surprise. "I didn't do anything! It just popped!"

"Being strange." Neema glided down. "Getting help. Here wait you."

Emma scowled while making a half-hearted attempt to move. *Where would I go?*

Neema zipped off, leaving a graceful, curving trail of white light into the endless green.

"Ow." Emma cradled her bleeding left arm to her chest and sniffled. A tickle in front of her ear made her grab for a bug, but her fingers came back with blood on them. Bites on the top and side of her head flared with pain, but her arm hurt the most.

Stuck to the middle of her chest in a sticky mess, alone, and in pain, Emma lost her battle with bravery, and cried.

11

THE WHY OF WHY

*M*inutes passed in silence, save for Emma's sniveling sips of air. She coughed to clear her throat and wiped her eyes. Each breath caused the gummy morass to tug at her stomach under her dress. She wondered if the Druid's Step would have let her walk across the bog like the foxes, or if the magic would only make it less sticky.

Deciding *not* to look around, Emma stared at her bloodied forearm, and held her hand over the wound.

"Uruleth, please grant me the gift of life."

Green energy manifested beneath her palm. She willed it into herself, and the burning pain of a deep fox bite became cool. When she lifted her hand away, the wound had gone. Emma repeated the spell, thinking about the healing magic mending her head and side. A pleasant chill spread over her scalp, as refreshing as a swim on a muggy summer day.

"Linganthas, please grant me the Druid's Step."

The faint tingle and telltale essence of mint in the back of her mouth told her he had heard her request. She struggled at the bog, which did feel less sticky. Under the effect of the spell, the muck behaved like normal thick mud, without the glue-like quality of enchanted tree sap.

Emma grasped the large root she had summoned, which true to Mama's word, had remained permanent. Grunting, she pulled, but still couldn't free herself from the spongy mire. The rubbery mud refused to let go of her. She struggled and pulled on the root for several minutes until she slouched, out of breath.

Every small *snap* or *pop* from creatures moving around in the forest became threatening. Those foxes had been small. What would happen if something bigger—like one of those cats Neema mentioned—found her here. Or worse, another bear like Mawr still enraged by the magic. Stuck in a bog, she wouldn't have the time to ask Strixian for help before it got her. She whimpered, but her weary arms could barely move her.

Deep *thuds* in the ground grew stronger and louder. Something huge crunched among the trees, heading toward her. Emma held her breath, staring with dread in the direction the sound seemed loudest.

Oh, Mythandriel, please let whatever's coming be smart enough for me to talk to!

Emma trembled, biting her lip to stop herself from screaming for her parents as the snapping of twigs and leaves got louder and louder. Maybe if she stayed quiet, it wouldn't notice her. A great shadow shifted behind the trees. She raised her hands in a feeble attempt to defend her face.

Mawr's huge silhouette emerged from the darkness, the bright silver-white spot of Neema's light orbiting his head. He emitted a low, sorrowful moan.

Emma exhaled with relief, and asked Strixian for the Wildkin Whisper. "Mawr!"

He crept up to the edge of the bog. "The scent of blood is in the air. Are you hurt?"

"I was." Emma wiped at her arm. "Not now."

Neema glided over and grabbed the root. She grunted and tried to fly upward, her wings glowed with a near-blinding brilliance from her effort to fly. "Ground in the root is?"

Emma tugged futilely at it again. "Yes. I thought I could pull myself out with it. Oh! I'm being forgetful."

At the thought of asking Uruleth for strength, a sudden exhaustion came over her. *Have I used too much magic too soon?* She thought back to Nan explaining how Mythandriel's healing magic would drain so much power from her at once that it would make her sleep on her feet. Perhaps the same held true for the thornvine she'd hurled at the fox. She hoped for an instant that Mama would be proud of her for being able to do it at all, but her mood crashed into a mountain of fear and guilt.

"I may be stuck here for a while." Emma grumbled. "I need to rest before I can ask for strength."

"I am here." Mawr attempted to smile. "I am strength."

Emma wiped her tears and grinned.

Mawr ambled around the edge of the bog and picked her root up in his mouth. He took two steps back, pulling until a sharp *crack* resonated in the muck. Neema dragged about six feet of slime-covered root out of the bog. She flew it around behind Emma's back, making a loop, and brought both ends over to the bear.

Emma wrapped her arms around and held on as Mawr eased himself backwards. The hard root dug into her back and armpits, but she rose up from the swampy mire with a deep slurping sound that would've surely made Tam laugh. Mawr pulled her clear and dragged her a little farther onto solid dirt. If Tam didn't laugh at noise the mud emitted when she slipped loose, he would have howled at what came from the bog a few seconds later when the hollow she'd made closed: a noise like Da after he'd had beans and onions broke the silence with a fluttering gasp.

It made Emma smile, but only for a second or two. Sticky slime coated her, all up under her dress to the middle of her chest. It felt as if she wore pants and socks made of ooze. She sat for a while scraping her hands down her legs and throwing glops into the foliage.

Why did those foxes pop into puffs of pink light? Nan would know.

Much to her relief, none of that awful mud stained the dress her grandmother had made.

"Is there a creek or stream close by?"

"Far not that way." Neema pointed.

Emma got up, cringing from the sensation of having slime everywhere, and walked. Moving made it even worse, as if she'd been dipped in glue that had started to dry. She crept forward, reflexively holding her arms up and to the side out of disgust.

Less than a minute later, she found a small stream sunken in a channel where it had carved a path in the earth. The water ran about six or seven feet below the level of the ground, lined on both sides by large rounded stones as well as slabs. Emma sat on the edge and braced her hands on the grass behind her. She stretched her leg until her toes found a rock, and lowered herself before turning to put her back to the water. Once she had both feet on the stone, she eased her weight down to another ledge. From there, she hopped to a rocky shelf that touched the creek's edge.

A toe test found the water warm.

Emma didn't bother taking her dress off, and jumped in. The stream only came up to the middle of her thighs, so she sat neck deep and got to scrubbing at the mud with her hands. Water dissolved it with ease, and soon, the sensation of being coated in stickiness faded. Hundreds of tiny silver fish appeared to find it delicious, and swarmed in the haze of green trailing away from her, snapping up particles of plant matter.

Neema sat on the ledge, letting her feet dangle in the water while Mawr waited above like a guard dog.

"Neema? Why did those foxes turn into light?"

The faerie shrugged. "Because did. Know must why humans always why?"

Emma blinked. "Why must humans always know why?"

"What I said that is!" Neema laughed.

"I don't know." Emma pulled her dress up underwater and ran her hand up and down her belly, chasing away the icky slime. "Because we do… and it might be important."

"Important? Nasty bad animals all's that doing."

"Does every animal in this place do that?"

Neema gave her a pathetic large-eyed stare. "Not Neema knowing. Killing not animals like. Hurting us they have done never before."

"Oh." Emma let her dress fall back in place and stood. The darkening effect of wetness drained out of the garment in seconds, leaving it dry. *What spirit helped Nan with this dress?* She glanced at the rocks and then toward the direction she thought the Elder Grove stood. *Nymira seems to know things. Maybe she will know what it means.* She scampered up the wall of the sunken creek, climbing back to the forest floor. "I need to see the queen."

Mawr bowed so she could climb on his back. "Then we shall see her."

Emma perched on his shoulders and held on. The great bear ambled forward at a brisk stride toward the faerie's home. Neema landed seated on the back of Emma's neck and picked at her hair.

Giggling, Emma squealed. "What are you doing?"

"Being happy not you hurt." The faerie zipped into the air, circled once, and landed draped over top of Emma's head, two tiny elbows poking her as she balanced her chin on her hands. "Important think you do the popping foxes?"

"Animals aren't supposed to burst into light. It has to mean something." Emma let her eyes half close. The motion of his stride came close to rocking her to sleep. "I hope."

12

FAERIE MAGIC

The journey back to the Elder Grove seemed to pass in mere seconds. Emma jolted awake at Mawr's abrupt stop and lifted her face out of his fur. She blinked heavy eyes and wiped a bit of drool from her lip on her arm. He'd stopped close to the Elder Grove, abiding their request he not attempt to enter. It struck Emma as silly they'd even asked him not to since the huge bear could not have fit past the gate. He emitted a low moan of tiredness, and trudged over to the canopied moss, where he lay down.

"Thank you, Mawr." Emma yawned.

"Mmm." He rested his chin on the ground.

She leaned back, swung her legs to the right, and slid down his shoulder. Faeries emerged from little doorways, branches, and dark spots between trees, drawn by curiosity at the massive bear. Emma blinked and stretched. A few quick breaths of fresh air woke her up the rest of the way. She approached the gate of woven vines and waited. In seconds, they untangled, opening for her. Faeries gathered around her in a glowing rainbow cloud, gliding along with her on her way into the grove.

The crystalline fountain emitted a musical series of chimes, fainter and sharper than the constant bell tones emanating from the faeries themselves. She hurried around the path to where Nymira's throne chamber occupied the hollow at the bottom of the immense tree. The Faerie queen glanced up, an expectant look on her face.

She knew I was coming to see her.

Emma curtseyed before kneeling and sitting back on her heels. "Queen Nymira, I think I have learned something strange."

"Speak, child. What is it you have seen?"

"Those foxes. I tried to follow them, hoping to find what is making them so angry. I fell in a bog and they attacked me. It wasn't what I wanted to do, but I had to kill one."

Faeries gasped; some bowed their heads.

"Go on," said Nymira.

"It didn't die like an animal should. It burst"—she held her hands wide, indicating a cloud—"into a big puff of pink light. It had no blood."

"Strike this creature with what did you?" asked Pimlin.

"A spell my mother showed me. A vine of sharp thorns." Emma gestured as if casting it again. "It cut the fox in two, but… pop!"

"A false creature, made of magic." Queen Nymira's ruby eyes flared with annoyance.

Emma blinked. "I couldn't talk to it. False? How can an animal be false?"

Nymira smiled the same way Nan smiled at Tam when he asked a question she wanted to laugh at. "As you summon roots, so do some who use magic summon creatures. They are made of energy, and return to energy when they are dispersed. The spell you use to communicate with animals did not work with them because they are not true animals. They have no spirit." Her eyes narrowed. "This explains much."

A few of the faeries got to rapid chattering.

"Burst the snakes it's why," whispered Neema in her ear.

"What about Mawr?" asked Emma. "I asked Strixian to free his mind, and it worked. I tried to do the same to the fox, but nothing happened."

"Mages who practice this art—I believe humans refer to it as conjuration—also have been known to cast charms upon animals to control them." Nymira gazed into the woods. "I know of a human in this realm who works such magic."

"Dangerous too it's!" said Rin, the black-haired male guard. "Child she is."

"Has idea of good does Nymira." Raa bounced up and down. "Hates faeries the conjurer-mage. Hurt not a little girl human would he."

"Talk human to the girl can," said Pimlin. "Learn his angry animals sending why."

"I shall accompany her as well," bellowed Mawr, from the gate.

Neema, hovering by Emma's shoulder, puffed up her chest. "Going me too."

Emma bowed her head. "I'm sorry, Queen Nymira, but you really should ask my Mama for help. I shouldn't go without her giving me permission."

Queen Nymira sighed and bowed her head. "You are in the Faerie Realm now, Emma. There is magic everywhere around you in this place. Magic that affects humans easily when they are adults. As a child, you have not yet closed your mind to all that is magical and fantastic."

Emma bit her lip, a twinge of embarrassment at remembering how urgently she had insisted faeries couldn't be real not too long ago.

"If your mother were to come here, it is quite likely she would not be able to leave. Such is the fate of the other human I speak of. He has been here far too long, and cannot return to your world." Nymira looked her in the eye. "I understand if you must return to your home. Our fate is not a burden you are required to bear."

Guilt hung heavy around her heart. The faeries would bring her home if she asked, but she would be leaving them to whatever that man wanted to do. Few people she knew of outside her family believed faeries real, and some of those who did regarded them as pests. Maybe this conjurer didn't understand faeries. If she could convince him they were not mere creatures, but small people, perhaps he would leave them alone. She bit her lip, staring at her toes. As much as she wanted more than anything to run home to her family, she couldn't let all the faeries die.

Not if she had a chance to help.

"I will talk to him." She looked up. Relief spread over the faeries' expressions. Some smiled, some clapped, and a handful cheered. "Are you sure he won't try to hurt me?"

The queen tapped her chin for a few seconds, lost in thought. "I believe it unlikely, especially if you are polite."

Neema let off a burst of rapid-fire words in faerie, gesturing at Emma.

Emma glanced at her. "What?"

"She says that she will not let him harm you. You freed her from the lantern, so she will do anything she can… even die, to protect you."

"No…" Emma grasped Neema in a gentle hug. "I don't want you to die."

Neema stared at her. "Want Neema die not either to."

"Queen Nymira," whispered Emma.

"Yes, child?"

She stooped lower, still whispering, "May I ask you a question that might hurt your faeries' feelings? I don't intend it in a mean way, but I am curious."

"Of course." Nymira smiled. "You are a child, and a child must learn when they are curious."

"Why do you speak properly, but the other faeries... umm... talk in strange words?"

Nymira grinned. "Because I am actually speaking your language. My people are using magic to make you understand ours."

"Oh." Emma sat up straight, smiling. "Thank you. I will go and speak to this mage, and ask him to stop sending false animals to hurt your people."

"You have my thanks, Emma." Nymira offered a slow, deep nod.

Emma stood and let Neema glide into the air. "Which way do I go?"

"Neema knows the path," said the queen.

"Unwise is this," said Rin before chattering at the queen in the faerie language.

"I won't do anything foolish." Emma folded her arms. "If he is mean or won't talk to me..."

The queen raised a hand. "Do not do anything that would imperil your life. If the man will not speak with you, do not make him angry. Return here, and I shall not hold you at fault. Neema will ensure that you return to your home."

Emma nodded.

Four Silverbells flew over, holding a sack made of knitted leaves radiating the sweet fragrance of faerie cakes.

"For your journey," chirped one.

Emma accepted the provisions. "Thank you."

"When going?" asked Neema.

"Now." Emma slung the leaf-bag over her shoulder. "Before he sends more false animals."

BRYNSHIRE

*A*top Mawr's towering shoulders, Emma rode into the woods. Within an hour of leaving the Elder Grove, the roperoot trees again dominated the forest, though the bear had little trouble stepping over them. Some of the roots crisscrossing the ground looked taller than Emma. Neema perched upon Mawr's nose like a lookout on the prow of a boat, pointing him onward.

Patches of glowing emerald moss dotted some of the trees, smeared among ordinary wintergreen lichen. Mushrooms as tall as men stood here and there, in shades of violet, blue, and white. Their heavy caps drooped and occasionally released puffs of sparkling violet dust. Though the sounds of life surrounded her, few animals showed themselves except for birds. Most bore a passing resemblance in shape to sparrows, jays, and ravens, though they had much more elaborate plumage, long tails that trailed like ribbons, and feathers awash with bright colors.

"How far away is it?" asked Emma.

"Days two or three." Neema scratched her head. "Will twice you sleep."

Emma's stomach churned with worry. "I'm going to be on punishment until I'm someone's Nan."

Neema giggled. "Being silly. Be you home in minutes few."

She's trying to make me feel better.

For hours they traveled, past thousands of trees and the occasional small pond or stream. One river proved deep enough to wet Emma's feet as Mawr swam across, the water as cold as where she had gone swimming back home. She spent a few minutes trying to understand why the other stream had been so warm.

Forest spirits wanted it to be warm? Magic? Bah. This is a faerie wood... anything could happen here.

Emma whiled away the time searching about for unusual herbs and flowers, staring at them until she felt sure she could describe them to Nan when she returned home. Perhaps talking about unique plants would buy a little time before they got to telling her how disappointed they were in her for traipsing off into the woods on her own again. Kimber's voice replayed in her head, talking about the 'faerie king's daughters' and how worried the younger one was when the elder ran off.

She nibbled on a cake, but dread at having to face her family's disappointment once she finally got home kept her from eating more than three. Mawr stopped to savage a berry bush, since the amount of food the faeries had provided for him amounted to one meal.

Daylight flickered in from narrow gaps in the thick tree cover, but gave no sense of the time. Whenever she looked up, she stared at a vast carpet of green, unable to figure out how far across the sky the sun had gone. Emma sang to herself in whispers to distract herself from missing home, but *Run Rabbit* made her think of Tam, and *Tamrin Brae* got her worrying she'd become the 'faerie king's wife' and would never go home again.

Hours ran into each other, though the wondrous sights: narrow waterfalls, huge green birds, a stark white stag with glowing azure eyes, a colony of bright pink frogs, and a silvery lake covered in gossamer hanging vines kept boredom at bay. It both frightened and relieved her not to see any more false animals, or malicious creatures that only wanted to kill.

Soon after the light began to dim, announcing the approach of night, human voices carried out of the woods off to the left. Emma leaned forward trying to listen, but couldn't pick out individual words—only the murmuring of a group of women.

She peered at the faerie. "Do you hear it? Who are they?"

"Who?" Neema leapt from Mawr's snoot to his head. "What?"

"I hear people talking." She pointed.

"Hmm. Know I not."

"I'd like to see. Maybe this conjurer is there instead of where you think he is? Or maybe those people know something that could help us."

Neema shrugged. "Not of knowing humans more one than in our forest. Strange. Strange is hearing them."

Mawr turned in that direction. The voices grew louder, and sounded much like ordinary villagers discussing ordinary things: a wife's health, a new calf, a chicken being slow with egg laying. After a few minutes of travel, the shapes of basic wooden buildings became visible past the forest ahead, all awash in an eerie light. A gathering of humans stood in the street of a small village, dressed like the people who would come into Widowswood each year for the Feast of Zaravex. Simple cotton dresses on the women, plain brown tunics or cloaks on the men, all well-worn.

Emma perked up, staring wide-eyed at a human settlement in the midst of the faerie world. Even the forest seemed to give it some space, with not a single enchanted tree or plant anywhere within the circle containing the village.

Something seemed off about the place, as if the town had a separate little sun that shone only on the houses and people, but not the trees at its edge. The modest hamlet did not appear to have an inn, or anything large enough to be a store. Small homes and smaller huts clustered around a village circle with a well at its center.

A group of children ran about in the far right portion, laughing.

The sight of kids, especially happy ones, calmed Emma's doubts at the unusual light.

Mawr's approach drew the notice of the villagers, who stared aghast.

"He won't hurt anyone," said Emma, holding her hands up and apart. "He's friendly."

A man pointed. "That poor girl has been taken by a bear."

"A giant bear," said a woman.

"By Yalem, someone do something!" A young, pregnant woman crossed her hands over her heart.

Emma patted Mawr on the head and whispered, "Maybe you should wait here. I'll be right back."

"I will be listening. Call out if you need my assistance." Mawr settled down to rest.

"It's going to sleep," yelled a man in a green cap.

Emma slid to the ground and walked closer to the townspeople. "Please, listen to me. His name is Mawr and he is my friend. I'm a druid."

"Oh," cried the same man.

The pregnant woman seemed to relax. "Hello, child."

Seven or eight other adults said hello one after the next.

"What brings you to Brynshire?" asked an older woman, pudgy and short, with dark-brown hair. She stooped forward over Emma. "And why are you all on your own riding an enormous bear?"

"Have you had anything to eat?" A man a bit younger than Da strode up next to her. "You're so thin and small."

"Umm, some faerie cake." Emma licked the flavor of fruit from her lips.

"Well, a girl cannot live on cake alone." He snapped his fingers. "Come lass, I shall offer you a plate of chicken and bread."

"Oh, Fenton... you're barely managing to feed yourself and that wife of yours. We can offer this little one some stew." The heavyset woman smiled at her.

"Nonsense," replied an old man. "I've got the hut all to m'self, and more than enough food to spare for a little mouth."

Emma offered an apologetic smile, feeling a bit awkward. "You're all so nice. Thank you. I'm looking for a conjurer. I think maybe some of his magic ran away and I need to tell him. Have you seen a mage here?"

The villagers conferred amongst themselves, each denied having seen any conjurers or mages.

"No, child," said Fenton, scratching at his hair before offering his hand. "Come, girl. You need to eat and it's almost time for a girl your age to be in bed."

Emma fidgeted. "Well, I suppose it *is* getting dark, and a bed would be nice."

"We'll give her food." The large woman took Emma's right hand. "Come, child."

When the woman started pulling her, Emma set her heels. "Umm..."

"Nonsense, Beatrice." Fenton took Emma's left hand and pulled her the opposite direction. "Millie has already cooked more than the two of us could possibly eat."

Emma grunted, feeling a bit like a wishbone. *What is wrong with them?* She twisted her arms and wriggled free, only to wind up with the old man's hands on her shoulders from behind.

"Poor wee lass. You look starved and tired. I've got a seasons' worth of venison ready."

He started to tug her backward, but she ducked out of his grip and darted a few steps away.

"You are all very friendly." Emma turned in a circle, staring up at a closing ring of villagers, all smiling at her with kindness. "Thank you."

The pregnant young woman seized her left wrist. "I'll feed her and give her a place to sleep."

"Pshaw, Margaret." Another man whom she'd not seen before reached for her right arm.

Emma spun around the pregnant girl's yellow dress and took a couple steps off to the side. *This is not right. They're fighting over who takes me home. People don't act like this.* "I don't want to be a bother to any of you. I've plenty of food with me already, and I shan't impose on you for a place to sleep." She edged backward, freezing once she realized she headed deeper into the village. "I need to be going."

"Nonsense, girl." Fenton blurred into a smear of color, and reappeared in front of her. "You are in Brynshire now. This is your home. You're welcome to stay here… forever."

"Like us," said Margaret in a lifeless tone while rubbing her hands over her gravid belly.

"New friend," said a little girl behind her, about Kimber's age. "Come and play with us."

Three boys blurred into existence next to the girl, each a bit taller than Emma. They smiled all at the same time.

"I have to go," said Emma, a hint of nervous timbre in her voice.

The villagers faded semi-transparent and the odd shimmery light around them intensified. Their friendly faces drew intense… hungry. Looming closer, all of them stared at her as if they *needed* her.

"You cannot go," said the old man. "You are here now, poor child. You must eat."

"Eat," said Fenton.

The other villagers all repeated "eat" one after the next.

"A child your age can't be alone," said the pregnant girl.

"Alone," muttered a man.

"Not alone," said the little girl. "You need a mommy and daddy."

A fortyish man with white hair smiled, reaching for her. "We can take her in. Alice has always wanted a daughter."

"You'll be happy here," said the heavyset woman.

Neema slapped into the side of Emma's head and clung. "Eat their don't food! Cursed it is."

"Such a pretty little girl." Margaret reached for her. "I would love another child, and my home has plenty of space."

Uh oh. "Sorry!" yelled Emma. She ducked the woman's hand. Too many of them stood blocking her path back to Mawr, so she ran for a gap between two huts. Grass whipped at her toes as soon as she left the dirt road, startling her into a stumble. She'd been walking on soft, unidentifiable plant matter since she'd arrived in the faerie realm—normal grass seemed out of place.

She caught herself against the wall of a small shack to avoid falling. A quick glance back over her shoulder made her shriek. The villagers rushed after her, all glowing like ghosts, their skeletons obvious as dark shapes within their bodies. Though they appeared to be moving at a slow walk, their figures rushed toward her with an unnatural speed, the adults all imploring her to eat, while the children invited her to play.

"Mawr!" shouted Emma as she darted around the back of the little house.

Emma circled the building, hoping to get back to the road and run for the forest while the villagers followed her. A boy Tam's age leapt up from the grass on the other side of the house and tried to hug her. His expression and grin appeared innocent, but she screamed at the sight of a dark shadowy skull floating behind the child's face.

She backpedaled as he leapt to hug her, and scrambled around to the left. A glowing farmer came out of nowhere and blocked her path.

"Poor little thing. C'mere, girl. Need ta get some food in ya."

Emma stared up at the man reaching for her hand, paralyzed in fear. His expression looked calm, pleasant even... but a sinister and dark feeling pervaded everything about this place.

Neema zipped left and right, trying to interfere, but the villagers walked through her like ghosts. The faerie squealed like she'd been dipped in freezing water and darted up out of their reach.

"I'm not hungry." Emma backed up and ran again as the larger crowd of villagers caught up, all telling her to come home with them and eat.

She raced past three wooden buildings and cut to the right, following a walkway around a fourth house. A boy almost old enough to shave caught her with an arm across the chest, halting her. His skin had a strong chill, making her shiver. Unlike the rest, he didn't seem eerily friendly, more like a normal person. Thick eyebrows drifted together over serious eyes.

"Flee this place, little girl. You must run. I... won't let them have you."

Emma gulped, staring at him. "Thank..." Her attention shifted to a thin strand of white energy trailing out from the back of his head.

The crowd swarmed into the alley behind her, filing the gap between houses.

"James," said the old man. "The girl is my responsibility."

"No." The teen pushed Emma behind him. "She does not belong here. You will not damn her as we are damned."

Hands on her belly, the pregnant young woman stared at Emma with sadness in her gaze. "I would love another daughter."

"Stand aside, boy," yelled Fenton.

Emma backed away. As the villagers drew closer, glowing threads became apparent with the onset of night. From each person, a thin white cord stretched off from their head into the sky. She looked up, following the glowing trails with her eyes. A cobweb of strands arched up and came down, converging at the center of town where they plunged into the well.

Mawr shouted, "Emma!"

The crowd didn't react to what had to have been a loud roar to their ears. They pressed forward, scuffling with James, who they easily shoved aside.

Before he disappeared into the sea of bodies, the teen shouted, "Run!"

Emma peeled her terrified gaze from the spectral townsfolk and darted into the village circle, heading for the well. She sprinted so fast she couldn't stop, and crashed headlong into the side, clinging to the well stones to keep from falling over. After a momentary daze, she stood up on tiptoe and peered over the edge at water a long way down, dark and black. Merely looking at it made her shiver from an unnatural coldness. A great bundle of white energy threads spiraled deeper into the murk, the light visible for several feet beneath the surface. Whatever they connected to had to be at the bottom, too far down to see.

Maybe Nymira can help them.

She pushed away from the well, spinning with the intention of running toward Mawr, but a wall of semi-transparent bodies blocked her off. Emma let out a clipped yelp of surprise and sprinted left, heading around the side of a thatch hut... and into the arms of a huge man in overalls with only two teeth left. He swept her up off her feet, cradling her like a baby.

"Pa!" yelled the man. "Ah got me a new li'l sis."

"No!" shouted Emma. She kicked into a backward roll, tumbling out of his arms, and landed on all fours.

He grabbed her under the arms and pulled her up off her feet again. "Easy, child. Ya don't gotta be 'feared o' nothin'. You been 'lone for while. Ya gots a family now. We tek good care yas."

"I have a family." Emma grabbed his icy finger and tried to peel his hands off her.

"Pa! Git on out here. This one's still wild. Been 'lone too long. Where's Maw?"

An old man emerged from the thatch hut, shirtless in overalls, wrinkled skin covered in dirt and bits of hay. "What you yammerin' 'bout boy? I's sleepin'."

The huge villager turned left, holding Emma up like a doll, his hands under her armpits. "Lookie."

"Put me down!" Emma kicked and flailed.

"We saw her first, Emmet," bellowed a heavyset woman, who ran over and grabbed Emma's arms.

Another man and a woman appeared, each grabbing one of Emma's ankles. She screamed, hands clamped around both her wrists, both ankles, and her chest. People pulled her in different directions like bratty children fighting over a doll until Mawr bounded around the side of the hut and let off an angry roar that blew the huge villager's hat off.

Amid the wave of panic that followed, Emma wriggled free and fell flat on her back. She evaded a few grabbing hands while scrambling to her feet and scurried back to the village circle, but another six adults blocked her in. Emma turned right, and stalled at a group of children, all reaching for her.

"Come play with us," said a little brown-haired girl.

"You kin 'ave 'alf me apple." A boy her height held up a transparent fruit.

"It's been long time since I hadda new friend." A black-haired girl Tam's age leapt at her. "My dollies wanna meet you!"

Four other children behind the first three also invited her to play.

Emma let out a squeak of surprise and dove to the left, avoiding the little girl's lunge to hug her. Rather than flop to the ground, the ghostly child blurred back to standing and whirled about, ready to pounce again.

The only exit from the approaching specters sent her into the village circle again, chased by a swarming throng of see-through people. Bodies blurred and reappeared around her. She yelped and ducked past a fat man's attempt to scoop her up—and smacked into the well.

Emma rolled around, pressing her back against the cold stones. "Please… I have to go. I already have a home. I don't want to stay here."

The crowd, which had grown to at least sixty or more, surrounded her. It seemed the only reason none had grabbed her is that they continued to bicker among themselves who got to take in 'the poor orphan.' Mawr squared off against a handful of men with pitchforks, swatting at their weapons as if trying not to hurt the people.

"I'm not an orphan!" yelled Emma. "I have a family!"

None but James reacted to her, though his effort to fight his way past the crowd didn't go far.

Trapped against the well, Emma shivered, her toes digging into the dirt. She looked around, but so many bodies packed so close together, she had nowhere to go but…

Down the well.

She looked up at the energy threads. Every villager had one—and they all seemed to connect to something in the water. Mawr ducked his head and bowled over the line of farmers. He bounded up to the group surrounding her, rearing back with his great claws.

"Wait, Mawr!" Emma held a hand up. "I don't know what will happen if you try to kill them. You might get cursed too."

The bear hesitated. "I will not let them harm you."

"Neema!" shouted Emma as she pushed herself up to sit on the edge of the well.

"Here!" The faerie's shout, from inches behind her head, made Emma scream from surprise.

"Where were you?"

"Behind you." Neema smiled.

Emma pointed at the winch handle and stretched out one leg, putting her foot in the wet bucket. "Lower me down. There's something in the water." She put her other foot in and balanced in the hanging bucket, swaying back and forth while clinging to the rope. *Is this stupid or foolish?*

"Sure are you?" Neema grabbed the handle.

"No, but if there's nothing there, you can make me light and pull me up. Maybe if I hide down here, the ghosts will forget about me."

"Try will!" Neema adjusted her grip on the handle, and shot a tiny bolt of magic at the latch that kept it from rotating.

The faerie screamed and spun into a blur of white light as the handle whipped her around and around. Emma plummeted straight down, also screaming. Her lungs about emptied when the bucket struck the surface of the water. She went under for a few seconds, paralyzed by the sudden jolt of freezing cold.

Air!

She swam up, gulping breaths once her head broke the surface, then shrieked at the cold. For a few seconds, she clung on the coarse rope as thick as her wrist, shivering and trying to breathe without choking. The thick mass of energy threads gave off enough light for her to see glistening grey stones, moss, and some tiny bugs crawling on the walls. Her teeth chattered.

This is colder than the creek. It should be ice!

"Sorry Neema!" yelled the faerie. "Dizzy Neema."

Emma treaded water, the bucket too deep for her to stand in without being submerged. She peered into the darkness below, but the energy threads didn't glow with enough strength to illuminate the bottom.

"M-M-Mythandriel, p-please lend me your light." Emma concentrated on the little glowing ball Nan had taught her.

Mythandriel's light manifested hovering around her head, many times stronger than the faint threads. The peach-sized sphere of white flames sadly didn't give off any warmth, though the tiny emerald faerie silhouette inside it made her smile. Even without sending the orb downward, the well bottom became visible. The orb's intense radiance blotted out the strands, but revealed a wooden talisman in the vague shape of a man laying upon the dirt about fifteen feet below. It reminded her of the enchanted figurines Nan had asked her to put in the trees around the emerald creepers' nest.

Emma stared at it. *It's a magic talisman.* While Nan's had felt strange, arcane, and powerful, this one gave off a much darker essence. Whoever made it must have had malice in their heart. *Nan said the spiders would be protected unless something broke the focus.*

Neema glided down the well. "Hurt are you?" When the light orb floated past, she stared at it. "Oooh. Pretty!"

"My foot is a little sore, and I think I banged my elbow, but I'm not really hurt." Emma poked the faerie in the stomach with one finger. "I know what I have to do. Wait here."

Neema nodded, still staring at the orb of light.

After a deep breath, Emma dove under and swam down. Pressure squeezed in on her, as if the talisman could sense her intent to destroy it. Emma ignored the feeling of drowning, knowing she hadn't been holding her breath long enough to be scared. She pulled herself farther and farther down, until her reaching hand grasped the lump of old rotting wood from the mud at the bottom of the well. Pain spread into her fingers, as if she'd thrust her hands into a fire ant nest. When she stopped swimming downward, her hair billowed out around her in an inky cloud.

Eep! As fast as yanking her hand away from a hot pan, Emma brought her leg up and rammed the talisman down over her knee, trying to break it—but it held fast. *Ow!* The burn in her hands intensified. She growled in her head, getting angry. Furious, she raised the talisman over her head and brought it down hard while driving her knee upward. That time, the ancient wood snapped in half over her leg with a *crack* that resonated in the water, loud enough for her to feel in her bones.

Pain stopped; the talisman pieces shuddered and released a black ichor.

Mythandriel, if you can hear me, please let your light chase away this dark!

The orb raced down to hover at her side and grew a little brighter.

With a great *bang*, all the water vanished.

Emma fell a few feet onto dry dirt, holding her ears. She continued shivering from cold, but not a droplet remained, not even in her hair. The oddity of going from water to air in an instant kept her staring for a few seconds at her pale feet burrowed in loose, dark soil. After collecting her thoughts, she looked up and gasped—even the stone walls had vanished. She stood on the floor of a narrow pit, peering past three stories of dirt at a tiny disc of sky.

Mythandriel's light continued to glide around her, casting great creeping shadows from all the tiny roots sticking out of the earth. Neema's faint whimper came from above. A little dirt fell on Emma's face, making her flinch and cringe away. After brushing her face off, she guarded her eyes with her arm and peered up again.

The faerie popped halfway out from the wall near the top of the former well, and spat a few times.

Emma shied away from the rain of soil. "Neema? What happened?"

"Magic boom." She pulled herself free and glided straight down to hover at Emma's eye level. "Where water put did you?"

"I don't know." She stared up again and yelled, "Hello?"

"Expecting what you were?" Neema tilted her head.

"I dunno." Emma ground her big toe into the dirt and tried to rub the shivering cold out of her arms. "But not this."

14

HOMESICK

*E*mma turned in place, studying the sides of the pit the well had become. Small swaths of earth fell in here and there whenever she leaned away from the wall, giving her the sense this hole objected to her being there. The section behind her rippled, appearing likely to cave in any second. She grabbed at the dirt and tried to climb, but pulled away handfuls of loose soil and dry roots. More crumbled down, covering her to the shins as the spot she attempted to take hold of fell inward.

"Care have!" shouted Neema. "Collapse careless and bury if."

Mawr's face blocked out the sky in the tiny hole far above. "Emma, it is good to see you are unhurt."

Emma stood as close to the center of the well as she could, feet together, arms clutched to her chest, too scared to touch the walls lest they collapse on top of her. "Are the villagers still acting strange?"

"No," said Mawr. "The villagers are gone."

"What?" Emma blinked.

"So is the village." Mawr's head swung to the right, exposing sky. A second later, he peered down again. "There is forest. No humans. No village."

Neema landed on Emma's back, arms and legs around her neck. A magical tingle spread over her body a second later. "Nothing weigh. Climbing now. Cave-in before go."

Emma crouched and jumped up, floating about twice her height off the ground before she hung in midair like a dandelion puff. She wiggled her toes, momentarily enamored with the almost-ability to fly.

"Up go!" yelled Neema. The faerie grunted, straining to pull her into the air.

Awe at weighing nothing shifted to terror at the thought of being buried alive. Emma grabbed at the roots along the wall, pulling herself upward with ease. The pit walls crumbled inward below her, the filling dirt causing the bottom to rise beneath her as she climbed, nipping at her feet, threatening to bury her any second. An uneasy, continuous wail leaked from her nose, fear driving her to pull faster and faster. Yet no matter how frantically she hauled herself toward the opening above, the racing collapse below her feet remained only inches away. She screamed when her hand slipped free, expecting to fall, but the rising ground didn't swallow her. Stunned, she gawked down at her half-buried foot standing solid.

It's not chasing me... it's following me.

No longer afraid, she climbed at a more cautious pace toward a circle of bright sky overhead that grew larger and larger. Mawr reached his mammoth paw as deep as he could, and as soon as Emma got close enough, she grabbed on. The bear swept her out of the former well and deposited her on the soft green of the faerie-forest floor.

Dirtfall reached the top of the pit with a dull *whump*, spitting a cloud of soil into the air. The carpet-like coating of plant matter and moss that covered everything in this place grew to hide the bare patch in seconds, as if the pit had never existed.

"What happened?" Emma gazed around at the lack of grass. Roperoot trees crisscrossed the entire area where the village had been. "Did I dream a village was here?"

Mawr reared back on his hind legs and shrugged. "The people all stopped moving at the same time… and they faded away, their houses as well."

Neema paced a circle around the former well, scratching her head. "Belong here not the deep well. You sitting in hole make stay the pit. Healed the forest did."

"The well wasn't supposed to be here?" Emma stood and crept over. She poked at the earth with a toe. The place where she'd been deep underground felt as solid as everywhere else. "You're saying the forest waited for me to climb out?"

"Magic." Neema flailed her arms. "You stone heavy sheet in like. Lift stone sheet flat become."

"Umm." Emma frowned. "I'm not sure what you mean." Trying to figure out whatever happened here would not get her home any faster. "We should keep going."

Mawr bowed so she could climb on his back, and they walked onward for another almost-hour. When it got too dark to see the trees ten feet in front of them, he stopped for the night and lay down. Emma stretched out on his back as if he were an enormous furry bed, and Neema snuggled up at her side.

She ate two more cakes and spent a while lying there, unable to sleep. The strong flavor of berry remained in her mouth long after she'd finished her meal. Thick tree cover blocked out the stars, leaving her in complete darkness save for the soft glow from Neema's wings. Emma stayed on her back for a time before curling on her side. That didn't help her sleep, so she rolled onto her belly and rested her head on folded arms. The wet-dog smell of Mawr's fur filled her nose, and despite the gentle up-and-down motion of his breathing, she still could not sleep.

Kimber didn't cling to her back. Tam didn't flop over top of her. Da's snoring didn't fill in the silence with his comforting presence. Mama's arm lay far out of easy reach to grab in the event of a scary dream. None of them knew where she'd gone.

Emma sniffled. The desire to go home built up to painful, but she'd promised to help the faeries.

"Emma?" whispered Mawr. "What troubles you?"

"I miss my family."

Mawr's body vibrated with a long, deep yawn. "I shall watch over you until you are home again, little one."

She rolled onto her back, fingers laced behind her head. A minty-leafy fragrance lofted by on a gentle breeze that made the bear's shaggy fur tickle her legs. "They're going to be worried because I'm missing and they don't know where I am." Tears gathered in her eyes. "I promised I wouldn't—"

"Few minutes," chirped Neema.

"What?" Emma rolled her head to the left, staring at the faerie. "You keep saying a few minutes, but I have been here for two days."

Neema sat up, a soft bell-tone emanating from her wings when they moved, and shook her head, flinging her gossamer silver-white hair back and forth. "Working not the same way does time in Faerie Realm. Circle magic Neema good at." She beamed. "Worried is not your family."

Emma furrowed her eyebrows. The faerie didn't seem in any way deceitful. "All right."

After a yawn, Emma snuggled into Mawr's fur. She focused on the deep rumble of his breathing, and the slow rise and fall of her furry bed. Neema curled up beneath her chin, making Emma squirm and grin at the tickle of little breaths upon her neck. She may be off on an adventure (foolish or stupid, she had yet to decide), but she was not alone.

15

DARBOLG

The journey brought Emma deeper and deeper into the vast fey wood the next day. Mawr walked without protest, following the direction Neema pointed. Trees gradually changed with each passing mile, their branches growing narrower, leaves becoming long, thin strands that dangled like the hair of forest giants. Sunlight filtered past the thinning canopy, lending the world an intense glowing green, though she still could not tell where exactly the daystar lurked overhead.

She guessed it to be afternoon when a dense white mist came into view up ahead. The low-lying cloud slithered among the trees like a living thing, perhaps chest-deep on her were she not atop the back of a huge bear. Soon after Mawr's great paws entered the fog, Emma coughed on a stink like spoiled meat. Two breaths later, the awfulness in the air reminded her of dumping out a chamber pot. This part of the forest smelled like the outhouse on a summer day. She gathered her dress over her mouth and nose.

Neema leapt from Mawr's snoot to land on Emma's shoulder. "Open keep your eyes. Is danger Darbolg has in lots."

"Darbolg?" asked Emma.

Sloshing water made her look down. Mawr's forelegs vanished to the elbows amid nasty grey water. Bubbles popped at random, each releasing more of the strange mist into the air. Emma shied away from the bear's side, and tucked her feet under her in warm fur.

"Swamp is Darbolg." Neema pointed around. "Conjurer on other side lives. Knows faeries afraid here."

Glops of brown and green floated by, dead leaves and rust-colored moss. Emma gazed at the fog, which concealed the shadowy forms of trees barely thirty feet away. She figured the bad smell came from rotting plants and whatever else died in the water. Feeling sorry for Mawr having to touch such dreadful things, she stroked the fur atop his head.

"Mmm," said Mawr.

The rhythm of his stride ceased. Confused at the trees continuing to move past them despite his seeming still, Emma looked down again. Foul water came up near his shoulders, leaving her sitting upon a drifting island of bear. He paddled along, swimming. Evidently, the water here had become so deep even this great creature could not reach bottom without diving under.

Emma gulped as a ripple went by on the left, a hint of snake scales visible. "Uhh... I think I saw a snake."

"Snakes will not bother me," said Mawr. "I am too big for them to find tasty."

Neema let out an "eep" and climbed under the hem of Emma's dress, hiding. Shivering faerie wings tickled her thighs, but she couldn't find the urge to laugh. She fidgeted instead, attempting to comfort the tiny woman with a pat.

"Eating will me one bite in snake do," whined Neema.

Emma stared at the water, but couldn't find any trace of a serpent. "I won't let a snake eat you."

A deep, droning buzz raced up from behind.

She whirled around and locked stares with a furry black wasp bigger than a housecat. Bright orange compound eyes regarded her with little detectable emotion. Emma bit back the urge to scream, especially at the sight of a dagger-sized stinger, also bright orange.

"Hello," whispered Emma. "Please be real."

The wasp's head rotated left, then right in rapid, precise motions. "Real. Yes. I real." His stinger throbbed, bobbing in and out of his rear end as if he couldn't wait to stab something. A droplet of transparent red liquid gathered at the tip.

"Please don't sting me." Emma smiled. "We aren't here to hurt your nest. I don't even know where it is."

"Hunting for lightmoth," said the wasp. "I will not attack you if you are polite. Did you see one? I thought I saw one over here."

"Neema, there's a big wasp here looking for a lightmoth. What is that?"

At the word 'lightmoth,' Neema trembled, making Emma jump and squeak from the tickle of faerie wings.

Emma pressed down on her dress to keep the faerie still, and addressed the wasp. "I'm sorry. I'm not from this place. I don't know what a lightmoth is."

The wasp looked around. "A moth that makes light. My favorite food."

She whirled about at another buzz from in front. A gleaming green beetle glided in to land upon Mawr's head. Nan had baked loaves of bread smaller than the beetle. It settled down like a nesting bird, a sharp *click* coming from hard shell plates closing over folded wings. Aside from being huge, and shiny metallic green, its overall shape reminded her of a ladybug.

"Hello," said the beetle, in a feminine voice.

The wasp drifted closer and picked at Emma's hair with his mouthparts. A steady breeze from huge thrumming wings cooled her head.

All the muscles in her back locked. "Umm. What are you doing?"

"Smelling you. Curious." The wasp backed off a few inches. "I saw light. Thought a moth here, but do not smell lightmoth on you. I know your smell now." His mouthparts clicked. "Stay away from nest, yes?"

Still rigid, Emma nodded. "I do not want to bother your nest, but I don't know where it is. If I get too close, it's an accident."

The wasp glided around in front of her, flying backward to match the pace of Mawr's swimming. "Nest is that way." He pivoted, pointing with his stinger to Emma's left.

She turned her head to look in that direction. What at first she thought to be a distant tree obscured by fog and surrounded by hundreds of floating, glowing spots, clarified in the mist to a paper-wasp hive bigger than some of the houses back home. At least one of the tunnels leading into it looked wide enough for her to crawl into. The moving orange lights shone from the eyes of forty or more wasps as big as the one hovering next to her.

"No. I am not going near that." *Never. No matter what. No.*

The wasp offered one leg. "Agreed."

Emma gingerly grasped the tip and 'shook hands' with him.

At that, he tilted forward and drifted away into the fog, toward the nest.

"Hello," said the beetle. "I am so tired from flying. I've lost my way and need to rest. I hope you don't mind."

Mawr grumphed.

"Hello." Emma smiled. Despite her size, a giant ladybug didn't scare her anywhere near as much as a wasp with a ten-inch-long stinger.

Loud buzzing from the fog on the right preceded a trio of bugs that resembled longflies, only about three times as big. One carried a mouse, which flailed and screamed for help. Emma looked away. She felt horrible for the little rodent, but who was she to decide his life meant more than the giant longflies' lives? Hurting the insects to spare the mouse or watching him carried off to be eaten felt equally bad.

The bear swam under a patch of swamp covered in dense-packed trees that bowed toward the ill-smelling water. Branches overhead formed a tunnel, with walls of willow strands. She reached out to touch the hanging thread-like leaves, which cascaded over her arm like the hair of a giant. Fog wafted about in puffs and whorls, dancing in the breeze.

Her moment of morose thinking about the mouse came to an abrupt halt as a thick, muscular coil wrapped around her in an instant, crushing her arms against her sides and lifting her off Mawr's back into a tree above them. Neema slid down her leg and clung to her left ankle, sitting on her foot.

Emma screamed, and struggled to breathe in afterward. She stared down in a panic at several bands around her middle covered in a diamond pattern of scales, black on green. The serpent's embrace tightened in a gradual squeezing, the coils sliding past each other in alternating directions.

She lifted her head and came nose to nose with a snake so large she had no doubt it could swallow her. The length around her appeared to be the thinnest part of its long tail. Its huge body draped over several branches, as it would surely break a single one.

Mawr stopped swimming and growled while treading water. He tried to stand on his hind legs, but sank out of sight with a startled bellow. The beetle floated on the water for a second, opened its shell, stretched out its filament wings, and lumbered into the air. Seconds later, Mawr surfaced in a flailing fit and roared in frustration.

"Mmm," said the snake, flicking his white tongue at her. "I have never had this before. You smell divine."

"Please don't eat me," wheezed Emma.

The snake blinked, as if surprised she could talk. His shock wore off fast, and he narrowed his eyes. "Why?"

"Because I'm only a child."

He flicked his tongue at her nose again. "If you are a child as you say, than I would not be able to eat one of your kind when they are full size. All the more reason to taste when I can." He grinned.

Mawr paddled to the tree trunk and pulled himself up to stand on the tiny island from which it grew.

"You really shouldn't eat me," rasped Emma. She struggled to push her arms outward to get a little more air in her chest, but couldn't move.

"Oh, and why is that?" His forked tongue flicked at her cheek. "Mmm. Oh, yes, you do taste rather delicious."

Mawr stood on his hind legs, looming up taller than eye-level with Emma behind the snake.

"Because Mawr will get angry."

"What is Mawr?" asked the snake.

"Mawr is behind you." Emma gulped.

"Behind me." The snake rolled his eyes. "I've never heard that before."

Mawr growled.

The snake lowered his head, peering at the bear while upside down.

Mawr bared his teeth, snarling.

The snake lifted his head again to look at Emma, eyes wide. "You bring up an excellent point."

His tail uncoiled as fast as it had snatched her. Emma tried to scream as she fell straight down into the water, but didn't have enough air inside her to make more than a squeak. She went under for mere seconds before revulsion propelled her to the surface, where she paddled, keeping her legs tucked, afraid of putting her feet down in some horrible slime. A second after she gasped for air, Neema landed on her head.

Emma tried to stare up at her, eyebrows flattening. "Why are you sitting on my head?"

"Bright fly makes wings. See wasps will. Lightmoth think me!"

As disgusting as it was to swim in, the water had a comfortable warmth, even if it would leave her hair stinking of rotting vegetation. Mawr gave the snake a final threatening growl before sliding into the water once more. Emma wasted no time pulling herself up onto his back. She sat as she had before, with her legs tucked to one side, wet and miserable.

Not that she minded the wet, but the smell…

Mawr continued swimming for the better part of the day. Emma fidgeted at her dress, wiped at her legs and arms, trying to rub off the nasty water that had long ago dried. Her hair remained sticky and she felt in desperate need of a proper bath. She couldn't tell over the overwhelming stench in the air, but felt certain that the same smell clung to her.

Perhaps an hour after leaving the snake behind, the bear made a meal of a few fish-like creatures. Emma couldn't watch, not so much for the idea of him eating them, but because they looked more like slime blobs with eyes than actual fish. Hearing the bear's contented "mmm" noises while chewing almost made her throw up.

Soon after the daylight showed signs of fading to evening, the lilting sound of a flute carried on the breeze. Emma sat taller, peering in the direction of an island up ahead where the fog did not cover as thick.

"What's that music?" asked Emma.

Neema shrugged. "Faerie not."

"It will be dark soon. Mawr's been swimming all day. We should rest." She pointed at the island. "That place looks big enough. Is it safe?"

Neema zipped across the water, zigzagged for a moment, and returned. "Safe looks."

"I would not mind a rest," said Mawr, his deep voice vibrating in her legs.

Mawr steered toward the spot, eventually rising from the water as his paws found earth. He grunted, pulled himself up onto land, and trudged onto the island. Emma slid to the ground with a *squish,* sinking to the ankles in muddy grass, surrounded by trails of water pouring out from the bear's fur. She stretched and yawned.

"Allow me a moment." Mawr wandered off to the left. At a safe distance, he shimmied, throwing a rainstorm of droplets in all directions.

Emma walked forward, heading in the direction of the island's center, hoping the ground dried out a bit more if she got far enough away from the water. Old stone up ahead suggested an ancient building of some kind had once stood here. A section of archway, a toppled column, and dozens of loose blocks littered the ground, all covered in a healthy amount of moss and ivy. The odd flute playing continued, louder, off to the right.

"Hello?" Emma approached the arch, and braced her hand on it to peer around at a wide clearing covered in lush grass and dotted with wildflowers. A huge fallen log lay at the edge of the woods on the other side ahead of her. Behind it, a tuft of chestnut-brown hair bobbed about, only the head of a small figure visible above the massive hunk of wood. Every now and then, a glimpse of a bare human shoulder peeked out as they weaved side to side in time with the song.

At the end of the clearing to her right, a bowl-shaped nest large enough for a wagon-sized chicken to sleep on hung between three trees. All manner of random shiny objects collected around it: stones, silver plates, a handful of knives, coins, and something that sparkled like a gemstone.

Emma crept across the clearing, approaching what appeared to be a boy standing with his back to her. "Hello?"

The flute playing stopped. The boy turned to look at her. Long, wild hair hung past his shoulders, framing a face she found most enchanting. Bright amber eyes held the innocence of a boy, but his roguish smile seemed like that of an older man. His nose, thin and pointed, matched his tapered chin and made her think of the elven man she'd seen at the Feast of Zaravex. His thick hair concealed his ears, so she couldn't tell if they came to points as well. At the sight of her, he grinned.

Emma gasped when she noticed small curved horns growing from his temples.

The boy stood taller, revealing he had no shirt. An amulet of cord and animal fangs circled his neck.

"You're not wearing a tunic," said Emma. Something about this boy made her feel strange. She trusted him right away, and the urge to become friends with him grew strong. The more she looked at him, the more she wanted to run over and hug him.

"I'm not wearing anything at all," said the boy. He leapt over the tree. From the waist down, he appeared to wear shaggy fur pants, but after a second of staring, the shock wore off and Emma realized he had the legs of a goat or deer, and a small tail to boot.

"Wow…" She blinked. "Are you a satyr, like Zaravex?"

He skipped over to her and offered a hand. She took it without hesitation, admiring the rich tan of his skin, deep compared to hers. "I'm a faun, and my name is Kes. What's yours?"

She gazed into his eyes, the amber so bright it sparkled like tree sap in the sunlight. She found herself grinning, and took his hand. "I'm Emma."

"A pleasure to meet you, Emma." Kes kissed her knuckles, released her hand, and swept an arm in front of himself with a deep bow.

Emma couldn't stop staring at him. "You live in this dreadful place?"

He sighed. "It is quite a bit less dreadful now that I have you to talk to."

"You're nice."

"I've a feeling you are as well." He grinned, arms out to the sides. "You are the first human I have not been frightened of."

"You? Frightened?" She peered up at him. "But you're... umm. Strong."

Kes laughed. "The others did not feel as you do. I can tell you are different. Closer to everything." He gestured at the forest.

Mawr lumbered up behind Emma and flopped on the ground to rest.

"Oh... he's quite big." Kes took a step back, tail twitching.

Emma blinked, dazed as if she'd snapped out of a fog. "He's helping me." She squinted at Kes. The odd desire to hug him had gone away, though she still wanted to trust him. "Were you doing something to me?"

"My apologies." Kes bowed again. "It is my nature, not something I mean to do. I have to think about not doing it... If we spend enough time together, it will no longer affect you."

Neema landed on her shoulder and whispered in her ear. "Faun he is. Charm girls do they."

"You're not going to hurt me, are you?" asked Emma.

Kes's eyes widened with alarm. "Oh, never! I have been alone for a long time. It is nice to simply have someone to talk to."

His roguish grin returned, and he lifted a small wooden flute to his lips. He played, dancing and weaving about her. When he stood still, his chin met about her eye level, but while he danced, he bobbed up and down. One moment he seemed shorter than her, the next, much taller depending on how far he stretched his legs. His necklace bounced off his chest as he spun, twirled, and leapt about. Despite being about the size of a twelve-year-old boy, his narrow hooves made only the noise of a baby deer scampering in the woods. Unseen insects and a bird or five joined in the melody.

Emma walked as his rapid, circling dance around her permitted, making her way to the fallen tree, careful not to bump into him. She pulled herself up to sit on the edge of the nest and let her feet dangle over the edge. He kept playing and dancing about in front of her while she nibbled on some of the faerie cakes from the leaf-pouch. Neema took one and perched on her leg, bobbing her head and clapping along with the music.

Minutes later when he stopped, Emma applauded. "You play beautifully."

He hopped up to sit next to her, not the least bit out of breath after all that dancing and cavorting about. He grinned. She grinned, and giggled. He laughed.

"Do you play anything?" asked Kes.

"No... but sometimes I sing to my brother."

Kes tilted his head. "Would you allow me the pleasure of hearing your voice, Emma?"

She thought for a second. The first song that came to mind she'd made up to calm Tam when he threw a fit at having to go inside one night. Emma thought back to the melody, took a breath, and sang.

"THE DAYLIGHT IS FADING, THE WIND TURNING COLD.
  A house, warm and waiting, the hearth burning gold.
  Through forests and fields, how far you did roam.
  Dear little brother, run far away home.

"MEADOWS STAND SILENT AS DARKNESS DRAWS NEAR.
  Your battle is won now, there's nothing to fear.
  The dragon is slain, the goblins have fled.
  Soon, the brave knight will sleep safe in his bed.

"YOUR SWORD AND YOUR ARMOR HAVE SERVED YOU TRUE.
  Tomorrow is brimming with promises new.
  Your journey has ended, you've finished your quest.
  Moonlight is coming, tis now time to rest.

"THE DAYLIGHT IS FADING, THE WIND TURNING COLD.
  A house, warm and waiting, the hearth burning gold.
  Through forests and fields, how far you did roam.
  Dear little brother, run far away home."

KES SMILED, HIS AMBER EYES GLIMMERING. "YOU HAVE A BEAUTIFUL VOICE. Never have I heard such wonderful singing."

A hint of blush warmed her cheeks. She fidgeted and tried to stop staring at him. "My brother Tam is still little, and I sing to make him feel better when he's upset."

He gave her a curious look. "What is a knight?"

"Umm, a knight is like a soldier, but instead of fighting in wars they do quests and things to help people." A knot of worry weighed in her gut, dreading the amount of trouble she'd be in when or if she ever made it home. "Tam thinks they spend all their time trying to kill dragons."

He scratched his head. "A knight is a human? I would think a dragon wouldn't be bothered by something so small."

"I don't know." Emma bowed her head, swinging her feet back and forth. "There's stories about knights and dragons."

Kes leaned against the nest beside her. "I know a few stories, but none are of dragons. Tales of maidens fair and brave men doing noble deeds."

"I'm glad I met you. I was afraid only the Silverbell Faeries were nice here." She looked up and managed a weak smile.

"Why are you in the world of the faeries?"

"Neema asked me to help her people because animals were attacking them. I'm a druid, so she hoped I could talk to them and find out why. I think a conjurer is sending false creatures to hurt them."

He grinned. "So you are a knight?"

"I'm not."

"Are you not on a quest to help someone other than yourself?"

She huffed. "Yes, but I'm not wearing armor and I don't have a sword."

He blinked. "Is that important?"

"Not to me, but… a knight has armor and a sword."

"Do they all?" He winked.

"Umm. I don't know."

"I would like very much to be friends, Emma." Kes offered a hand. "But just friends now since I am young… only 204."

She gawked at him, but took his hand. "You're… wow. I'm ten."

He held her hand for a moment in silence. "Humans are different from fauns, but I still would like to be your friend."

"You're not charming me now, are you?" She grinned.

Kes shook his head. "No." His eyebrows perked up with a sudden idea and he took two steps back. "Follow me. I'd like to show you something."

"I should be sleeping soon. I have to find the conjurer."

He bowed. "This will take only a few minutes."

She narrowed her eyes. *I've heard that before.* "Are you sure?"

"Yes, it isn't far."

I've heard that before too. Against her better judgement, she jumped down from the nest and took his hand.

Kes led her into the small patch of forest on the island in the midst of the swamp. She caught herself staring in wonder at his tail and legs, and the line about his waist where goat fur stopped and human skin started. He looked like a farm boy, thin but strong, and moved with the grace of an elf.

"What is it like to have hooves?"

He grinned at her. "What is it like to have toes?"

She looked down at her feet. "Umm… I can wiggle them and stuff, and sometimes I jam them into the bedpost and it hurts."

"Not a bad answer." He laughed. "You can't really describe it because it's all you know."

A faint hissing noise up ahead grew to a mild roar as they walked. He led her a little ways deeper into the bushes and ducked a low-hanging vine. Emma followed, holding on to mossy tree trunks for balance while stepping over and around huge roots.

Neema followed close by, though the faerie didn't seem worried at all, so Emma kept calm.

"Not much farther," said Kes.

"All right."

He led her to a spot where a pair of trees had grown close together, with a 'staircase' of lumpy root gnarls leading up to a narrow gap between them. Without hesitation, he leapt up and through the gap, landing out of sight on the other side.

Emma braced her hands on the trees and tried to climb the roots, but her feet slipped off the slick moss. *Linganthas, please grant me the Druid's Step.*

"Do you need help, Emma?" asked Kes.

She smiled in thanks at the plant spirit and raced up the roots, her footing as sure as a dryad's. Kes started to reach through to offer his hand, but jumped back with a yelp of surprise when she barreled into the gap and nearly crashed into him. She sprang off the top, landing beside him upon a carpet of dark green grass as soft as cat fur.

"I'm a druid, remember." She held her chin high.

"So I see." Kes laughed at himself. "You are a most interesting friend."

Emma reached up and brushed a fingertip at one of his horns. "You are as well."

"Almost there." He grinned, and gestured at a small pond not far away, lined with wildflowers.

The flowers started off a deep reddish purple nearest them, and shifted to blue before becoming green and white toward the far side. At the back of the pond, a waterfall cascaded down rocky steppes covered in moss of metallic gold. Deep-red flowers perched upon green stalks near the cascading churn. Long petals ringed by another set of broader leaves made them resemble dragon's heads.

"Wow…" Emma stared at the scenery. "This is so pretty. Thank you for showing me this."

Kes crouched low and fussed with something. "I thought you would like it."

"Wait… isn't this an island? Why is there a waterfall here?"

"It's a tiny mountain at the very center of my island. The water bubbles up inside it and spills over the top."

"This is *your* island?" She leaned back, eyebrows up.

He laughed. "Well, I live here right now. So, it is mine."

"I suppose that makes sense." She turned her head to watch a passing butterfly that appeared made of amber glass.

Kes stood, hiding something behind his back. Emma narrowed her eyes at him in playful suspicion as he trotted over.

"What are you hiding?"

Kes grinned and produced a crown of wildflowers.

Blushing, she ducked a little so he could put it on her head. "They're pretty. Thank you!"

He bowed before taking her hand. "As promised, only a few minutes."

Emma smiled at the beautiful waterfall pond for a little longer before following him back to his hanging bed. He brought her to the side of the 'nest,' and gestured at it.

"You may sleep here tonight."

"I don't want to steal your bed."

Kes shook his head. "It is fine. You will need strength for your quest."

She fought the urge to roll her eyes, but pulled herself up into the giant swaying bowl. Kes caught her left ankle, and tickled the bottom of her foot.

Emma squealed and rolled onto her back, laughing. "Stop! Stop!"

He kept tickling her while she writhed and giggled, until she sat up and tried to grab his hand. With that, he let go, and they touched foreheads, his horns pressing against the sides of her temples.

Eye to eye, nose to nose, he winked. "So that's what it's like to have toes."

Emma's laughter subsided to a broad grin. "That wasn't fair."

He tilted his head, his horns making hers tilt as well. "What will you do when you finish your quest?"

Her sad eyes turned downcast. "I'll go home."

"You long to be with your family. I can feel your love for them."

"Yes." Emma sniffled.

"I would travel with you then. When you go home, you will no longer be in the faerie world. While you are here, I would like to spend time with you."

Emma reclined, curling up in a ball at the deepest point of the bowl-shaped nest. "All right, but I don't want you to get hurt."

"I don't want you to be hurt." He winked and pulled a blanket of woven grass over her.

Emma smiled. Neema draped herself over Emma's head, one arm dangling in front of her eye.

"Friends?" whispered Kes.

She yawned, nodding. "Friends."

16

GOLEM

The next morning, Kes offered her a pale white tuber. He demonstrated snapping it in half and eating the insides, which tasted similar to mashed potatoes and butter, only cold. The lack of sweetness made it a welcome change from the faerie cakes she'd been eating for three days. He fed a few of the same vegetables to Mawr, who ate them whole. Neema turned her nose up at them, and devoured an entire cake herself. Emma blinked in disbelief as the tiny woman polished off a cake larger than her head.

After finishing her meal, Emma hopped up on Mawr's back with Kes sitting behind her. He seemed less comfortable about the idea of riding upon a bear, and fidgeted about until finally putting his arms around her from behind. Emma smiled to herself. Sometimes, she found it annoying how everyone in Widowswood, especially all the grownups, felt it necessary to constantly pat her head, squeeze her shoulder, or full-on hug her. However, for some reason, she didn't mind Kes clinging to her.

Not even a little bit.

Neema hopped off her shoulder, slid down the front of Emma's dress, and marched over the bear's head to stand almost at the point of his snoot. "There almost are we."

"How much more swamp is there?" asked Emma.

"Darbolg is vast," said Kes. "But it is long to the north and south, and we are heading west. If we keep going this way, we'll reach the edge in a few hours."

Emma nodded. *Strixian, please let my family know I am okay.*

Mawr traversed deep pools that forced him to swim, shallower water that let him trudge, and short patches of solid ground between waterways. A few hours after they'd left Kes's island, a cluster of hawk-sized moths went by, each radiating a dingy white glow. They corkscrewed about as if they couldn't manage a straight line. One slapped into the side of a tree with a distinct "oof." He clung for a few seconds before mumbling, "Oh, where did that tree come from?" and taking wing again.

Emma giggled.

Swaths of solid ground became more and more frequent as they continued west. A bit over two hours after the lightmoths went by, Mawr pulled himself out of the water at what appeared to be the edge of the swamp. He caught his breath and got walking again. The fog lessened over the next several minutes, and soon the familiar roperoot trees surrounded them.

Mawr marched onward, navigating the crisscross of thick wooden tubes with little effort, pausing here and there to feast on berries as big as Emma's fist. She reached out and grabbed a few after Neema assured her a human could eat them without worry. They resembled plums, and smelled sweet. She took two, and gave Kes three.

The inside flesh had a dark purple color and tasted like blackberry. A fibrous strand in the middle connected the top to the bottom, ringed with lots of hard seeds. Emma nibbled around them, pleasantly full after finishing her two. Neema ate a hair less than half of one, and Emma finished it off. Kes ate his in three bites apiece, consuming everything—including the seed thread.

Soon after the berry stop, a moving patch of bright pink caught her eye up ahead beyond some trees. She perked up, staring in that direction, stunned at the idea she might've spotted a walking flower. Before she could ask Kes what she'd seen, a creature wandered into view, seeming in all ways but color a goat. It lifted its head in curiosity, staring at them as if it couldn't quite understand the meaning of an enormous bear carrying a human child and a faun.

"Hello," said Emma.

Another goat appeared, this one lemon yellow. Behind it two more, one green and one blue.

The pink one let out howling laughter like an insane man.

Emma jumped at the sudden piercing noise. "Ack!"

"Aaaaaaaaaah!" screamed the green goat.

"Bwahahahahah!" roared the yellow goat.

The blue one threw its head back and cackled.

"Hello?" asked Emma.

Eight goats stared at her with blank expressions. As she opened her mouth to speak again, they all shrieked at once with a noise like a crowd of people screaming in terror, though their expressions remained... bored.

Emma jumped again. "What's wrong with them?"

"Being false I think." Neema scratched her head. "Talking to you can?"

"Ahhh! Ahhh! Ahhh!" The purple goat sounded like a man being boiled alive.

"No. They're only laughing and screaming."

"They don't feel like animals," said Kes.

Neema giggled. "Know them do you?"

Emma winced.

"No." Kes laughed. "I've not met them before."

"We must be getting close," said Emma. "I think the conjurer made them."

"Aaaaaaaaaah!" shrieked the red goat. Though it sounded like a terrified man, the animal stood there chewing on a branch with a sleepy expression.

Mawr kept walking, and soon the continuous manic laughter and screaming of goats faded to silence. Pine trees appeared every so often among the more unusual faerie-world trees, and after perhaps another hour of travel, became the majority.

At a distant *thump*, Emma jumped. "What was that?"

"What?" asked Neema.

"I heard it too," said Kes. "A heavy sound, like someone dropping a rock."

Every few seconds came a *thump... thump... thump.*

"Or something big walking." Emma huddled down low to Mawr's back, pulling Kes forward such that he almost lay on top of her. "Maybe we don't want to let it see us."

"Mawr is huge." Kes chuckled. "I don't think he can hide."

"There," whispered Neema.

Emma looked at where the little woman pointed. A man-shaped being, seemingly made of bronze, approached from ahead and a bit off to the right. The right arm ended in a blade the size of a broadsword, while its left arm had a human-shaped hand clutching a shield. Its head resembled a knight's helm with a T-shaped opening. It had no mouth, and two amethyst-colored spots glowed where eyes should be.

"What is that?" asked Emma.

"It looks like a golem," said Kes.

"What is a golem?" Emma blinked.

Kes let go of her with one arm and pointed at it. "That is a golem."

She sighed. "I mean is it going to hurt—"

Its helmet rotated to face them as a bright glow welled up inside it. Kes leapt off Mawr's back, dragging Emma with him. Before they hit the ground, a beam of pale purple energy shot forth from the golem's eyes, singeing the fur where they had been sitting. Emma landed into a somersault, and bounced up to her feet.

Mawr grumbled. "Ouch."

"Run!" she yelled, taking a few hesitant strides to the left.

The golem raised its blade arm and lumbered toward Mawr. While it did not move alarmingly fast, Emma had a feeling it would never get tired… and would follow them until they dropped from exhaustion.

"Golem," said Emma. "We don't want to fight."

It ignored her, continuing to tromp after them.

Kes stretched his left arm out and made a gripping motion at empty air. In a flash of green-yellow light, a fancy recurve bow appeared in his hand. Dark polished wood engraved with elven patterns gleamed in the light of an arrow forming from the same magical light. He raised the bow, barely seeming to aim before firing. The arrow streaked for the large bronze helmet, striking the metal a mere half-inch from one of the glowing eye spots.

The golem shifted direction and tromped toward Kes.

"Linganthas, lend me your strength." Emma gestured with both arms toward the golem, imagining a tangle of vines as thick as her arms rising up and ensnaring its legs.

The roots erupted from the ground as she had pictured them, winding around the bronze boots and dragging the false metal man to a halt. It strained against the bonds toward Kes, evidently unaware of why it couldn't move forward. He raised another arrow, but the helmet rotated to the side, protecting the eyes.

Kes darted to the right, circling about.

Mawr charged at it.

The golem raised its blade and shield.

"Mawr, stop!" yelled Emma.

Roaring, the great bear lunged into a downward paw whomp that caught the golem square in the shield, knocking the towering monstrosity to the ground and sending it sliding backward, snapping free from the ensnaring roots around its thick metal legs. Fortunately, the bear hit the bronze man so hard, he knocked it away before the sword swiping for his head came around.

Kes, a ways off on the right side, fired again. Alas, the golem got its shield up, deflecting the arrow with a dull *clank.* He readied another arrow, but before he could loose, the golem projected a beam of purple energy from its eyes, forcing him to dive to the side as the magical ray seared a long streak of fire on the ground.

Emma sprinted away from the clearing into the brush, darting around a tree for protection from the energy beam. She clung to the trunk, peering around the side at the golem chasing Kes about in circles. The faun ran in long, bounding strides, jumping whenever the golem let off a blast from its eye gems. Mawr lumbered after them, but didn't appear to be working too hard to catch up.

Kes jumped into a twist, shooting an arrow backward at the pursuing golem, but again, it deflected off the shield.

"Linganthas, please send forth your strength." Emma gestured upward with both hands.

Roots lanced up from the ground and tangled the golem's legs, tripping it flat on its front with a resounding *clank.* Kes skidded to a halt, his hooves spraying moss, and raised his bow with an arrow at the ready. Emitting an eldritch buzzing, the golem's upper body rose up like a trapdoor, bending at the knees. Kes fired, but again, the shield got in the way. Mawr traipsed up behind the golem.

A brilliant yellow-white bolt zipped out from among the trees, bounced off the golem's back with little visible effect, and careened into the brush. Neema blurted a loud, single word in the faerie language that sounded like "*Nyzbix!*" Her apparent anger faded in an instant.

She stared at Emma, blushed, and covered her mouth. "Telling the queen I said that not please be don't."

The bronze man pushed itself standing, tearing the writhing roots from the ground.

Emma focused her attention on the largest of the strands she'd called, about as thick as her leg. She reached out with her mind, feeling for a sense of control. Her thoughts touched the essence of the magic within, and she willed it to grow longer.

The root shot upward at her direction, wrapping around the golem's shield arm and yanking it down to the side.

Kes let off a short laugh of delight, and fired.

His arrow struck the golem in the helmet, setting off an explosion of purple energy with the twinkling crunch of smashing glass. The golem flailed its blade arm and staggered back, tugged to a halt by the root around its shield arm.

Emma growled, pushing her hands down in the air. The root creaked, straining to drag the metal construct to the ground. She shook from the effort, straining and grunting as trying to lift a weight too heavy for her to bear. Her vine mirrored her gesture, struggling against the golem's might.

Mawr reared up on his hind legs and bashed the golem in the back. The strike knocked the bronze contraption off its feet. It swung around on the root like a tetherball, careening into the side of a tree and bouncing away with a great clamor before crashing to the ground. Emma directed the root to keep pulling on its shield arm. Kes darted to the left and leapt clear over Mawr, his legs tucked up tight, letting an arrow fly while he sailed through the air.

The shot struck true, smashing the second amethyst eye into a burst of crystalline fragments. Twitching and buzzing, the golem lurched to its feet, violet lightning sparking from its joints. It slashed downward, stepped forward, slashed sideways, pivoted, thrust the blade forward, and took a step back while executing a wild upswing. A second later, it repeated the same sequence of attacks.

It looks like one of the Watch in training, doing the same moves over and over.

Mawr watched for three repetitions of its routine. As it slashed downward for the fourth time, he reared up on two legs and swatted the golem with a double-paw slap that bashed it flat. He lurched forward and bounced his full weight on it, crushing the chest like a poorly made cauldron.

A dazzling orb of violet lightning swelled up from the golem, growing brighter and larger.

"Uhh…" Mawr scrambled backward as fast as he could move.

With a brilliant flash of purple light, the golem blasted apart into loose pieces. A wave of energy rolled over Mawr, making his fur stand on end and turning him into an enormous brown puffball.

Emma let off a nervous giggle, but screamed and ducked when a fragment of smoking metal shot over her head.

"Ouch," said Mawr. He sat back on his haunches and huffed.

Her mirth flashed to concern. She sprinted out from her hiding place and hurried past twisted scraps of bronze littering the soft green moss-carpet, many of them still smoking. Glittering spots flickered here and there from scattered shards of its smashed eye gems. As soon as her hand touched his fur, her hair fluffed out. A faint metallic scent lingered around him like the air after a thunderstorm.

"Are you hurt?"

Mawr sneezed. "I do not believe so, but that did not feel pleasant."

Emma exhaled in relief. She stooped to grasp a small piece of metal, but yelped, dropped it, and stuck her finger in her mouth, whimpering. The fragment had been as hot as a pan from the stove. Once the pain faded, she wandered around the wreckage, both curious and horrified at such a thing. She kept her gaze downward to avoid stepping on anything sharp or hot. Sunlight glinting in the moss drew her to where the creature's broadsword blade landed, still attached to a length of forearm.

Dried blood caked around the hilt.

She shivered. "Oh, no… it's hurt someone."

Kes walked up and put an arm around her. "Are *you* hurt?"

"No. Are you?"

He smiled. "I'm too fast for such a clumsy thing."

"You're quite a shot." She smiled.

"I'm okay. My parents were much better… I've only had this bow for forty years or so."

She stared at him and folded her arms. "Oh. Only."

He used the tip of the bow to scratch the side of his head next to a horn. "What?"

"I keep forgetting how old you are. You look like you're maybe ten or eleven."

"Well." He shrugged. The bow disappeared in a flash of magic. "If I were human, I probably would be. We don't grow up as fast as humans. You may think I am old, but I'm really not so different from you."

She crouched over the broken metal arm. "Who do you think it hurt?"

Kes squatted at her side. "I don't think anyone lives here but animals."

That thought didn't cheer her up at all. "Do you think the conjurer will try to hurt me?"

"I cannot say until we see him." He took her hand. "As soon as I look into his eyes, I will know what sort of man he is. If I think he would hurt you, I will distract him so you can get away."

Her eyes widened. "I don't want you to get hurt either!"

"He won't catch me." Kes flashed his rogue's grin, and disappeared.

Emma stared at her hand, which still felt as he held it. "Kes?"

"Right here," he said, sounding no farther away. "I'm invisible."

"That's amazing," whispered Emma.

"Pff." Neema scoffed, and turned invisible. "Turn can't who invisible?"

"Umm. I can't," said Emma.

Kes reappeared. "That's why I'll distract him so you can hide." He stood and tugged her upright. "But we don't know if he's going to be mean yet. There are not many humans here, so he will probably at least want to talk to you first."

Emma nodded. "I hope so."

"Is far not," said Neema, also reappearing.

Mawr ambled over. "Shall we continue?"

"Yes. Before he hurts anyone else." Emma climbed onto Mawr's back.

Kes followed, again encircling her with his arms. Neema stood upon Mawr's brow in the pose of a captain commanding a warship, and pointed west.

With a soft grunt, Mawr lurched into motion. Emma gripped his fur, staring ahead into the trees, hoping that this man would not be anything at all like the last mage she'd run into.

17

CHILD OF LINGANTHAS

*P*erhaps an hour later, the forest grew dim despite it being the middle of the day. Emma gazed upward at the abundant canopy, which blocked most of the sunlight and left the woods cool and dark. No longer pines, the trees in this place had gnarled trunks as wide as houses at the base, but tapered narrower near the top some fifty or sixty feet overhead. Most of their branches clustered at the upper reaches, with only a few jutting out farther down. Glowing pale-blue lichen clung to the furrows in the wood, seeming to thrive in the dark conditions nearer the ground.

The mossy undergrowth she'd become so accustomed to did not continue into this shrouded wood, rather the ground appeared made of roots, smoothed and flattened by weather and the passage of creatures. Wavy patterns reminded her of noodles packed tight together. Gouges in the roots every so often put her on edge. Whatever creature had claws big enough to create furrows she could stick her entire arm into seemed like the sort of creature she should probably avoid.

Mawr lumbered onward. Neema pointed to the right and seemed satisfied after he turned a little in that direction. A few minutes later, they entered a clearing around a most unusual large hill, covered in moss and brambles. It swelled up from the ground quite all of a sudden, in the middle of an otherwise flat area. The rounded shape stood three or four

Mawrs tall, and appeared made of the same mushed-together roots as the forest floor.

"How odd," said Emma.

"What?" Kes leaned his chin over her right shoulder.

"That hill. It's quite fat and round." She traced a pumpkin shape in the air with her hands. "It looks like a ball of roots. Maybe it's a strange kind of tree?"

"Fat and round?" said a voice so deep it made the very air shake.

The hill moved, uncurling. A long tail covered in green leaves and moss stretched out to the right, while the left end extended into a neck. Four powerful legs pushed the entire mass off the ground, and a dragon's head made of intertwined roots with trails of hanging plant matter for whiskers swung around to face her. Patches of 'hill' slid apart, evident as folded wings. Eyes of solid green light regarded her with a curious expression; bushy moss eyebrows climbed. The dragon's whiskers twitched, and he huffed a chuckle that carried the fragrance of mint and herbs.

Emma's jaw hung open. *Run! Don't stare at it. Run!*

"Well. Hmm. I'd return your most ungracious comment, but there is nothing to you." The dragon leaned his nose in close. Roots creaked as his lips peeled back into a grin. "Fat and round indeed."

"Umm." Emma trembled. "Please forgive me for calling you fat. I didn't realize you were a... dragon?"

"Hmm." The dragon scratched at its jaw with a single claw of dark, polished wood. His eyes flared, and he offered a quick nod. "Apology accepted."

That's a dragon. A real... dragon. And he's looking. At. Me.

Kes squeezed her.

"I sense the spirit's favor within you." The dragon smiled. "Your fear is needless."

Emma swallowed. "What spirit?"

"Why, Linganthas of course." The dragon's eyes widened, glowing brighter. "I am an embodiment of his essence. Your kind often refer to my kind as his children."

"Are you a dragon? Or a tree? Or..."

"I am a Child of Linganthas." The dragon bowed his head in reverence. "My body is that of wood and leaf, my soul that of a dragon. You have called to him for aid many times. He knows you."

Emma nodded. Her trembles stilled as awe and wonder filled her. "I was in trouble and asked him for help. He was kind enough to hear me."

"Mmm. Yes, I can feel that you are unaccustomed to his gift." The dragon lowered himself to the ground in a rather catlike posture. "The Spirit is within everything that grows from seed or spore. In this place, he is around you, beside you, under your feet. Respect him and he shall always favor you. Indulge me, human child. How have you called upon him?"

She grinned and told the dragon of getting stuck in the bog, and of calling a thornvine as Mama had, and of tripping up the golem. All the while, the dragon nodded.

"You are starting to see. You call upon his favor, but do not allow the essence into your thoughts. Too much like a wizard. They beckon fire and throw it, no longer caring what it does once they've made it." A root emerged from the ground beneath her, coiled around her waist, and lifted her up. Smaller roots branched away from it, seeking her feet, which they supported like steps.

Emma waved her arms for balance, grinning with delight as the roots carried her up into the air.

"You asked for a root and tried to pull yourself from the bog, but you could have done this and been lifted free. The roots of the spirit are more than common branches for climbing."

Emma nodded. "I'm sorry. I did not know."

Twisting and creaking, the writhing root lowered her to the ground and receded out of sight.

"Learn. Now, you try." The dragon pointed at a raindrop-shaped pod some thirty feet high in a nearby tree. "Do as I have demonstrated, and retrieve the fruit."

Emma walked over to stand below the branch. Kes followed, as did Neema. Mawr flopped on his side, figuring it a prime opportunity for a nap.

"When you diverted that walking junk heap's shield, you started to learn." The dragon offered a sagely nod. "Do the same now. Allow the life energy of Linganthas' growth to touch your own. Share with it your thoughts and actions. The roots shall become as another limb."

"Linganthas, please send forth your energy." She focused on the desire to create a long, winding root, thick enough to support her weight.

As it took shape in her mind, she sensed living material sprout from the ground between her feet. It coiled around her leg, winding higher until it wrapped around her hips and chest. Emma concentrated on the living presence within the magic, exploring the energy until it no longer felt like a root grasping her, but another part of her body that had grown down into the earth. Scratchy wood embraced the bottoms of her feet, supporting her weight. She swayed forward, then overcorrected to the right, waving her arms while a whine of alarm leaked from her nose.

The dragon's whispers at the back of her mind nudged her along, shaping how she perceived the magic and teaching her how to guide her thoughts to merge with the essence of the life energy in the root. Emma opened her thoughts to Linganthas, and within a moment, the point where her toes ended and roots began blurred in her mind. The roots themselves took on the sense of being extensions of her legs, carrying her upward, no longer an outside force. Gliding upward became almost as natural as walking. Higher and higher she stretched, raising her arms to grasp the dark purple fruit. When she reached it, she gawked at its size—larger than her head.

"Is it all right to take this?" asked Emma. "Can I eat it and will it harm the tree to pick?"

The dragon raised its head toward her. "You may eat it, and the tree will not miss it."

Emma wrapped her arms around the fruit and gave a tug. It snapped free and sent her swaying with its weight. She caught herself as easily as if she'd taken a step back. Gradually, she willed the roots to recede, lowering herself to the ground. Once her feet met the smooth interwoven floor of the grove, she sent the root back where it had come from.

A bit tired from the use of this new magic, she sat in place with the fruit between her knees. "Thank you for teaching me."

The dragon smiled. "I sense that it is not within your nature to cause harm, but there are times when such actions are inevitable. The magic you know as 'thornvine' or a 'whipthorn' is somewhat different. In that regard, you do not touch its essence, but concentrate on a single instant of need to defend yourself."

Emma nodded.

Kes sat next to her, produced a small knife from apparent thin air, and cut the rind of the fruit open. He divided it into sections: a tiny one for Neema, a small part for Emma, a similar-sized one for himself, and the bulk of it for Mawr.

The fruit's insides had an iridescent purple-blue color with stringy threads that got stuck between her teeth. Sweet and tart in equal measure, the fruit burst with flavor inside her mouth, making her cough.

"Are you all right?" asked Kes, nibbling.

"It's like eating blueberries and lemons together." She cleared her throat and coughed once more. "Strong."

"Neema like." The faerie took great chomping bites of her piece.

The dragon settled himself like a cat curling up for a nap, though he didn't close his eyes.

He's a giant... Emma stared. *Shrub Dragon. Tam would come apart at the seams if he saw him.*

Mawr appeared to like the fruit as well, and continued licking the rind well after any trace of its flesh had gone.

"Dragon, do you know where all the crazy false animals are coming from?" asked Emma.

"Yes." The dragon pointed with his tail in about the same direction Neema had been going. "There is a small house some distance that way, on the far side of a canyon. A bridge lies nearby, but it is old. Be careful when crossing."

She sucked at fruit bits in her teeth, smacking her lips.

Kes laughed. "Your lips and tongue are dark blue."

Emma glanced at him. "So are yours."

He stuck his tongue out at her.

She responded in kind.

Neema raspberried them both.

Emma giggled. Her moment of levity faded fast, and she let out a long sigh. "Do you think the conjurer will want to hurt me?"

"Hmm. I believe this man has lost his mind. He is not... oh, what is the word in the human language..." The dragon waved a clawed hand about in the air for a second. "Sane. Yes. I believe he has become not sane."

"Is he dangerous?" Emma drew her knees together at her chin.

The dragon scratched at his chin. "Erm... most likely not to you, since you are a child, and human as is he. No... I do not believe he would be a threat to you, but be wary. Those who are not sane may become angry at the slightest offense."

"All right." She looked at his wings, folded against the length of his back. "Can you leave the faerie realm?"

"Of course." The dragon smiled.

"Were you... maybe flying around the other day in my world? Really high up?"

His grin turned whimsical, thin roots like whiskers around his chin perked up. "Perhaps."

Emma twisted her big toe at the ground. "Great Child of Linganthas, might I ask of you a small favor?"

He tilted his hand toward her, palm up. "That would depend entirely on what it is you ask."

"Oh…" Emma clasped her hands together. "I was hoping you would be willing to say hello to someone."

"Hmm." The dragon settled into a napping posture and closed his eyes, resting his chin upon a great paw. "Perhaps I can do that."

18

OLD ENOUGH

*M*awr resumed his walk across the dark forest, leaving behind the clearing in which they'd met the wood dragon. She grinned with anticipation at how Tam would react to seeing a real dragon up close. *He'll either be thrilled, or need clean breeches.* She hoped for the former. Balancing surprise with not wanting to scare him to death, she decided to arrange the meeting where Tam could see the dragon from a distance first.

After a few miles, sunlight strengthened among the trees. A clear line between dark and light approached, as if they left an area where magic had shaped the woods as a deliberate shelter. The oddity of it brought Emma's thoughts back to the matter at hand, rather than daydreaming of how happy her little brother would be. Perhaps the dragon had done that? Of course... a dragon made of wood lairing in the forest would want some privacy. He wouldn't crawl under some stuffy mountain.

Past the edge of the heavy shade, the trees resembled those of Widowswood, only many times the size and covered in white bark. Leaves of green and gold concealed the source of musical birdcalls with melodies that made Emma imagine faeries playing flutes. Mawr trekked onward, an unstoppable titan crossing ground at a dizzying pace. Emma stroked the fur at his neck, grateful for his help. Walking to this place on her own would've taken ten times as long... and required she swim that awful swamp. The bear seemed to sense her gratitude and affection, and hummed contentedly.

A few hours after entering the well-lit forest, the ruins of white stone structures came into view among the trees. A scattering of large blocks on the left, overgrown with moss and shrubs, appeared to be the ruins of a long-ago collapsed building. Farther ahead on both sides, crumbling spires reminded her of the Elder Grove, only much larger, as if built by faeries as tall as humans.

"This must have been an elf city," said Emma.

"I've not been here before, but it does look like that." Kes gazed about, his awestruck grin contagious. "'Tis a magnificent sight to behold, is it not?"

"Yes." Emma leaned back against him, momentarily overcome by a strong belief that nothing could go wrong if she stayed close to him. She tilted her head, gazing at him with an adoring expression.

He looked from the spires to her, noticed the way she stared at him, and made a face like she'd caught him stealing cookies. The need to lean on him disappeared. "Sorry about that. I lost my concentration while admiring the ruins."

Emma sat up straight, realizing she'd been charmed. He hadn't meant anything bad by it, so she kept smiling, though nowhere near as adoringly. "It's all right. This place is quite a sight."

She glanced up at a seven-story tower made of decorative stone swirls. Whoever had built it had possessed such skill that the walls appeared to be a single piece of stone rather than individual bricks, even after sitting in ruin so long. A strong sense of melancholy hung over the place, like a home the day after a holiday meal when all the guests had gone away.

"Live here not do anymore the Astari." Neema glided back and forth, studying some carvings on the stone. "Gone other place have to the tall fey. Much long ago."

"The forest is taking over again," said Kes. "I wonder why they abandoned this place."

Neema shook her head. "Know I do not."

"I hear water." Mawr nosed to the right. "I believe there is a chasm ahead, with a river at the bottom."

"Cross must we," said Neema.

They followed a path of glimmering chromatic stones set in the earth to form a road. Grass and spongy moss had mostly overtaken the path, but it connected to similar paths all throughout the ruin. Much like the faerie's city, the Astari had made their buildings open and airy, using nearby trees without uprooting or cutting into them. She figured they had druids who could guide the trees around the structures, but since the Astari had abandoned the place, nature grew as it desired. Without their influence, branches had broken or pushed aside many walls, floors, and roofs.

Emma's roaming gaze stalled on a twin set of tall white stone spires gleaming in the distance, beyond a star-shaped courtyard and a crumbling fountain. A series of pointed arches in two rows rose high over the greenery, hinting at the shape of a decorative bridge hidden behind a sloping hill. To her left, the elven buildings continued for a fair ways. Perhaps a mile to the south, a huge white dome peeked above closer buildings. Lines formed from green gemstone traced the shapes of leaves down the walls from the top of the dome, and a watery shimmer flickered along the bottom suggesting a pool of water at its base.

I wonder what's in there... it looks important.

At Neema's urging, Mawr headed for the bridge, following the ancient stone path to avoid rubble as best he could. The roar of distant water grew louder as they approached, and within a few minutes, they came to a halt few paces from the bridge.

The spires towered five stories overhead, great beams supporting hundreds of thin white roots that held up the walkway. She had a feeling the beams had been made of stone, but couldn't tell if the 'roots' had been actual roots or more stone worked by a master artisan. Dense ivy covered both sides of the bridge, hanging down in wavering trails into the chasm. Cracks and holes covered the entire span, filling Emma's belly with a sick, worried weight.

"Uhh... That doesn't look at all safe." She gulped.

Mawr paused. "I do not think I should set foot upon it."

"Make lighter." Neema hugged the top of Mawr's head.

He wobbled, emitting an uneasy groan. "I... what have you done?"

"As leaves weigh the bear does," sang Neema.

Emma threw her leg up and over his head and slid to the ground. "She can only make one of us light at a time. We shouldn't ride him across."

Kes slipped off. For an instant, he seemed in the throes of a clumsy fall he didn't expect, but he recovered in midair and landed with grace. "Come, Emma. We're light enough already."

He darted out onto the bridge, hooves tapping with a gleeful prance upon the stone slabs.

"Wait! No… one at a time with Neema making…" She sighed and hurried after him.

Hundreds of tiny rocks scattered across the bridge surface, likely debris from all the holes. Emma gasped at the coldness of the stone beneath her feet and almost decided to turn back when she spotted a sharp thorn that had no doubt broken off one of the supporting cables. Much to her dismay, the wind made the entire bridge sway and wobble. The *click, click, click* of Kes's hooves got faint enough to be alarming. Emma snapped her gaze up and almost gasped at how far away he'd gotten. She kept looking between him and where she stepped, terrified of putting her foot in a crack or hole.

"I feel like I'm flying," yelled Kes, his voice echoing.

Emma stopped short at what she thought to be a pit in the bridge surface, but her toes curled over the edge of a hole big enough to swallow her. Paralyzed, she stared at a perfect view of churning whitewater a long… long… way down.

And screamed.

Kes stopped and spun to face her. "What's wrong?"

Emma backed away from the hole, her legs refusing to bend more than a little bit. "I don't like this bridge. We need to find another way."

"The canyon goes for miles. It would take a week to go around." He walked backwards three steps, arms wide to the sides, grinning. "Come on."

Emma forced herself to keep going around the hole. *I'm a small girl. I don't weigh much. Everyone says I'm little for my age. I'm not going to break the bridge.* A sharp gust of wind flipped her hair to the side and made her clutch her toes at the smooth stone. *Nan isn't scared of heights.* She smirked at herself. *Nan is a raven. Birds can fly.* The odd thought of a bird being afraid of heights made her giggle.

Kes laughed and pivoted around to trot. "Someone's slooooow."

"Stop it." Emma avoided another deep crack and crept around a wide pockmark. "Don't be careless."

"I'm not being careless." He whistled. "I'm being adventurous."

Emma yelled, "Adventurous and foolish are often the same thing. Da says that."

He laughed.

She looked up again and wanted to scream at him for getting so far away, almost to the middle of the span. *Ooh! He's just like Tam. What is it with boys!?* Part of her wanted to move faster, part of her wanted to curl up into a ball and sit tight.

He spun to face her again, walking backward. "Hurry up. It's—"

Kes' hoof came down on a chip of rock that shot out from under him. His legs flashed into a blur of motion, his hooves making a *clickety clickety clickety* noise as he careened to the left, kicking small stones around in a spray, unable to find traction. Screaming and stumbling, he slipped over the side, barely managing to catch the edge.

"Kes!" shrieked Emma.

She bolted to a sprint, trying to run as light as possible on the balls of her feet. When she came within two steps of where his hands clung to the edge, the whole slab shifted downward. Shrieking, she flailed her arms and skidded to a stop. Massive root cables on both sides creaked and groaned, stone flaking from them in chips. Emma stared up at the narrow cords, shivering as hundreds of tiny cracks spread all over them. They seemed ready to snap from even a mouse's weight.

With a nervous groan, Mawr pulled himself onto the bridge. "I am coming. Hold on, boy."

Emma almost shouted for him to stop, but remembered he didn't weigh anything as long as Neema stayed touching him. She whirled back to Kes, and cupped her mouth with both hands. "Kes! It's okay. Mawr's almost here." *Wait. No!* "Neema! Make Kes weigh nothing! He's going to fall."

Mawr stopped, groaned, and ambled backward to get off the bridge so the faerie could let go of him.

"I... I'm sorry, Emma." Kes struggled to pull himself up, but slipped back farther than he'd climbed. "You're right. I suppose I was reckless."

His fingers continued to slip.

"No!" screamed Emma. She leapt into a dive, sliding on her chest, and grabbed his wrists.

The twenty-foot-long slab of bridge beneath her broke apart from the rest of the walkway, bobbed, and dropped two inches. The support cables cracked, puffs of dust raining from above as a creaking groan made the entire bridge shudder. She stared down at him, goat legs futilely trying to step on ivy and snapping it. Hundreds of feet below, rocky water churned white and deadly. Cold wind whipped her hair into her face.

Tiny, distant shouting came from Neema, but Emma's brain didn't make sense of any words.

Kes, bright amber eyes wide with fear, tried to put on a brave face.

"Let go... Let me fall. I don't want you to die too." He grunted and tried to get a better grip, but his fingers slipped on the disintegrating stone.

Emma squeezed his wrists with all her strength. The slab upon which she lay lurched down another inch and jerked to a stop. It wouldn't matter if she let go. Their section of bridge was about to break and send them both falling. Even if Neema got there fast enough, she could only make one of them weightless.

"Linganthas!" shouted Emma "I need your aid. Lend your power to the ivy."

She stared intently at the spread of vines all over the side of the bridge. At her urging, they came to life. Slender runners coiled around Kes's legs. Leafy tendrils of ivy came up over the bridge and wrapped around her whole body, drawing them up in a cocoon of leafy cords, the vines embracing and lifting them. Neema zoomed into her chest, clinging. Concentrating on the plant's essence, Emma opened herself to the vines, making them an extension of her body. A sense of having grown wings lessened her fear of falling—somewhat.

The support cables broke with a great rippling series of *cracks*, revealing the 'thorny stems' to be artistic stonework. The slab of walkway swung downward like an opening door, hanging vertically. Emma shrieked as she fell, swinging into Kes and colliding chest to chest.

Neema squeaked.

They swayed in the nest of still-moving ivy that tightened in response to her fear. The twenty-foot-long piece of bridge hung for the span of two breaths before it snapped from the other side and plummeted, tumbling, into the abyss below. Chunks of stone rods from the disintegrating cables tumbled end over end on their way into the churning rapids.

Faint muttering came from between them, Neema struggling to wriggle upward. She disappeared in a puff of silver-white energy, and shouted at her from a short distance above and behind.

Emma's terror urged the ivy to keep grasping at them. Moving plants lashed her and Kes together in such a firm weave that it became difficult to breathe. Their clasped hands dug into her chest, his chin rested on her shoulder, their cheeks touching. The ivy gripped them so securely, she couldn't move any part of her body except for wiggling her toes.

"Emma! Kes!" bellowed Mawr.

Neema shrieked something she couldn't understand, part scream of horror, part faerie language.

"We're alive," wheezed Kes, his voice vibrating her chest.

A tremendous *boom* echoed up from the river below as the slab crashed into the water. Emma startled, and the ivy cocoon clenched for an instant in response.

Wrapped in vines, dangling like a bees' nest over a fatal drop, Emma couldn't think. Every ounce of her concentration went toward keeping the ivy holding them secure. Kes squirmed.

"You are getting quite good at that vine magic, but perhaps it is a bit *too* tight. We must breathe."

She whined.

"Can you move us back to the bridge?"

Emma gulped. She loosened the upper part of the vine so she could pull her head away from his shoulder and look to her right at the next section of bridge. One by one, idle strands of ivy came to life and reached out to join the snarl on that side, while others to her left released. Their bundle migrated sideways, gliding to the west to reach the next slab of walkway. Emma directed the ivy to lift them up onto the surface and set them flat upon solid stone. Shivering with fear, she lay motionless while Kes squirmed and wriggled.

"You can unwrap us," wheezed Kes.

Emma turned her head left and right, staring at the stone on which she lay. "Sorry. I'm still scared."

He hummed the melody she had sung to him the other day, *Far Away Home*. Squeezed as tight as she was to him with her chin over his shoulder, she couldn't see his face, but he had to be smiling. Soon, thoughts of home as well as her new friend eased her mind, and the ivy released them. The vines receded, sliding back off the edge to hang as they had done before Linganthas had sent his aid.

Emma remained flat on her back, out of breath and too terrified to move.

Neema landed standing on her chest, rattling in Faerie so fast she made no sense.

"I thought I was going to die." Kes lifted her hand, kissed it, and clasped it firm. "You are both brave and beautiful."

"I'm not sure panic counts as bravery." She gasped for air.

Neema pounced on Emma's cheek, hugging her, and burst into tears.

Kes smiled. "My father once told me that humans will always put themselves first, but you didn't hesitate... you wouldn't let me go."

"No..." Emma sat up and cradled the sobbing faerie. "You're my friend... even if you are careless. Where are your parents?"

Mawr ambled back and forth on solid ground near the start of the bridge, emitting a nervous moan.

Kes looked off into the sky. "I don't know."

"How can you not know?" Emma glanced at Mawr. *No wonder he's scared. He's as wide as the whole bridge.*

Neema said something too low to hear over the howling wind.

Mawr backed up a few steps.

Kes chuckled. "They decided I am old enough to be on my own, so I am on my own."

She looked down at stone chips by her foot. "That's sad. I'd be so lost without my family… I wouldn't even know what to do."

"Fauns are different." He lifted her chin with one finger and made a silly face at her. "Don't be sad for me. It is our way."

"Too fast fall. Time in get to you not I could." Neema sniffled. "Thought lost you were."

Emma shivered and closed her eyes. *So did I. Thank you, Linganthas.* "We're okay. Can you please take Mawr safely across before he is consumed with worry?"

"Yes. Do I will." Neema hugged Emma's face again before zipping over to the bear, leaving a long trail of silvery light.

With the faerie sitting on his head, Mawr pawed at the ground, pulling himself up to the speed of a run. When he reached the edge by the missing slab, he hooked his claws on the edge and hauled forward. Like a massive, furry balloon, he glided over the twenty-foot gap and kept on drifting.

"Going keep," said Neema as they floated past. "Here stay Emma and Kes. Return Neema will time at one Mawr after across."

"Yes. That is what I was going to say before." Emma smiled at Neema before tilting her head at Kes. "When you grow up and find a faun woman, and have a baby, are you going to abandon them too when they're still little?"

Mawr drifted off across the bridge, occasionally swiping at the stone to keep up his speed.

Kes showed all his teeth with a big grin. "I'm sure my parents made up their minds not to do that when I was born… but after living with me for two hundred years, they got tired of my pranks."

"That's sad." She hugged him. "That you're all alone."

He tapped a fingertip on her nose. "Well… after you live with someone for two hundred years, you can tell me if you find them annoying."

Emma stuck out her tongue at him.

He grinned, then frowned and rubbed his right hoof. "Not the best for walking on smooth stone. Much better on dirt."

"Umm." Emma pulled a foot up into her lap and brushed dust from her sole. "I don't think it matters whether you have hooves or toes. This bridge is falling apart. You didn't slip; the stone turned into dust."

"When Neema returns, you go first."

"I can catch myself on the ivy if it breaks. You go."

Kes shook his head. "Nope. Don't make me charm you."

"You can't." She folded her arms.

"I know I can."

Emma scowled. "What makes you so sure your charm will work on me?"

"I'm a faun. You're a girl. That's how it works."

"It made me want to be your friend and trust you, not do what you tell me." She held her nose in the air.

Kes scratched his head. "Hmm. Father said it would change when I got older."

"Change? How?" asked Emma.

"I don't know. When I asked, he laughed and said 'you'll see.'"

She rested her chin on her fist, thinking. The women always gave the pretend satyrs flowers during the Feast of Zaravex. Maybe flowers had something to do with it... "Are fauns and satyrs the same thing?"

"Not entirely." He smiled. "I'm a faun now, but when I am grown, I'll be a satyr."

"Oh. Like 'boy' and 'man.'"

He nodded.

Neema glided up to them. "Safe is Mawr."

Emma pointed at Kes. "He's next."

He batted his eyes at her. "Oh, sweet faerie, how can you leave Emma all alone on this bridge?"

Neema grabbed his left horn. "Work on Neema don't your charms. Come Neema with, Goat Boy."

Emma covered her mouth and giggled.

He rolled his eyes. "All right... all right."

As Kes skipped off to the other side, Emma scooted to the edge and grabbed an armful of ivy. She held as still as possible, barely even breathing until Neema landed on her shoulder almost ten minutes later.

"Time walking to." Neema's wings kicked off a faint puff of light and sparkles, and the tingle of faerie magic spread over Emma's body.

She pulled herself upright using the ivy, and made her way across the bridge with Neema pushing at her back. As soon as she reached solid ground, Emma fell to her knees on the moss and allowed herself to shiver from all the fear she couldn't let out on the bridge. Kes crouched at her side with an arm across her back.

"I'm sorry for scaring you," said Kes.

Emma pulled her hair off her face and tucked it behind her ears. "I forgive you. I've been more scared than that before."

"You have?" Kes raised an eyebrow. "Do you make a habit of crossing ancient bridges?"

"No." She leaned her head back and took a few full breaths, trying to relax. "A Banderwigh took me."

Kes scowled. "I hate those things." He blinked. "Wait... *Took* you? And you're not trapped?"

"I got away..."

He cringed. "Nasty things."

"What?" She stared at him. "You've seen one? Did it try to put you in a cage?"

"No." He clasped her hand and pulled her standing. "They wouldn't be interested in collecting a faun since we're too full of mirth." He winked. "Alas, that makes them angry, so if one saw me, it would surely try to hurt me."

Emma nodded. She'd seen firsthand how Banderwighs reacted to children who didn't stay sad. "Yes. But you could outrun it easy."

He walked with her to Mawr's side. "Are you so sure? They are cursed creatures."

"Yes." She pulled herself up onto the bear. "*I* could outrun him, and you're faster than me."

Kes sprang up and landed behind her. "Oh, this I simply must hear. Tell me the story, Emma?"

She frowned at the forest, knowing a long trip awaited. "All right."

19

FIRE CHICKENS AND LIGHTNING CATS

From the far end of the bridge, they followed a dirt path across a narrow grassy plain, which gave way to another forest of roperoot trees, much smaller than the others. Emma figured this to be a newer section of forest that had not been growing for as long. While still larger than any trees she had seen back in the world of humans, compared to the forest around the Elder Grove, they looked like babies.

Along the way, she told her story of the Banderwigh. Kes cringed at the description of the false girl who tried to make Emma sad by convincing her she'd burned the town. He cheered at her escape, and clung to her with nervous anticipation as she described the creature chasing her with an ax. The way he hung on her every word made her think of Kimber and Nan's stories... and that brought to mind the idea that she someday might be telling her children about the Banderwigh.

Should I do what Nan did and make it sound like it happened to someone else?

They stopped for a brief drink at a stream not far from the edge of the forest and continued on their way.

"Close now," said the faerie, pointing. "Way that go."

Mawr followed her directions for another few minutes. "I smell smoke."

Emma sniffed at the air. "I don't."

"You are a human. He's a bear, and his nose is as big as your whole head." Kes gestured at the giant nose.

She sighed. Having nothing to say back to that, she folded her arms and fired an annoyed stare at the trees.

A short while later, the scent of burning wood reached her, and she perked up. Mawr curved to the right, following a hint of dirt path up the side of a hill. When they crested the top, a human-style house came into view in the distance, complete with a fenced-in yard, water pump, and a few chickens.

"Please stop here." Emma patted the bear on the head. "He might be scared of you."

Mawr lowered himself so she could climb down. "I will stay close in case you need me."

Emma slid to the ground and adjusted her dress back into place before walking on. Neema floated along behind her.

She paused, eyeing the faerie. "Nymira said he hates faeries... you might not want to—"

Neema vanished. Seconds later, a giggle emanated from thin air.

"Right. I forgot you can do that."

Emma marched up to the gate.

"Bwaaaaa!" screamed an enormous scarlet chicken, tall enough to be eye level with her. It charged straight at her, flapping its wings while screeching.

Emma let off a cry of surprise and scrambled into a backward run.

Rapid soft *thumps* came up behind her. Kes dove, tackling her to the side as the chicken leapt into the air and exploded in flames.

Emma hit the ground on her back. They bounced, rolled over each other twice, and came to stop with her flat on her chest and Kes upside down a few feet away. He'd knocked the wind out of her, but she had no great desire to stand up yet. She lay, arms and legs splayed, happy to breathe in and out.

"Was that a giant exploding chicken?" asked Emma a moment later.

"Not a chicken at all. Magic," said Kes. "But yes, it appeared to be a giant exploding chicken."

Emma caught her breath and stood, brushing forest mulch from her dress. "What is *wrong* with this place?"

"It's not this place. It's the conjurer." Kes grasped at the air, and his bow appeared. "I think he may be as mad as your faerie queen says if he is making such strange creations."

"Try not to shoot him, please." She grabbed his hand in both of hers.

"Unless you *have* to."

"Of course."

Again, she approached the gate. An equally huge orange chicken rotated to face her, a wild glint in its glowing red eyes. She leapt back and started to run, but hesitated when Kes's arrow streaked by. His shot struck it in the center of its chest, and the oversized bird exploded in a fireball where it stood. A blast of warm air laden with the smell of cooked eggs washed over her.

She peered around in search of more fiery fowl. The rest of the chickens milling about the front yard appeared normal sized, and not the least bit interested in immolating themselves. With cautious steps, Emma advanced toward the gate. As soon as she pulled on it, the metal cried out with a rusty *squeeeak* that made her back muscles tighten.

Two large panthers burst from the branches of nearby trees, gliding out from a flurry of leaves on vast dragon-like wings. They landed in front of her, snarling. The air took on an electric quality that prickled at her tongue with the taste of copper.

Emma jumped back, gawking at the pair of great cats with glowing green eyes and lustrous black fur tinted dark violet. Their tails, longer than seemed natural for felines of that size, swished side to side with irritation. They growled at the same time, tiny snaps of lightning dancing over their lips. She got the sense they wanted to scare her off more than attack.

Emma raised her hands. "Hello."

Their aggressive glowers faded. Small whitish tufts of eyebrows rose, and the one on the right tilted its head.

The one on the left looked at the other and spoke in a male voice. "This creature talks."

"It does," said the other, sounding female.

The male sniffed in her direction. "Go away."

She risked taking a step closer. "I mean no harm. I must talk to the conjurer who lives here."

"Another human... most unusual." The female advanced, her sinewy body undulating with each stride. She folded her wings down from their threat display, tucking them against her sides. When she stopped close, the top of her head came up to Emma's chin. Tingling spread over her cheeks as the cat's nose neared her face. Small sparks lapped at her skin like the fingernails of a dozen faeries scratching.

"That tickles," said Emma, unable to resist a grin.

"Indeed a human. And only a cub at that." The female huffed. Hot breath scented like the air after a heavy rainstorm puffed in her face.

She raised her arm slow, and scratched under the female's chin. Within seconds, a purr so deep her lungs felt like they rattled inside her came from the strange winged cat. The animal's eyelids drooped half-closed, and her tail swished about in contentment.

"Oh... this one knows how to negotiate," purred the female.

"Hmm." The male also relaxed his wings and approached.

Emma offered her other hand, which he sniffed before tilting his head enough to grant access to his chin. She obliged, spending a few minutes skritching the pair while they purred.

At a faint *snap*, the male's tail fluffed. He pulled his head away and stared into the trees behind her. "I hear something else."

Emma looked back at where she'd last seen Kes, but he'd vanished. *He's gone invisible.* Saying nothing probably wasn't the same as lying, so she kept her mouth shut, hoping they didn't ask if she came alone.

"How can you speak?" asked the male, still eyeing the woods.

"I'm a druid." Emma brushed cat hair off her hands. "Almost."

The cats backed to the side, making an opening between them.

"Thank you." She smiled and walked in.

The male glanced back, his ears twitching.

"It sounds like a boar," said the female. "A small one."

He chuckled. "Now you're making me hungry."

"You wouldn't be if you didn't sleep all day." The female raised her head.

The cats escorted her to the door of a burgundy house that appeared somewhat wrong, but she couldn't quite place why. After staring at it for a moment, she realized the angles didn't line up straight like they should. One end seemed wider than the other, and the second story tilted opposite from the first. None of the windows—or even the door—managed to be straight rectangles, all skewed or slanted. It didn't seem possible for a house to remain standing with such strange lines, but stand it did.

It must be magic.

Emma stepped up onto a tiny doorstep with a plain brown welcome mat between a pair of potted plants, pink tulips a few inches taller than her. She cleared her throat, dusted a few stray bits of leaves and forest debris from her dress, trying to seem as regal and proper as she could.

And knocked three times.

20

THE HOUSE THAT DOESN'T BELONG

*E*mma clasped her hands behind her back, waiting patiently for someone to answer the door. At a sudden slimy sensation like a giant dog licking the bottoms of her feet, she squealed, jumped, and stared down.

"Hello," said the welcome mat.

Emma babbled. "What... what was that?" She took a step back and raised her right foot to examine her sole, finding it dry... and completely free of dirt.

"Your shoes are clean," said the welcome mat.

"I'm not wearing shoes!" She cringed and wiped her feet on the grass. Despite appearing dry and ooze free, they felt... like a dog had drooled on them.

"Your *feet* are clean then," said the welcome mat.

She grumbled, and raised her arm to knock again, but the door opened out from under her fist. A wizened man with wild white hair going in all directions spent a moment staring at the air above her head with an annoyed scowl. Right before he slammed the door, he glanced down and spotted her. His right eye seemed larger than the left, and both brows resembled wads of cotton glued to his head. A robe the same shade of burgundy as the house covered him from neck to shoes, blotched with stains.

"Humm," said the man. "What are you doing here?"

"I've come to talk to you." She curtseyed. "I'm Emma."

He leaned down, grasped her by the shoulders, and spun her to put her back to him. "No wings... not a faerie."

"I'm not a faerie. I'm human."

The man pulled her about to face him once more and lightly pinched the tops of her ears, giving a mild pull.

"Eee!" Emma squealed and grabbed the sides of her head.

"No points... you're no Astari either."

She fought the urge to scowl. "I'm Emma Dalen, a human girl from Widowswood, looking for the conjurer. Are you the conjurer?"

He grasped the shoulders of her dress and tugged at the fabric. "Hmm. Well made. You've not the look of a beggar about you."

"I'm not a beggar. I must speak to the conjurer." She sighed. "Are you the conjurer?"

The man gazed into the clouds, transfixed by something. He snapped out of it a short while later and smiled at her. "I don't know if I could claim to be *the* conjurer... but I am *a* conjurer."

Emma folded her arms. "How many conjurers are there in the Faerie Realm?"

"Only me. I suppose that makes me the only conjurer here." His eyes sparkled with sudden glee. "I *am* The Conjurer of the Faerie Realm!"

She pursed her lips, stared down, and flexed her toes twice, letting irritation fade before opening her mouth. "Then I am here to see you."

He raked his hands through his beard, attempting (without success) to set it to order. "I have not had guests in some time." He whirled to face the house and yelled, "We have a guest!"

A chorus of voices rang out from inside:

"Fresh the floors."

"Corral the clutter."

"Tidy the table."

"Wipe the windows."

"Tip the tea."

"Drat the dust," moaned a voice like an old woman. "I shall never finish."

The man took a step in. Emma leaned forward to peer into the house, staring open-mouthed at brooms, rags, chairs, and plates flying around on their own. All the whispering came from objects rushing to clean up the most slovenly, messy, disorganized place she had ever seen. A disembodied pair of white gloves floated around, plucking clothing from the floor, while a feather duster zipped back and forth as if it couldn't decide where to start. Two rags flitted about the furniture in a rush to wipe everything, and a broom worked itself about in front of a stove that grabbed wood from a nearby shelf and gobbled it up. The oven door slammed after three logs went in, the eye-shaped holes in the door made to resemble a pudgy human-like face glowing with fire. Its arms that it had been using to grab wood folded up into handles.

Emma crept inside, blinking at the chaos.

"Comb!" shouted the man.

A hairbrush flew out of a drawer and attacked his unruly mane. With it still working, he faced her again with a smile. "Hello, child. Forgive the mess. It has been some time since I've had visitors."

Emma let off a yelp as a chair galloped over and swept her up before carrying her to the table. She grabbed the sides of the seat, holding on tight in case it moved again. A plate sailed over and landed in front of her, a teacup and saucer close behind.

He cleared his throat and adopted a formal posture. "Greetings, young lass. I am Danithar, conjurer of no small talent."

"You made all of these things alive?"

A teapot with four stubby legs galloped from one end of the table to hers, skidding to a halt hard enough to upend itself and pour steaming tea into her cup, which rattled and whispered, "Ow, ow, ow, ow. *Oooooh*, that's warm."

Emma leaned back, staring wide-eyed at the cup, somewhat horrified.

Danithar smiled. "Of course. How many other conjurers do you think dwell in this silly place?"

"Not a moment ago, you said you were the only one here. Have you forgotten?" She blinked at him.

"Forgotten? No, I quite remember that I am a conjurer." He moved to the table and started to sit on nothing, but a chair rushed under him before he fell. "How have you come to be here?"

"Someone asked me for help." She paused, staring at a towel flying over like a stork with a baby. It dropped a freshly baked potpie on the plate in front of her.

The plate vibrated. "Alas… that's hot."

"Thank you for giving me food." She picked up the fork.

"Of course, child. What are you, nine? Why are you out here alone?"

Her worry lessened. The man seemed friendlier than she'd expected.

"I'm ten, but you are right. I shouldn't be alone... A friend asked me to help her. Some of your magic animals are hurting people."

"I don't think so." Danithar tapped a finger to his chin. "There are no people here to hurt aside from yourself and me."

The teapot trotted over to fill the conjurer's cup, which hissed and gasped.

She took a bite of the potpie, and winced. "Mmm! It's hot!"

"Told you," said the plate, sounding self-satisfied. "Be glad it's not sitting in *your* lap."

"Let it rest a moment." Danithar offered a grandfatherly smile. "Tell me... what makes you think my creations are causing harm?"

"The Silverbell Faeries asked me to help them because strange animals were trying to kill them. They knew I could talk to the animals and hoped I could find out what had made them so angry, but the animals wouldn't talk."

"A druid?" He blinked. "You?"

"I said that not a moment ago as well." Emma blew on a forkful of potpie. "I'm learning. Maybe I'm not a full druid yet."

"Ahh, grand. An apprentice! Pity you are trapped in this place, but at least we do not have to be alone."

"What about the faeries?" Emma tested the food with her tongue. Satisfied at the temperature, she ate.

He waved her off. "Bah. Winged rats is all they are. Pests and vermin."

Faint grumbling came from a little behind her.

"The Silverbells are really sweet and nice. Why would your creations want to harm them?"

"Thieving rats!" he shouted. His eyes flared with a frightening anger, making her cower. The fear radiating from her seemed to surprise him, and he quieted. "Forgive me, child. I mean you no harm. Those horrible little sprites are a plague on this forest and ought to be wiped out."

A sniffle emanated from closer to her ear.

Emma gasped. "Why? They're people... just small. They didn't even want to kill your creations after some of the faeries had died, because they hate hurting animals."

Danithar folded his arms and grumbled. "I bet they've charmed you into believing them. Oh, how did that go...?" He muttered nonsense words to himself.

Emma ate a few more forkfuls of the chicken potpie after blowing on them a little, while watching him talk to himself.

"Aha!" He raised his hands and muttered, *"Ano mar dor vrakkun, inar orun keth."*

Weak white energy flew from his hand, wrapped around her head, and dissipated.

Emma froze, her toes curled in alarm. Nothing felt different. "W-what did you do to me?"

Danithar smiled. "A curse removal spell. Do you still think of the faeries as friendly?"

"Yes." She nodded, and raised another forkful of potpie to her mouth.

"Hmm. I suppose that's why I didn't feel the energy break."

"I'm not under a curse." Emma took two more forkfuls. "This is quite good. Thank you again. It's been days since I've had real food."

Neema let off a mildly offended "Hmmph!"

"I mean human food," said Emma.

"Is food not real. Conjuration is," whispered Neema. "Eating as same. Worry not do."

"You're welcome, child." He glanced around. "I suppose I can add a loft or something for you. Whip up a bed in an hour or so."

Emma bit her lip. "I'm not an orphan, sir. I did not come here hoping you would take me in. My family is waiting for me to come home, and the sooner you change your mind and stop trying to hurt the faeries, the sooner I can go home."

"If you've got a family... what are you doing here? Those faeries stole you, didn't they? Just like they stole from me."

The hairbrush stopped grooming him and flew back to its drawer, landing in a pile of random junk.

"A faerie brought me through a ring, because they needed help. They're frightened of those magic animals. Can you please stop them from attacking the faeries?"

"Why should I?" He set his fists on his hips. "Thieving winged rats they are."

"What did they steal from you?" asked Emma, nibbling on a bit of crust.

Danithar waved his hand about. "A rare, rare crystal from the plane of Aether. That's where the energy for magic comes from. Auracite... it's quite difficult to obtain because it only exists in an alternate plane, you see. Only learned mages can hop between planes. It takes a lot of reagents, powders, power, time, effort..." He sighed.

"Auracite," muttered Emma.

"It's quite rare." He smiled. Something at the window in the back of the room caught his eye, and he stared at it.

She bit off another hunk of crust, chewed, and swallowed. "You mentioned that."

Danithar snapped his head around to look at her. "From the plane of Aether."

That too. She overdid a smile. "Wow."

"Auracite is a crystal that is essentially solidified magical energy. It can be used as a focal point for powerful spells." He gazed upward, raising his hand. After a second, he dropped his arm in his lap and grinned at her. "It's also rather pretty."

"I don't think..." *Don't call him wrong. He might get angry.* "I mean, if I get your Aurcite back from—"

"Auracite."

"Sorry. If I get your—"

Danithar wagged his eyebrows. "It's pronounced Aur-a-cite."

"Yes, I—"

"Would you please say it properly?"

Emma forced herself to keep a polite face. "Auracite."

Danithar bowed his head at her. "Thank you."

She sighed in silence. "If I get it back from the faeries, will you please stop trying to hurt them?"

His expression melted into one of worry. "Oh, child. You shouldn't go near faeries. They will keep you prisoner forever, like a pet." A blue flash at the window got him staring again. "You know the blue-feathered hookbeak only lays eggs once every nine years? And only two at a time. They mate for life by the way." He grinned. "A pair of those birds become so close, that if something happens to one, the others have been known to become so sad, they drop dead."

"That's... umm wow..." She set the fork down on the plate next to the empty dish. "Sir, I don't think you've seen the truth in the faeries. They're sweet and innocent."

He continued smiling at the window. "Poor girl. They've charmed you and I can't stop it. If you're so foolish as to run off to them, I suppose the world would be better off with one less unintelligent person in it." Danithar gave her a sad stare for a moment before glowering at the floor. "Damnable faeries. Winged rats." He startled and gasped downward. "Why is the floor in here brown?"

Emma peered down. "It's made of wood."

"The house is wood, and it's burgundy."

"Painted," said Emma.

He nodded. "Oh, yes… I suppose you have a point."

"Sir, I've already been to the faerie's home. They aren't keeping me. They have asked for my help and promised to send me home when I am finished or if I can't help. Please consider it?"

He stroked his beard. "I don't know."

"You think the faeries want to trap me, but if I go to them and come back here… that will prove they don't want to keep me forever, wouldn't it?"

Danithar blinked. "Well, yes, I suppose."

"So if I come back with your crystal will—"

"What kind of crystal?"

"The magic one."

His right eyebrow climbed. "What's its name?"

"Auracite," said Emma, in a flat tone.

He clapped and grinned. "Forgive me. I adore the sound of that word." *Nutters.* "It's pretty."

"So is the gem. Milky white with striations of pink, purple, and blue. It emits a little light as well and tingles if you touch it." He held up his finger, staring at the tip. "I miss it. Of course, if you have no magic, it doesn't tingle much, but if you're a druid, maybe it would tingle for you."

"Mythandriel, please lend me some of your light." Emma cupped her hands and summoned a glowing orb.

The intense light sent long shadows crawling over the interior of the house. "Oohs" and "Ahhs" emanated from most of the furniture, plates, and animated tools. A curious broom handle peered out from behind a curtain.

"Pretty." Danithar stared at it.

Mama, this man has lost his mind. "If I get your Auracite back from the faeries, will you tell your creations to leave them in peace?"

Danithar bowed his head. "A pity you wish to leave. I fear you shall not return. The land is not safe for a child your age."

"I traveled from the Elder Grove to your house… and I'm not alone. I have friends waiting for me outside."

He squinted at her. "Did you bring a faerie to my home?"

Emma took a deep breath, held it, and let it out slow. "A faerie is following me to keep me safe. I know you don't like faeries, so I asked her to wait outside."

"Hmm." He raised and lowered his eyebrows back and forth for a moment. "Very well. If you manage to steal back my Auracite from those faeries, I will agree to leave them be."

"Please stop sending magic animals to attack the faeries until I come back." Emma stood and walked over to him, arm extended. "Deal?"

After a suspicious squint, he took her hand and they shook. "I accept your terms. But, if you are not back in a month, I shall take revenge upon them for whatever they have done to you."

Emma forced a smile. "I won't be that long. Thank you for the food and for your hospitality." She curtseyed. "I shall come back as fast as I am able."

Danithar sprang from his seat and hurried to a cabinet. He took a sack of muffins, two loaves of bread, and a handful of salted meat out. He mumbled something inaudible and a child-sized backpack appeared in his hand, into which he stuffed the provisions. "I am being foolish allowing you to go out there, but you seem convinced."

Emma took the pack. "Thank you. The faeries are nice."

"Hmmph." He put his fists on his hips. "I shall hope you are…" He gazed at the window, and all the annoyance in his expression faded to the wonder of a small boy. "Scarlet-tailed frostbelly… I haven't seen one of those in decades."

Emma edged backward. "I'll let myself out. Thanks."

Danithar scurried to the window, and proceeded to make bird noises while Emma headed for the door.

She peered over her shoulder at him, whistled, and hurried outside to where Mawr waited.

"Aurcite floorcite!" shouted Neema.

Danithar wailed as if he'd been stabbed with a knife. "Who said that wrong?"

Emma gasped, giggling despite it being a poor idea to antagonize the man. Neema, still invisible, flew into Emma's back hard enough to knock her forward a step, and pushed her up to a jog in the direction of the bear. Leaving Danithar shouting demands to "say it right," Emma hurried over out of the yard and into the woods. She scrambled up to sit on Mawr's back. Neema appeared in a flash of silvery-white light, and flounced down in her lap, fuming.

"Believe can't I mean says things he did!" She glowered. "Talking why like about us that did he?"

Emma reached to pat her on the head, but stopped. *She's not a pet rat.* "I don't know. He seems nutters."

"Oooh!" Neema balled her hands into fists. "Stop to if not didn't I want attacks, I tricks playing years for on him!"

Kes appeared from behind a tree and trotted over. Emma grinned at him as he bowed to her. He leapt up to sit behind her.

"What then, Emma?" asked Mawr.

"Please take us back to the grove." She leaned forward and patted him.

As the great bear rose to his feet and got underway, Emma stared down, filled with worry and sorrow. *This is going to take forever. I'll never get home. And what if the queen won't give me the crystal?* It seemed a poor idea to even ask about it. If she did, the faeries would think she accused them of stealing. There had to be a way to ask without asking. If nothing else, she had a few days' time to think of something before they arrived.

21

FAERIE TRICKS

For the first four hours of the journey back to the Elder Grove, Neema fumed and ranted about what a rude, obstinate, smelly, ugly, wrinkly, disorganized, stupid, ungrateful, disheveled, nasty old man Danithar was. It helped her mood when Emma clarified by 'real' food she had meant the faerie cakes tasted so wonderful they reminded her of treats and desserts more than vegetables or meat. The faerie's anger had mostly faded by the time they stopped to sleep for the night.

Kes sat next to Emma, both of them leaning against Mawr, and asked her to tell him about her home.

She got a little weepy while describing Widowswood to him, and all the people she knew there. He held her hand and kept smiling at her, which stopped her from breaking into crying. Soon, her rambling about home trailed off to a half-awake mumble, and the next thing she knew, morning had arrived.

Mawr carried them back across Darbolg. Emma stayed low on his back the whole time, wary of more snakes. Neema crawled down the neck of her dress to hide from wasps, which she feared would mistake her for a lightmoth. Kes spent most of the second day playing his flute. When they stopped to sleep again, he perched at the base of a tree, crossed his legs, and played a low, haunting melody.

"What are you doing?" asked Emma.

He stopped, grinning. "My song tricks creatures and harmful things so they stumble right on by without noticing us."

"How could they not notice *music?*" Emma laughed. "You're making *more* noise than we would sleeping."

He winked. "It's magic." And with that, he resumed playing.

Emma shrugged and cuddled against the bear. Tomorrow, they would reach the terrifying bridge, but she would insist they allow Neema to ferry them across, weightless, one at a time. If Kes tried to run again, she'd wrap him in a ball of roots. The music lulled her into a daze, and soon, a fitful sleep. She dreamed of exploding chickens, giant floating bears, and rainbow-colored screaming goats.

THREE DAYS AFTER LEAVING THE CONJURER'S HOUSE, THEY ARRIVED BACK AT the Elder Grove. While Mawr headed for the patch of moss he used for a bed, Emma plucked Neema from her shoulder, holding her up like a doll.

"Will you please ask the faeries to bring him food and water? He's been *so* great to us. He needs our thanks."

"Do will yes." Neema nodded and zipped off.

Emma hugged Mawr's head, stroking his fur and thanking him over and over for all his help.

"I am still in debt to you for freeing my mind, little one. I would walk forever if you asked."

She choked up and stood there for a while, clinging to him.

Faeries swarmed over, bearing bowls of water, berries, nuts, and breads.

Emma wiped her tears and headed into the grove, around the crystalline fountain, and stopped by the throne chamber in the hollow of the great tree. She knelt out of respect and waited for Nymira to finish talking to Imril. The snow-haired faerie man raised a hand in a 'one moment' gesture, and hurried along in his conversation.

Soon, Nymira nodded to him and looked up at Emma. "I am pleased to see you have returned unharmed. What news?"

Emma folded her hands in her lap. "Queen Nymira, the conjurer believes that a faerie has stolen a magical crystal. He's angry about that, and wants to hurt all the faeries out of revenge."

"Nonsense!" Nymira's glowing red eyes flared brighter. "We have stolen nothing from him!"

"I apologize, queen. I don't believe the Silverbell Faeries took his crystal, but he is convinced. Why might he think that?"

Nymira stood and stormed back and forth before her throne, her flame-red hair dragging like the train of an elaborate gown behind her. "When the man first appeared, we sensed a human in our land. I sent scouts to determine his intentions. He seemed friendly enough, so, as a gesture of welcome, we tidied up his disaster of a home."

Pimlin cringed. "Messy! So messy was it."

Emma narrowed her eyes. "He didn't put out faerie cakes to say thank you, so you played tricks on him."

Nymira flashed a coy grin. "Perhaps tricks were played."

"And?" Emma folded her arms.

"We didn't take anything… simple tricks. Clothing up in the trees, knotted his hair into his beard, took all the nails out of his chairs… things of that nature. We did not steal anything."

"Hmm." Emma stared at the ground in front of her knees. "He's quite angry, and also a bit… nutters."

Nymira flopped on her throne. "It is possible the magic of this realm has affected his mind. This world is not made for humans, and they do not fare well here past a certain age. Brief visits are tolerable, but too long within this place and it will become part of a person. A young child such as yourself…" She winked. "Especially with a little fey in her family, would notice nothing… but a grown man… it is quite likely he has already become bound to this place, and his mind has broken."

"How can I convince him that you don't have the Auracite? I know you didn't take it, but do you have any Auracite?"

Nymira shook her head. "Such a thing is beyond even my ability to obtain. My powers are limited to this realm. I do, however, know of a possible salve for his mind."

"Umm." Emma scratched above her ear. "How does one put a salve on the mind? It's inside the head."

"Hah!" Nymira laughed and flew up to kiss her cheek. "You are precious!" She glided back, hovering at eye-level. "I meant salve in a figurative sense. There is an Astari ruin part way between the Elder Grove and where this conjurer has made his home. At its southern end, a shrine to Mythandriel yet stands."

Emma nodded. "I think we found those ruins. By the bridge." She blinked. "The dome with the green leaves decorating it?"

"That is correct." Nymira raised her eyebrows. "Please tell me that you crossed with Neema's assistance."

Kes whistled innocently.

"Eventually." Emma shot him a scolding look.

"Within that shrine," said Nymira, "is a lifespring. Collect the blessed water from it and give it to the conjurer to drink. It should clear his mind."

Fila and Raa carried a glass bottle out from behind the massive tree and dragged it over to her.

"Be careful, Emma." Nymira floated up to eye level. "Do not drink this water yourself, or you will become bound to this realm and unable to leave."

She nodded. "Won't it do the same to Danithar?"

Nymira let off a sad sigh. "The man is already bound to this place, though he does not realize. He has been here so long, if he should set foot back in your realm, he would dry out to a pile of dust. Humans who cannot accept magic become bound to this place within days, but he is a practitioner of magic, so he should have been able to endure for a while. However, he has been here for over five hundred years."

Emma cringed and took the bottle. "I understand."

"One more thing I must warn you." Nymira's expression became one of motherly concern. "When you find the temple, do not simply take the water. If any power remains within the guardian, they will regard you a thief and surely seek to harm you."

"What should I do then?" asked Emma.

"Be respectful. Wait for a sign from the spirits. If they do not permit you to take from the spring, return here and I shall try to think of something else we can do."

"All right." She gazed longingly up at the sky, wanting to go home. "We should wait until morning. Mawr is exhausted."

"Of course." Nymira spoke to the faeries around her in their language. "Food will be brought to you. By all means, take some rest. Know that I am grateful to you for all your efforts."

"Danithar has agreed to stop sending magic animals to hurt you for a month at least while I 'get his crystal back.' I want to go now so I may return to my family sooner, but Mawr is tired and it would be cruel of me to press him."

Nymira glided up to her face and caressed her cheek. "Worry not, child. Your family is as you have left them. They do not fret or worry over you."

Emma tried to believe it, but couldn't squash the nugget of homesickness in her gut. "I'm sorry for being so nervous. I promised I'd be good, and here I am, away from home for days."

Nymira patted her cheek. "Trust us, and do not let worry cloud your dreams. Now, rest. As the bear is, so are you exhausted."

After bowing, Emma walked back to the snoozing Mawr, and sat. Kes flopped at her side on his stomach, flute at his lips.

Another few days. She tried to believe the queen's words that her family hadn't fallen into a storm of worry. Soon, a small army of faeries brought over cakes, fruits, and water. She ate and lounged in the grass, passing the remainder of the day in uneasy stillness.

22

TRESPASS

*a*t morning light, Emma asked Mawr to take her back to the place with the ruined buildings and the scary bridge. He agreed without protest, and Kes scrambled up to perch behind her. Having spent days upon his back, the faun no longer seemed nervous, nor did he cling to her constantly, though he did sit close.

Emma asked about his life. He described it as far more boring than her home, days spent frolicking in the woods, hunting for berries and such to eat. She thought it odd for a being so fond of the company of others, especially girls, to be all alone in a place without anyone, but didn't say anything.

The journey back to the Astari ruins again required they cross Darbolg. Depending on how Emma shifted, Neema either hid under the hem of her dress between her knees, or zipped down the neck and huddled against her chest. After almost a full day in the foul-smelling bog, they neared the edge. Off to the left, a trio of huge wasps set upon a cloud of lightmoths, taking three of the hapless dinner-plate-sized insects as meals with relative ease. She watched in horror, but kept quiet, so as not to frighten the faerie. Seeing how little time it took for the wasps to come out of nowhere and take their prey made her understand why Neema desired to stay out of sight. She cradled her hands to her chest, holding the lump Neema made in her dress with a gentle embrace.

Kes played a new song, which he'd made for her. Notes part way between cheery and haunting echoed over the swamp for a short while, bringing a smile to her lips, and getting Mawr to hum along.

"Is that song magical like the other?" asked Emma.

"It has magic in it, yes." He winked.

"What does it do?"

Kes put a hand on her cheek and traced a thumb beneath her eye. "It will always remind me of you."

Emma blushed. Having a friend was a new experience. No one in her life fit the word. Not her brother Tam, nor Kimber, her new sister. Both of them occupied a place in her heart quite different from a friend. She had never spent much time in the company of any other children from town, but she liked being with Kes. While he played, Emma let her mind wander, trying to imagine what sorts of things friends might busy themselves doing if not for being in the faerie world. *He would create mischief and get me in trouble, no doubt. He'd play tricks on Hadrath, probably set his pigs loose. He'd flip the brake on the fruit cart and watch it roll out of the town square. Maybe he'd go make a mess of Mr. Carrow's bakery!* Emma grinned. Not that she'd dare risk doing the sorts of mischievous things she suspected he'd want to, but it amused her to *think* about them.

Mawr continued walking even after sunset, so they could leave Darbolg behind and find solid ground upon which to sleep. In the dead of night, he found a spot of firm ground where three of the white-barked trees grew close and their thick drape of leaves offered shelter. There, the unlikely group bedded down to sleep.

Emma awoke, groggy and in dire need of a privy, long before the sun came up. Kes sat next to her, teasing a soft, lilting melody from his flute.

Emma grunted and sat up. "You're not sleeping?"

"Neither are you." He wagged his eyebrows.

"I have to go…" She dragged herself to her feet and wandered off to find a secluded place. Once she finished, she stumbled back to Mawr and collapsed upon her bear-bed. The music continued, and after a few minutes, she opened one eye. "Aren't you going to sleep?"

"Fauns don't always have to. The song I'm playing is the same as sleeping."

Emma yawned. "What will you do all night then if you'll be awake?"

He smiled. "Watch over you."

"Mmm." She smiled at him, closed her eye and let sleep take her.

LATE THE NEXT DAY, THEY WANDERED INTO THE CRUMBLING REMAINS OF the elven city, but took the southerly fork in the ancient road instead of going to the bridge. The ruins spread over a larger area than she'd expected at first glance; the city had been many times the size of Widowswood Town. For half an hour, Mawr walked past collapsing buildings, spires, and vast gardens on elevated tiers connected by white stone walkways. Statues of elves stood or lay fallen, some in robes, some in armor, some with nothing on at all.

Emma gazed in awe at the beautiful craftsmanship left to sit in a place where no one would ever see it. "I wonder why they decided to leave?"

"I don't know." Kes yawned. "Is that the temple?"

He pointed ahead and left, at the dome-shaped structure carved from pure white stone. Leaf shapes drawn in jade circled the outside, spanning from the ground to the top. A circular pool twenty or thirty paces wide surrounded the building, littered with small, flat stones. The dome, and especially the ring-shaped reflecting pool, radiated a sense of warning.

"Yes, that's the building I saw. It feels bad," said Emma.

"Badness, yes." Neema glided forward, paused at the pool's edge, and returned. "Curse in the water. Strong it is. Deadly. No touch."

Emma warned Mawr not to touch the water due to a curse.

He stopped nearby, and flopped down to rest.

"No drink," said Neema.

Again, Emma warned him what Neema said.

The bear chuckled. "You expect I would drink water you've said is cursed not a moment before?"

Emma giggled. At a quizzical look from the faerie, she translated bear.

"Sure making." Neema nodded.

After sliding off the bear, Emma walked up to the edge and peered in. Close to her, the water didn't reflect the sky as strongly and she could see beneath the surface of a shallow pool. A floor of flat grey stone tiles covered in dark moss looked close enough that she'd only be in water up to her knees if she dared enter. A sinister presence radiating from the pool filled her with dread, awakening inside her an instinctual desire to run away. Even if Neema hadn't called it cursed, she wouldn't have wanted to touch it. Perhaps she too could sense curses, or maybe being a child somehow offered her senses adults lacked.

"This is a temple," said Kes.

She glanced at the flat stones. From a distance, they had looked like floating pads, but up close, she made out the forms of small columns a mere inch taller than the water. "I think these are stepping stones."

"They're small," said Mawr.

Emma leaned one foot out and set it upon the nearest stone. With her heel at the edge, her toes hung over the front. Da couldn't have fit half his foot on it.

"Even at your size, you cannot find a solid perch," said Mawr.

Kes crouched beside her. "The Astari were known to be fast and agile, more so than humans. I bet they hopped across with ease, and used the magic in the water as a way to protect the temple."

Emma backed off to solid ground. While the stones near the edge looked easy enough to hop between, they got farther apart closer to the interior, and it wouldn't take much to slip and fall in.

"Climb on my back." Kes patted his shoulder. "I'll carry you across."

"Maybe you can skip across, but not while carrying me."

"Nothing weigh!" Neema wrapped herself around Emma's neck.

Emma stared at the temple. "Can you carry me across while I weigh nothing?"

Neema sighed. "At a time one. Fly can magic make or light."

"You always glow." Emma tilted her head.

"Light!" shouted Neema. "Heavy not."

"Oh." Emma grinned. "I understand. Your magic can make you fly or it can make me lighter… not both at once."

"Said already I that did." Neema sighed in exasperation.

Emma wrapped her arms around Kes and gripped her wrist before hopping up and lifting her legs. He grabbed her behind the knees and took a few steps to each side before a few quick hops. She clung to his back, his shaggy brown hair brushing her cheek, heavy with the scent of sandalwood and clove.

"Are you dancing?" asked Emma.

"Checking balance." He gazed at the pool for a while before walking to the left around the edge.

"Now what are you doing?"

"Looking to see if there's a path. There might be a set of stones that are easier to cross than others."

"Oh." She perked up to stare at the pool, but all the pale grey dots on black water seemed the same to her.

"I think I found it," said Kes, about a quarter of the way around from the doors. "In front of the doors and right in back would be the first place someone looked. But... maybe I am seeing an illusion. Ready?"

She squeezed herself tight to his back. "Yes."

"Ready am yes," said Neema, clinging to the back of Emma's neck.

Kes sprang into the air, alighting on the first stone for only a second before jumping again. Each time his hoof came down, a sharp *click* broke the solemn stillness of the place. Emma clenched her jaw, staring at their reflection racing by on the water. He leapt from stone to stone to stone, laughing the whole way as if falling wouldn't kill them.

Of course, a curse could be many things aside from death... but this water felt *bad*.

He stopped about halfway across, balancing on one leg while studying the stones around them. Emma yelped when he jumped up, switching hooves on the same stone.

"There it is," said Kes, sounding confident. He grunted and leapt again in a series of rapid jumps—*click click click click*—and stopped at the three-quarter mark. "Almost there."

Emma, breathless, looked back at the pool behind them. "I hope we don't have to run away from this place fast."

"Well then"—Kes hopped two stones one after the next—"You should try not to make whatever is in here angry."

Another leap put them on the grass surrounding the domed building. He walked forward a few steps before letting go of her legs. She held on to him for a moment more, trying to calm her breathing.

"Are you all right?" He put his hand atop hers where she held tight to his chest.

"Yes. Just... a little frightened. The magic in that pool is scary." She unclasped her hands, but kept holding his.

Kes pointed to the right. "The doors are over there."

She led the way around the building. A short hallway with a pointed arch roof jutted out from the dome, ending at a pair of double doors that appeared to be made of amber and bore a carved likeness of an Astari woman, hands outstretched as if offering solace. The massive entrance towered over her so high she had to stand on tiptoe to reach the handles. She strained to get her fingers around the bar. Kes crouched, wrapped his arms around her legs, and lifted her so she sat on his right shoulder.

"Thanks," said Emma.

She grasped the handle, expecting the giant doors to ignore her little arms pulling, but when she tugged, the door moved as if it weighed less than a quill. Kes set her down, and she grabbed the edge, pulling the door to the side before walking in.

Two-story-tall statues of Astari elves in garments made of leaves stood against the inner wall, each in line with one of the leaf shapes in the stone. The translucent jade outlines caught the sun, flooding the entire chamber with dim green light. Four male and four female elves held their hands upward, gazing at the central point of the roof in reverent awe. A scattering of long-rotted tasseled cushions atop a faded blue and silver rug occupied the otherwise empty central floor.

An enormous bowl of plain white stone, much larger than the tub she bathed in at home, sat at the feet of the statue facing the entrance. Glowing water within painted the Astari woman above it in wavering ice-blue shadows. Emma gawked at the luminous water.

That has to be the lifespring Nymira told me about.

The female elf statue standing astride the bowl wore an elaborate crown of leaves and vines, but none of the others had anything upon their heads.

Is that Mythandriel?

Emma gulped. It felt wrong for her to be in the elves' sacred place. The hair on the back of her neck stood on end. She expected someone to show up out of nowhere and scream at her for daring to enter.

"You're shaking," whispered Kes. "What's wrong?"

"I..." She looked up at the huge elven statues, terrified one of them might come to life and glare at her. "Feel like I'm doing something wrong. Like I'm going to get in a lot of trouble for being in here."

"You don't usually do mischief, do you?" He grinned.

"No." Emma shook her head.

"Well, you're not here to do anything bad. You're trying to help a sick old man."

She breathed in her mouth and out her nose. "Yes."

Emma shrugged her backpack off and took out the glass bottle Nymira had given her. She left the pack on the floor by Kes and approached the pool of glowing water, careful not to step on any of the ancient cushions on her way across the room.

Nymira told me to ask... It's wrong to steal, but there's no one here.

She stopped at the pool and gazed up at the huge statue, unable to see its face past the body. After a moment of thought, she knelt, set the bottle on the stone in front of her knees, and bowed her head.

"Lady Mythandriel, I have come here seeking a way to heal the thoughts of an old man. He wants to hurt the faeries because he believes they stole something from him, but they did not take the stone he prizes. Please show me a sign if I am allowed to collect some of your magical water."

Emma closed her eyes, opening her thoughts the way she'd done when trying to reach out to Ylithir. Minutes passed in silence with no spectral wolf or elf appearing inside her daydreams. She repeated her plea, and continued her effort to touch the spirits, concentrating on the image of the light orb, the way the inner core of it, darker green, resembled like a tiny faerie.

Kes gasped.

Emma opened her eyes a split second before something cold and metal touched the ridge of her jaw. She froze, shifting her gaze to the left. A woman's bare foot appeared at the limit of where she could see without turning her head. The sharp edge of a blade tickled at her neck.

"Eee!" shouted Neema.

"Human," said a melodic voice. "I should slay you for trespassing here, but since you are a child, I will allow you to return the way you came. Your kind has no business here."

The blade retreated from her throat.

Emma gulped. After two breaths and a hand to the chest to make sure her heart hadn't stopped, she peered up.

A stunningly beautiful woman with long lemon-yellow hair, pale skin, and eyes like dark emeralds stood over her. Leaves of brown, burgundy, and green clung to her skin in the shape of an airy robe that left most of her stomach bare. The delicate silver longsword she held seemed too thin to be a real weapon, but the edge had not felt fake when touched to her neck. Smaller than Mama, the top of her head might've come up only to her mother's chin.

Emma bowed deep. "A-are you Mythandriel?"

The woman chuckled. "No, child. My name is Lorandrien. I was chosen to guard this temple when my people embarked upon the great crossing. I am timeless, but I am bound to her shrine. You needn't bow to me."

Emma sat back on her heels. "Do you know Queen Nymira of the Silverbell Faeries?"

"I do," said Lorandrien.

Neema glided over and chattered away in faerie. Lorandrien replied in the same language, albeit slower, and smiled.

"She has sent me here to ask for some of the lifespring water. The faeries are in danger. A conjurer has gone nutters and believes they stole a gem from him, so he is summoning false animals to harm them." Emma paused to catch her breath. "Queen Nymira believes this water can restore his mind and stop him from killing all the faeries."

Lorandrien's weapon glowed until it became a sword-shaped outline of light and faded away. "You do not seek this water for your own use?"

"No." Emma shook her head. "I don't want to drink it. It's not for me. I only ask for it so the faeries can be safe."

Neema blurted a few words, pointing emphatically at Emma while flashing the same pleading face that convinced Emma to follow her to the faerie circle in the first place.

The Astari guardian took a knee and brushed a hand over Emma's head. "You are so small, yet your heart is so large. Spirits speak of humans, but seldom of anything other than greed and desire for power." She smiled. "I do not sense these traits within you."

Emma bowed her head. "I'm sorry for trespassing here. Nan has taught me a little of Mythandriel's light, and my Mama calls upon her often. I am not like most of my kind. This is her temple and it is an honor that you have let me visit."

Lorandrien took the glass bottle and dipped it into the pool. After filling it, she closed the stopper and set the glowing vessel on the floor beside Emma. "Mythandriel has granted you her favor. She knows you are capable of protecting the Silverbell Faeries. Take this water with her blessing."

"Thank you." She bowed.

The Astari woman stood and gestured at the door. "Your path from this place is clear, child. May Mythandriel guide you."

Emma cradled the bottle in two hands, surprised to find it as cold as snow. She shifted her weight off her knees onto her feet and got up, then curtseyed at Lorandrien, bowed deep at the statue of Mythandriel, and hurried over to where Kes waited. She eased the bottle down among the remaining provisions, careful to seat it at the bottom of the pack.

"Thank—" Emma glanced back toward the pool, but the woman had vanished. Her voice dropped to a whisper. "You."

Kes tugged on her arm, hurrying her out onto the grass. Emma pushed the doors closed as she had found them. When she faced the reflecting pool, a line of bubbles appeared, stretching from the near shore across the pool in a line to the other side. Amid a froth of mist and splashing water, a mass of living vines emerged, knitting together to form a footpath straight away from the entrance.

"Well, that was nice of her," said Kes.

Emma glowered at him. "Be respectful."

She pulled the backpack on and scurried across the bridge. Neema flew at her side, Kes running a step behind. Within a second of their reaching the far end, the bridge unraveled to separate vines that sank below the murky water. Emma closed her eyes. *Thank you for the bridge, and for allowing me to bring some of your water to Danithar. Please let it grant reason to his mind.*

Emma grabbed Kes's hand and ran to Mawr.

"It is good to see you," said Mawr. "Were you able to find the water? Do we return to the faeries or to that strange man?"

"To Danithar, please." Emma climbed up atop the bear. "Mythandriel allowed me to take some of the water… I hope it works."

"Too me," chirped Neema.

Kes nodded. "To the crazy man who makes his plates talk and his chairs prance about, and says unkind things about faeries."

"Did why remind me him of you?" Neema fumed. "Messy, rude, clumsy, smelly, old, wrinkly, mean…" She continued spouting off random insults for the next few minutes.

Emma laughed and settled in for a long trip, hopeful she would soon be able to return home.

23

PARTING WAYS

*E*mma curled up atop Mawr's back, but the great bear's gentle snoring would not lull her to sleep. Everything she had seen in the days since following Neema into the woods replayed in her thoughts. The fear of being attacked by the not-foxes, the awe of seeing the wood dragon, the horror of almost falling from the bridge, and the majesty of Mythandriel's temple overwhelmed her. More than anything in the world, she wanted to have her family around her.

The faeries had kept assuring her she would only be gone for a few minutes, but many days had passed. It didn't seem as though they had been lying to her, but what they said didn't make sense. *What if the conjurer is right? He was friendly, but a little nutters.* Emma shivered as she argued with herself. A five-hundred-year-old mage who specialized in studying creatures telling her that the faeries would keep her forever on one side, and innocent-faced tiny people on the other. Tiny people who would play pranks and tricks on someone who didn't thank them for thanking them. That did feel like a mean thing to do.

Neema had done nothing to make her think she'd been lied to, but... what if the man was right?

She covered her face and cried, terrified of never going home again. Her body shuddered with sobs she tried to keep quieter than the faint notes of Kes's flute. Tomorrow, they would reach Danithar's house and she would find out if the lifewater would do as Nymira said. Tomorrow, she might go home—well, after a three-day trip back to the Elder Grove.

Unless the faeries kept her forever.

The music stopped.

Emma went still, holding her breath to keep from making sound. Fur shifted under her a second or two before Kes tugged on her arm.

"Why are you crying?"

She didn't want to let him see her in tears, but he sounded close. He had to have seen her wet face already. "I miss my family."

Kes climbed up to sit next to her. "Tell me about them."

Emma opened her eyes and rolled flat on her back, squinting up at him. "What?"

He smiled. "Tell me about them. Sometimes, when I get lonely, I talk about my parents even if there's no one there to hear me."

She scrunched up her nose. "Why?"

"When you think about someone, they're with you." He grinned. "Whenever I talk about them to myself, I remember them, and it's like they are still there."

Emma sniffled and waved her feet absentmindedly back and forth. "My Da is brave. He's in charge of the Watch, and has to protect everyone in Widowswood Village. He's strict, but fair, and I know he loves me a lot. I used to think he didn't believe in magic, but he only pretended not to. His mother and family are stuck up and snotty, and they think our magic is 'for peasants.' I love my Da, even if he does eat cheese and apple together. Bleh."

Kes laughed. "How is that a bad thing?"

"I don't like mixing them. I don't know how he can stand to." She shivered at the thought of it. "Tam, my little brother, can make him angry sometimes." She grinned. "Tam's a handful. He's got so much energy, and he doesn't listen. He's only six, but he's not afraid of anything... except this older boy, Rydh."

Kes grinned. "I hope that older boy didn't hurt him."

"No, he stepped on his toy and laughed at him." Emma scowled. "I thumped him for it, but I think he's sorry for doing it. Tam wants to be a knight when he grows up. He's always playing with his wooden sword, or Stick Knight and Shrub Dragon."

"When I was little, I had a lump of wood I pretended was an Eldritch Walker," said Kes. "They are living trees who guard the forest against darkness."

"I have a sister too." Emma grinned. "Her name is Kimber and she's eight. She's got *thick* red hair that's so long she sits on it sometimes. Mama didn't have her, but that doesn't matter. She's my sister."

Kes nodded.

"Her other dad... at least she thinks he was. I don't know if I believe it. The man was so mean to her. Hit her a lot and made her hunt for apples all day and beg so he could get Faeberry wine. Sometimes I don't think he was really her da, 'cause a da wouldn't be that cruel to his daughter."

"Bah. Pity my father never saw him. A man who strikes a woman, especially a little one, ought to be put to the knife." Kes draped his arm across his knee. "My father would've been happy to do it."

Emma picked at her fingernails. "He hit me too when I told him to stop hittin' Kimber. It made Mama angry. She put something in his wine that... umm."

"Sounds like he deserved it. My mum and your mama would probably be friends." He gazed at the sky for a few seconds. "What's Kimber like?"

The gloom around Emma's heart faded. "She's as pale as me, but maybe a little more pink. And she talks a little funny too, but I can understand her. Da said it's the umm... district she came from in Calebrin. Poor people live there and they all talk like that. She likes fancy things and faeries and tea parties and dolls. She loves having a family, and I'm glad she's with us. I hope she's not scared since I'm missing. Mama's going to be upset too."

"I bet your mother is pretty." He winked.

"My Mama is really good at making potions. Everyone says I look just like her, only small. She's a druid too. So's Nan. She's my grandmother. She can turn into a raven and fly around."

His eyes went wide. "I'd love to see that. Can your mama turn into an animal too?"

Emma folded her hands over her stomach and gazed at the stars. "No. Mama doesn't have an animal spirit. Nan says not every druid can do it. It depends on if the spirits favor you. I'm pretty sure Ylithir likes me. If I can ever turn into an animal, I bet it's going to be a wolf."

"You'd make a good wolf," said Kes. "Brave and fearsome. I bet you'd have black fur like your hair, and sparkling blue eyes. Sapphires worthy of a king's crown."

She grinned, a wash of warmth spread over her cheeks. "Nan makes the best pies in the whole town. She loves telling us stories. I used to think they were silly, but now I want to know how it ends."

"How what ends?" asked Kes.

Emma explained the story of Princess Isabelle that Nan had been reading to them for the past several weeks. She almost felt the warmth of Tam and Kimber at her side under the blanket, safe in their bed listening to Nan. "What are your parents like?"

"Oh, they're nothing like what you'd expect." He grinned. "They're satyrs. They both love to drink wine and dance. Mother plays the mandolin and father has a big flute. When I was smaller, they used to play music together and I'd dance. Sometimes we'd find travelers in the forest and entertain them for a night."

"Travelers? Here?" Emma looked around.

"No, not in the Faerie Realm."

Emma blinked at him. "Fauns can go through the faerie circles too?"

"Yes. A few notes to open the gateway."

"Oh." She stifled a yawn. "What do your parents look like?"

Kes reclined. "Well, like me I suppose, only taller. Father has a long, pointy beard. He says I'll have one someday. Mother likes jewelry, but nothing made of metal, and only things given to her in gratitude or when nothing is expected in return. If someone gave her something, she'd be their friend forever."

"I still think it's sad that they've left you." Emma rolled on her side, one arm tucked beneath her head. "Don't you miss them?"

"I do, but that's why I talk about them. Satyrs are different from humans. They find each other, and stay together only until a child is old enough, then they part ways... my parents will likely never cross paths again."

Emma gasped. "Don't they love each other?"

"I suppose they had enough love to let each other go to find happiness."

"Wouldn't they be happy together?" Emma felt queasy at the idea of Mama and Da not being with each other.

"Satyrs are different from humans, in more ways than our legs. Most humans don't understand."

Emma chuckled quietly. "You're right. I don't understand. I think it's sad. What about you?"

"Don't look at me," said Mawr. "I'm merely a bear."

Kes threw back his head and howled with laughter.

"Mama and Da love each other a lot and would never run off. They wouldn't leave me alone at ten years old either."

"I'm not ten years old." He stuck out his tongue. "I'm 204."

"You look like you're ten, so maybe that's faun years for ten."

He shrugged, grinning. "Maybe. It's beautiful how your family is. I can feel the strong love you have for them. It glows from your dark-blue eyes." Kes leaned over and grasped her hand. "I am happy for you that you have such a family waiting for you. I'm sure you'll be with them soon. We have the healing water. Tomorrow."

"Tomorrow," whispered Emma.

"Mmm," mumbled Mawr. "You should both sleep so you have strength."

She sat up and pulled the glowing bottle out of the backpack, staring at it. Though the lifewater had possessed a weak glow in the day, in the dead of night, its brightness made her squint. Emma traced her thumb back and forth across the bottle, still as icy cold as it had been when she'd first touched it hours ago.

Lady Mythandriel, please watch over me. I beg thee let this water heal Danithar's mind.

Emma tucked the bottle into the pack once more, lay on her side, and snuggled into the fur.

"You toss quite a lot in your sleep," said Kes.

"I sleep in a bed with my entire family. My spot is against the wall. Tam used to sleep behind me with Mama behind him and Da closest to the door, but now Kimber's usually between me and Tam. She sleeps *so* hard. I don't know how she can do that. A dragon could tear the roof off our home and she wouldn't wake up." Emma brushed her hand back and forth over Mawr's fur. "It's strange not having my brother squishing me into the wall."

Kes stretched out at her back and reached an arm around her. "It would do my heart a wondrous boon to make your rest feel safe."

Emma grasped his arm, taken by a sudden feeling of safe contentment. "Are you charming me?"

"Perhaps a little. You will need your strength and wits tomorrow."

Grinning, Emma closed her eyes and let the slow rise and fall of Mawr's breathing lull her to sleep.

24

PROMISES

*A*round noon the following day, Mawr carried them up to the conjurer's house and stepped over the fence. The winged panthers leapt from their treetop homes, snarling in their guard poses.

They took one look at him and zoomed straight back into the branches out of sight.

A hint of cinnamon and spice hung in the air, mixed with the scent of burning wood. From inside the house, many tiny voices chattered back and forth. Some discussed chores, others complained of not having enough time, one cried "too hot, too hot" over and over, while a feminine voice professed it a beautiful day.

Mawr stopped a few steps from the stoop and flopped on his belly. Emma climbed down with extra care, so as not to risk spilling or breaking the bottle of lifewater. She neatened her dress, took a breath, and walked up to the door.

Kes leapt to the ground and scampered up behind her. Neema remained somewhere in Mawr's fur, invisible.

"Confidence, Emma," said Kes. "Stop trembling."

"I'm not scared. I'm nervous." She raised a hand to knock, but hesitated when she saw her fist shaking.

"He won't hurt you."

She steeled herself and knocked. "I'm not afraid of being hurt. I'm afraid of it not working."

"Don't you trust Mythandriel?"

Emma whirled to face him. "I do!" she yelled before whispering, "It's old nutty mages I don't trust."

"Hello," said the welcome mat.

She grimaced as the feeling of wet dog-tongue slid across her soles. "Must you?"

The door opened, revealing the wild-haired old man. "Child… You have returned." His expression of surprise melted into the anticipatory stare of a little boy on his birthday. "Have you found the Auracite?"

"The faerie queen is sure that her people have not taken it."

"Blast," yelled Danithar, growling at the floor. "Deceitful winged rats!"

"Wait." Emma held her hand up. "I'm not finished."

"Oh, aren't you now?" Danithar reached forward, grabbed her under the armpits and carried her inside. After setting her in a chair, he folded his arms. "I should not have let you run off. You're not old enough to be running around. Unless your parents show up looking for you, this is your home now."

Kes crept in, looking around.

"Friend of yours?" asked Danithar. "Be wary of his kind, girl. Tricksters, all."

Kes put on an innocent smile.

"He's my friend."

Danithar rolled his eyes and wagged his eyebrows at the window. "Oh, I'm sure he is."

"He is," said Emma in a flat tone. She slid out of the backpack, set it on the floor between her feet, and retrieved the bottle. "You need to drink this. It will help you."

"The man's correct. Satyrs are known for being tricksters." Kes bowed at Emma. "But I have not tricked you, nor do I intend to."

"What is that?" Danithar started to reach for it, but his attention shot to the window. "The frilled thornbeak returned! I think it's laid eggs, too."

"Danithar," said Emma.

He stared out the window mesmerized.

"Danithar," said Emma, louder.

"There has to be five or six eggs… oh to get a look at them." He squeed.

"I have something for—"

The conjurer leaned close to the window, muttering and waving at the birds like an elderly woman cooing at newborn babies.

Emma raised her voice. "Excuse me, sir, but—"

"It has! There are eggs in there." He waved his fists in excitement.

"Aurcite," said Emma.

"It's Aur-a-cite," snapped Danithar, whirling to face her. "Please enunciate it properly."

"Auracite," muttered Emma. "Nymira said this will help you."

Danithar crept over and gave the bottle a suspicious squint. "And who is this Nymira?"

"The Faerie Queen."

"Oh, I am sure she would adore me drinking this." He shook his head. "What foul trickery have you been charmed into participating in?"

"No trick. You're in the Faerie Realm now, correct?"

He grumbled. "Yes."

"And you know faeries charm people. So don't you think the Faerie Realm can charm people too?"

"I suppose that makes—oh, my… look at the plumage on that—"

Emma stared at the ceiling. "Aurcite."

He spun back from the window. "Child, please pronounce the word properly."

"Auracite." Emma held up the bottle. "This will take the curse from your mind."

"I'm not drinking anything a faerie made." White cotton eyebrows knitted close as the wrinkles across his forehead deepened.

"The faeries didn't make this. Mythandriel gave it to me."

Danithar rolled his eyes. "I'm to believe a goddess handed you a bottle of—my pumpkin bread is done." He started across the room toward the oven.

"Aurcite."

He whirled to glare at her.

"Auracite," said Emma. "There's an Astari ruin east from here. We went to an old temple and a spirit let me take this from the fountain. It will help you."

"Hmm." Danithar took the bottle and peered into it.

"My, my," whispered Emma's chair. "This little one could use a bath. She reeks of ten-day-old cabbage stew left to sit in someone's boots."

She gasped, mortified.

Two other empty chairs snickered.

"I fell in Darbolg swamp." Emma frowned.

Danithar leaned over and sniffed at Emma's hair. He coughed. "My word…"

Emma blushed and stared down.

"To the bath!" said Danithar, pointing.

Emma's chair galloped down a hallway. She clung to the seat to keep from falling off, wide-eyed and screaming. It burst past a curtain (which pulled itself up out of the way) and stopped short, launching her into a large wooden tub. The curtain closed itself, encircling the tub, an instant later.

"Umm." Emma looked around at the biggest bathing vessel she had ever seen.

"Touch the blue gem," said Danithar from the far end of the house. "Boy, would you care for something to eat. Oh, look! A speckled firetail in the tree!"

Kes laughed.

Two disembodied white gloves floated in, as did a brush and a washcloth. The gloves reached to her expectantly. Emma studied her surroundings, still turning in place, and found a large, blue gem set into the edge on the side where the tub met the wall. She pushed on it, yelping as a magical burst of energy leapt from the gem to her feet. In an instant, she found herself standing in a tubful of warm water, which came up a bit past her knees. A haze of steamy fog settled on the surface, and a faint scent of lavender filled the air.

The gloves tapped her on the shoulder, pointed at her, and held out a hand.

Emma removed her dress, and the gloves snatched it before zipping off.

"Hey! Where are you going?"

"I'm not going anywhere," said Danithar from down the hall.

Emma growled under her breath. "The gloves took my dress!"

"To wash it," said Danithar.

The cloth wrapped itself around a blob of soap, and attacked her. The brush followed suit. No matter how she moved or flailed, both cloth and brush evaded her arms and scrubbed. Emma yelped and dunked herself to the neck, the brush and cloth hovering over her, waiting. The oddity of her situation wore off eventually, and she went under to get her sticky hair wet. When she sat up, the cloth and brush resumed cleaning her. Biting her lip, Emma stood with her arms out to the sides and allowed herself to be washed like a royal with servants attending her bath. Soap leapt onto her head and invisible fingers massaged her scalp, cleaning all the swampy foulness from her hair. As odd as it was to have animated objects attending her, the comfort soon won her over, and she relaxed, allowing herself to enjoy the bath.

When the cloth wrapped around her knee and tugged, Emma sat and raised her feet out of the water. Unable to help herself, she giggled at the cloth sliding back and forth across the bottoms of her feet and between her toes. A few minutes later, it plunged under the water to rinse before flinging itself to drape over a peg on the wall, hanging limp like an ordinary rag. The brush landed on a shelf and stopped moving.

Emma sat neck deep in the lavender-scented water, waiting, tapping her foot. "Where is my dress?"

"The speckled firetail is an interesting creature, boy," said Danithar. "They have litters of two to four, and they stay together for their entire lives."

"Aurcite!" yelled Emma.

"That's not how you say it," shouted Danithar.

Will Nymira be angry with me if I thump him? "Auracite! Now, where is my dress?"

"Being washed," said Danithar. "One moment."

"I'm done with the bath!"

Danithar sighed. "Push the blue gem again. Have you never used a bath before?"

"Yes, but not a magic one."

She pressed the blue gem and the water burst into fog, leaving her sitting in an empty tub. A towel plucked itself off another peg. Emma got to her feet and let it dry her, feeling like she'd gone back to being three years old and needed Mama to give her baths again. After a few minutes of standing there with her arms impatiently folded, the gloves returned with her dress, which looked no different from when it had floated away, though it did have a faint scent of flowers. She swiped it and gave the gloves a glare before pulling the garment on. The curtain rushed to the side before she could grab it, making her yelp with surprise and almost fall over. Annoyed at the delay, and more than a little bewildered by the experience of flying objects bathing her, she stormed out to the main room.

Kes sat on a bench by the windowsill, listening to Danithar ramble on and on about speckled firetails, frostbellies, and thornbeaks and how the different types of birds lived, hunted, and went about their birdly existence. Danithar took great delight in describing the firetails, which turned out not to be birds at all, but squirrel-like creatures with bright orange fur and ruby eyes. When Emma walked in, Kes looked at her and made a face like he'd been hung by a noose.

She laughed. As awkward as it had been to take a bath in this mad house, she adored not smelling like rotting plants. She ran her fingers through her no-longer-sticky hair, smiling. "Danithar. Please trust me. Drink the blessed water from Mythandriel. It will help you find the Auracite."

"You said it correctly!" He clapped, glee clear in his tone.

"I'll never say it wrong again if you drink that."

He tapped a finger to his chin, wagging his eyebrows up and down. "Hmm." Danithar picked up the bottle and studied it.

Emma tapped her foot.

Four chairs approached like sniffing dogs.

"Much better," said one.

She made a fist as if to punch it, but the chair didn't react.

Kes chuckled.

"Very well." Danithar opened the stopper and drank. He stopped with a refreshed gasp, put the stopper back, and slammed the bottle down on the table like a man with an ale mug. "That was cold!"

She nodded.

Danithar stared into space, his look of confusion growing. Brown swam into the grey from the top of his head down to his beard. The wrinkles in his cheeks and around his eyes faded in seconds as his posture straightened. When he stopped changing, the man appeared to be in his early twenties. He raised his hands, gazing at them. "What… what is this?"

Emma leaned back, eyebrows rising at the change in his voice. He sounded stronger, more confident, even powerful. "I think this place made you a little nutters. Nymira said that water would cure you."

"A little?" muttered Kes.

Danithar patted himself down before running to a cabinet and flinging open the doors. He rummaged among bottles and jars of powders, blue, red, yellow, green, and gold. He slammed that cabinet and moved to the next, picking among potion bottles and a leather case packed full of wands. "Bah. It's gone!"

"The Auracite?" asked Emma.

"Yes." He scowled. "Those faeries… They'll regret stealing from me. I'll wipe them out to the last."

"No!" wailed Emma. "You promised!"

He squinted at her. "You're not a goblin are you? Under an illusion?"

"No. I'm a girl." She ran over and tugged on his arm. "You can't hurt the faeries. Please! They didn't take your crystal."

Red-faced with anger, Danithar stormed for the front door. "Animals aren't working. They're too vulnerable to eldritch magic. I'll send another bronze footman. No! A bronze colossus!"

"Please don't!" Emma grabbed his arm, but he pulled away and rushed outside. "Keep her safe," he muttered as if speaking to the door, which slammed itself.

She tried to follow, but the door refused to open. Emma grunted and struggled at the knob for a little while before giving up and darting to the window. She stared out at the front yard where Danithar dragged a hunk of bronze across the grass. It had the overall shape of a boot, but came up to his neck. If he made something like that metal horror they'd seen in the forest out of that, it would be taller than a house.

"I could shoot him," said Kes.

"No!" Emma whirled away from the window. "He'd hurt you. You're just a boy. He's a powerful mage. No... we can't fight him. We don't have to fight him. We have to prove the faeries didn't steal."

"How do you prove something to an insane person?"

Emma scowled. "He doesn't seem insane now, does he?"

"Perhaps not as much as before, but he is quite angry." Kes scratched his chin while thinking.

"There's got to be something..." Emma paced around the table, dodging the self-sweeping broom. "The faeries *were* here, but I believe them."

He shrugged.

Emma stopped, glancing out the window at a bright orange squirrel zipping along a branch. "Nymira said they came here to welcome him to the Faerie Realm... They cleaned his house for him, but he didn't thank them."

"So they played tricks on him."

"Right. Maybe they hid the crystal somewhere in the house or outside?"

"That door won't let you out."

She glared at it. "You can get out. He told it to keep *me* safe. You look outside. I'll search inside."

"All right. Yell if you need me." Kes approached the door, which opened for him. Once outside, he grabbed the knob in both hands and held it. "Come on."

She bit her lip, and ran for it.

The door slammed an instant before she got there, accompanied by a loud *thump* as Kes crashed into it.

"Ouch," said Kes from the other side.

"Are you all right?" Emma pressed herself into the door.

"Yes. My horns are stuck in the wood." He grunted, and a faint *pop* followed. "Follow your first plan?"

She glared at the knob. "Fine."

"If you really want out, I'll tell Mawr to break it down."

Emma laughed. "He would, too."

"Right. Searching." Kes scampered off.

Metal clanking outside lit a fire of urgency in Emma. Danithar would make something awful to stomp the Elder Grove into bits. She *had* to stop him.

"Hmm. What did they do?" She headed for the cabinets. "They cleaned. Let's start with the cupboards and the drawers. The man was so scatter-brained, maybe he didn't look."

She climbed up to stand on the countertop and opened the first cabinet. Bottles and jars of powders inside gave off powerful fragrances of mint, metal, and earth. One smelled like energy, which is to say it didn't smell like much of anything but fizzy tingles. She moved the jars around, searching behind them, but found no glowing white crystal.

After closing the doors, she sidestepped and checked the next cabinet. Again, no crystal. The third cabinet held dishes, which all cried out "pick me, pick me!" at the same time. She moved them enough to look under and around, before proceeding on to the final cabinet. Pots and pans inside kept suspiciously quiet.

When she lifted one to look under it, it screamed, "No, please!"

"Eep!" yelled Emma, dropping it. After two breaths, she calmed. "No what?"

"Don't cook with me!" wailed the pot. "It hurts!"

She shivered. "Why would he enchant pots to be able to feel? That's cruel. I'm not going to cook. I'm searching for something."

Two small cauldrons, a soup pot, two pans, and a deep skillet all exhaled with relief.

Finding nothing, Emma closed the doors and jumped to the floor. She opened each drawer in turn: silverware in the first, wooden rods she assumed the man intended to make wands out of in the next. Another drawer held tools and the one after it contained nails, screws, nuts, sprockets, and springs.

Emma blinked. "What is all this stuff?"

The fifth drawer had been packed with shiny stones, all organized by color in little bins. She picked over quartz, several different crystals, agate, cat's-eye, tiny diamonds, rubies, emeralds, some chalky white rocks, and four bins of black stones.

"Hmm." *He said it was white like milk, with pink and blue and purple on it... and it would tingle!*

She plucked a stone from the bin of milky ones. Cold, hard, nothing. One by one, she touched the stones, holding them for a second or two before putting them in a pile on the counter out of the way. After testing fourteen of them, a glint of white light flickered from the bottom of the half-full bin. Emma plunged her hand in, fishing for the bright stone, and unearthed a big crystal the size of a man's thumb.

Solid white like frozen milk, its eight facets had bands of faint lavender and blue. Both pointed ends appeared pink at the tips. Holding it felt as if an army of nibbling bugs crawled over her hand. All the little hairs on the back of her arm stood on end.

"The Auracite!"

Gripping it tight, she ran to the door. "Let me out."

"Sorry, child. I must keep you safe," said the door in the voice of a grandfather.

"I'm only going to the front yard. Danithar needs to see this. He's been looking for it."

"Patience, girl. I will ask him if it is allowed."

She sighed. "I'm ten, not three!"

After a long, frustrating moment, the door opened.

Emma ran forward. Danithar rushed from where two seven-foot-tall bronze legs held up the beginnings of a set of metal hips.

"You have the crystal?" He blinked.

"Is this the Auracite?" She held it up.

Danithar's eyes widened as if he gazed upon his stolen child returned. He cradled it in both hands, seeming near to tears with joy. "Yes!"

"*Now* will you stop trying to kill the faeries?" She folded her arms. *And acting like a spoiled little boy?*

25

CONJURATIONS

*D*anithar cradled the Auracite crystal in his hands, smiling. Emma stared, hands on her hips, foot tapping. Impatience grew each time her toes touched grass. She'd found the source of his anger. He would have to stop his mad effort to kill the poor faeries. Soon, she would go home.

"Well?" asked Emma.

"Hmm? What?" He looked up as if startled.

"Were you even listening?" She paused, forcing herself not to sound too petulant. "The faeries did not take your crystal. They were trying to be nice to you and cleaned your house. I don't think they understood that crystal belongs with your magical supplies, so they put it with the rocks."

He made a face like she'd spilled cold soup in his lap. "It was… with the stones?"

Emma nodded. "In with all the other white rocks, at the bottom of the bin."

He sighed. "I have been so angry and confused. This place… it does things to a human mind."

"Please stop trying to hurt the faeries. They only wanted to be nice to you." She let her arms fall limp at her sides. "I would like to go home. If you promise not to hurt the faeries, I can go home to my family."

"Of course, girl. Of course." He nodded and tucked the Auracite into a pouch on his belt. "I shall recall all of the creatures I had summoned to attack them."

Danithar took a step back, closed his eyes, and held his arms out to the sides. "*Va druthan il arben lor.*" His voice echoed, deeper than normal and magically loud. The air tingled with arcane power. Lavender orbs of energy swelled from his outstretched hands. Rapid-fire threads of pink lightning shot into the sky, mostly heading to the east. One tiny bolt of lightning struck Mawr in the nose.

And he evaporated in a cloud of pink mist.

Neema's shriek came from nowhere, followed by a soft *plop* in the grass.

Emma gawked at the dissipating cloud. "Mawr! No! What did you do?"

"Oh, that huge bear?" Danithar glanced over his shoulder. "He was one of the creatures I created to… harm the faeries."

"No!" Emma sank to her knees, sobbing. "You killed him! You killed Mawr."

Kes ran over and slid to sit beside her, wrapping her in a hug.

Emma bawled, heartbroken. Every kind thing Mawr had said replayed in her mind. Images of his warm fur, the gentle sway of his tireless walk, and his selfless desire to help her weighed heavy upon her heart. "He was my friend!" She sobbed. "Why did you kill him?"

"Child," said Danithar in a soft, soothing tone. He took a knee and put a hand on her shoulder.

She cringed away. "You killed him!"

"That bear wasn't real. He was merely a conjuration. Magical energy, nothing more."

"You're wrong!" shouted Emma, glaring at him despite tears she couldn't stop. "He *was* real! I could talk to him, but I couldn't talk to those stupid foxes. He was kind, and strong, and patient, and he did so much to help me… It's not fair! He didn't deserve to die!" She bowed her head and sobbed into her hands again.

Danithar exhaled. "Ahh. Emma… Those foxes were lesser conjurations. They exist to fulfill a task. When the task is done, they return to the nothingness I created them from. The bear was a greater spell. It remains like a real creature until dismissed or destroyed."

"Don't call Mawr an 'it!'" shouted Emma. She succumbed to a fit of bawling, clinging to Kes. Eventually, hard tears gave way to sporadic sniffles and mournful staring at the grass where her friend had been. "You didn't have to kill him!"

"I'm sorry, child. The bear wasn't real. I didn't kill him, any more than a spell that ceases function is a life ending."

Emma pulled her face out of the crook of Kes's neck, glaring at Danithar in disbelief. Tears dripped from her chin. "But he was my friend. He was real to me."

Danithar reeled from her expression, his eyes downcast with guilt. His eyebrows drew close, his eyes shifted side to side as he nibbled on his lip. Emma looked again at the spot where Mawr had been only moments ago, and surrendered to deep fits of crying. If not for Kes holding her, she would've flopped face down in the grass.

The conjurer, a mere blurry cloud of burgundy to Emma's teary eyes, glided off to the side. Soon after, a *clonk* came from the house door.

Neema landed on her shoulder, appeared from invisibility, and hugged the side of Emma's head. "Real was he, magic but too. Must to have be for safe faeries are. Together tied magic."

Emma wanted to leap into Da's arms and cry. That she couldn't made her weep harder.

Kes patted her back, murmuring comforting sounds.

"Go time is home now." Neema's eyes held sadness, but she smiled. "See family soon. Want see, yes?"

Emma nodded. "It's not right. Mawr didn't deserve to die."

Neema shook her head. "No. Not alive ever was."

"I don't believe you." Emma wiped her face. "He was alive. He had feelings."

26

A BURDEN TO BEAR

*E*mma cried, mourning the loss of her friend. Kes rubbed her back while Neema tried without success to cheer her up. Not even the thought of going home pulled her to her feet. She kept seeing Mawr curled up in the grass, patiently waiting for her to ask him for a ride yet again. Her friend, protector, and companion had not deserved to die. Guilt stabbed deep, little different from if she had been responsible for his death.

Danithar emerged from the house a few minutes later. He strode past her to the spot where the bear had been, crouched, and raked his fingers over the grass. Emma calmed enough to watch him, wiping her face on the back of her arm. He grasped at the ground once again, this time smiling at whatever sat in his hand. She wiped at her cheeks again, annoyed at herself that she couldn't stop crying.

"What are you doing?" asked Emma past her sniffles.

Danithar walked closer, holding his left hand palm up, staring into it. "Mawr you say?"

Emma's face scrunched up with sorrow. "Yes."

The conjurer plucked the bottle she'd brought the lifewater in from his belt, and shook it over his hand until a few drops fell. A faint fizzling noise came from his palm.

Emma stood, but couldn't see into his hand. "What are you doing?"

"I've been working out some calculations."

Danithar took the Auracite crystal from his pouch, pinched it between his thumb and forefinger, and aimed it into his hand. *"Us vondar ma dorann. Cha-ahn mor'sekh inar."* A thin beam of light shone from the crystal into his palm. Seconds later, bright amethyst energy appeared on the ground in front of his boots. It swelled up into an orb the size of a man's head, and split into four smaller spheres, which crept apart in straight paths.

Emma backed up, as did Kes. Awestruck to silence, she gawked, the last few tears still sliding down her face.

The creeping orbs stopped two paces from Danithar and shifted to rotate in a circle, burning a glowing violet ring into the ground.

Danithar chanted, *"Ourin ves mahr dorann,"* four times.

In a flash, mystic sigils and strange patterns appeared within the circle around Danithar. He rubbed his thumb over the Auracite crystal, which glowed blinding white.

"Indranor sil an."

A *snap* like a lightning strike slammed the air and sent Emma to her knees, hands clamped over her ears. A bear-shaped mass of violet energy appeared, lingered a second, and darkened into Mawr—or at least a bear of similar size.

Danithar seemed tired, but held his body rigid as if fighting against some intangible effort. "Child," he wheezed. "You did something. You must have done something to him to give him awareness. Do it again if you wish him back."

Emma's heart swelled with joy. She leapt to her feet and darted to the edge of the circle. The bear sat motionless, like a fine-detailed statue. She reached to touch him, but her fingertips burned as soon as they crossed the circle. With a gasp, she pulled back.

Danithar grimaced from the effort it took to contain the magical forces swirling around. "Be quick."

"Strixian..." Emma widened her stance and held her hands out at the bear. "Great Strixian, please grant Mawr the wisdom to know he is Mawr." Her memory leapt back to when she had first scrambled up a tree to get away from him, replaying the moment her magic had taken the fury from his eyes, leaving him confused. She gathered up all her sorrow at missing her friend, wrapping it into the desire for him to live. "Please heal my friend."

A tug of energy pulled from her being and she swayed to her knees from exhaustion.

Tiny changes, a tilt in the eye, thickening of the cheek fur, a subtle adjustment to the shape of the mouth, gradually made the ordinary bear's face once again into a being she had come to regard as the dearest of friends.

Mawr blinked and shook his massive head side to side.

Danithar's eyebrows rose. *"Va duril."*

A great *bang* echoed into the forest, scattering an explosion of birds in every imaginable color to wing. Both lightning panthers poked their heads out from the branches, wide-eyed, ears back. The glowing energy circle vanished. Danithar slouched with relief. He hastily dropped the Auracite into his pouch and waved his hand to cool it.

"Mawr?" asked Emma.

"Are we to walk again?" asked the bear, in a familiar scratchy, resonant voice. "I am rested and ready."

"Mawr!" Emma burst into joyful tears and flung herself into a hug, barely able to get her arms quarter of the way around his neck.

"I feel as if I have missed something of importance," said the bear.

Kes laughed.

Once she collected her emotions, Emma pulled away from Mawr and looked up at Danithar. "Thank you for bringing him back."

Danithar smiled a weary smile. "I almost feel sorry for your father. Surely, no man could suffer the weight of guilt while those sweet blue eyes beg for anything."

Emma hugged Mawr again, crying and giggling at the same time.

He gestured at the bear. "This bear is as real as a bear can be. Between the enchanted water you brought, the power stored within the Auracite, and whatever it is you did to give him a sentient mind… he is not tied to my essence as a conjuration. This bear is no longer merely a coalescence of magical energy, but a true creature."

"A coa-what?" Emma blinked.

"Coalescence," said Danithar. "Umm. A gathering… or collection."

"Oh." Emma nodded.

"What did he say?" asked Mawr. "I am confused."

Danithar glanced at him. "What did he say?"

Emma grinned. "He doesn't understand what happened." She hugged Mawr again. "The magic that made you angry is gone forever."

Mawr nodded. "That is good indeed. Are we to walk?"

"I don't know." She looked at Neema. "What do we do now?"

"Walk Elder Grove to." She beamed. "Return home Emma."

Emma faced Danithar and offered a hand. "Thank you. Can I tell Queen Nymira that you won't hurt them?"

"Yes, child." Danithar stooped forward, seeming out of breath. "You mean to wander off again? I dare not permit it. Many dangers lie in wait among these woods."

"I've been back and forth twice. My friends will protect me." She kept her hand out. "I must return to my family. Why don't you come too? This place is not for humans." She cringed inside as soon as she asked it, remembering Nymira telling her he couldn't leave.

He took her hand and shook it. "I shall be no threat to the faeries, but alas I cannot return to our world. I have been here for too many years, and I shall surely fall to dust on the other side. The enchanted water has bound me even more to this place." He chuckled. "Fear not. I have become rather enamored with the birds."

"Yes, you have." Emma grinned. "Farewell, Danithar."

Kes leaned to the side and covered his mouth with one hand. A beautiful whistling trill came from the forest nearby, making Danithar whirl around and gasp with delight.

Emma stifled a snicker.

Finding no bird, the mage held out a finger toward Neema. She landed upon it, standing. "Please convey my deepest apologies to your queen."

"You should offer them treats," said Emma. "A gesture of apology. They are fond of Faeberry cakes and mead."

Danithar made a face as if obligated to do something unpleasant, but nodded. "Perhaps that is wise. So I shall."

Emma climbed upon the bear's back, taken by tears of joy yet again. "Thank you for being such a wonderful friend, Mawr."

"I am glad to have met you as well," said the bear.

Kes waved at the conjurer and sprang up behind Emma.

Neema took her post standing on Mawr's nose, and pointed. "That home way."

FAERIE CIRCLE

*E*xcitement at going home made the three-day trek back to the Elder Grove feel like three months. Kes spent the first day telling her a story of when his parents and he followed a group of forest bandits. He described with great glee how inept and clumsy the humans were, how they always fell into streams or broke the perches they built in the trees to watch the road for travelers to ambush. He grinned each time he described the thieves' misfortune, giving Emma the idea one or both of his parents had cursed the bandits with bad luck.

Each night, his father would take their wine while his mother made herself look human and went into their camp to distract the men. Kes raided their food supplies, and later they would eat and drink, while listening to the confused humans try to guess why their stuff kept disappearing.

Emma laughed, and told him of her own experience with thieves.

When they reached the bridge, Neema took care to ferry them across one by one while her magic made them light. The following day, Emma huddled at the center of Mawr's back while he swam the murk of Darbolg. Finally free of the stink in her hair, she didn't want so much as a single toe to come in contact with the awful grey water.

Emma couldn't sleep on the night of the second day. Tomorrow, they would reach the Elder Grove, and after a brief meeting with the queen, she would be home again. In an instant, she went from staring at the stars to draped across Mawr's back, groggy, gazing over brown fur at passing trees.

"You magicked me to sleep, didn't you?" mumbled Emma.

"Sleeping no without help." Neema kissed the side of her head. "Needing much sleep, Neema helped so."

"Thanks," said Emma, her voice as dead as her body felt. "I think you used too much magic."

Kes lifted her into a sitting position and held her up.

She laughed. After about twenty minutes, the magic faded, allowing her body to wake. A little less than half a day later, the Elder Grove came into view. Mawr walked, tireless as ever, and brought her up to the gate. Emma slid to the ground and ran inside, scurrying around the crystalline fountain. She rushed over to kneel before the queen, grinning.

Nymira looked up with a warm smile. "From the amount of time you have been gone, and the happiness radiating from you, I trust your tidings are good?"

"Yes, Queen Nymira." Emma nodded. "The water from the temple made Danithar young again, and he isn't quite so nutters. He still didn't believe me, and was going to build a giant metal man to hurt you all."

The Silverbell Faeries emitted a collective gasp.

Nymira raised one eyebrow.

"I remembered what you said, that the faeries wanted to be nice to him and cleaned his house. I found the Auracite in a drawer with common stones. He expected it to be with magical reagents, but I think the faeries mistook it for a rock and put it with other rocks."

Nymira buried her face in her hand. "The man is a fool."

"I showed him the crystal, and he is sorry. He promised not to attack you again, and is going to put out treats as an apology."

The faeries erupted in cheers. Fifty or sixty tiny bodies flitted over to hug her at once in a cacophony of bell tones, except for Nymira and her guards, who remained regal and composed. Emma giggled and cringed at the tickling flutter of wings.

"You have done far more than I ever expected from a human child." Nymira glided up to eye level. "I grant you my favor, Emma. You have returned our Neema to us, and you have safeguarded the lives of all my faerie kin. For as long as you remain our friend, you have our loyalty."

The faeries erupted in cheers.

Emma smiled. "Thank you."

Music, flutes, and the singing of tiny voices filled the forest. Faeries came from everywhere, dancing and zipping around. They tugged at Emma's hands, and she soon found herself dancing as a celebration took over the Elder Grove. Kes leapt in, adding his flute to the chorus while jumping and twirling about.

She frolicked, laughing along with the revelry, but gazed every so often into the woods toward the faerie circle. While she wanted to go home, she did not dare refuse the Silverbells' gratitude. One hour stretched into the next, and before she knew it, she collapsed upon a carpeting of thick mossy undergrowth, too tired to stand.

Faeries brought her cakes and water, continuing to dance upon her as they sang her name and cheered. Emma ate a bit, and drank. Bright colors trailed from their wings, glowing lines against a dark green forest. Dizziness swam in her head. The music blurred into the tiny voices, the sound twisting as if she drowned in it. In an instant, all became quiet.

SHE SAT UP FAST, LOOKING AROUND. A DEEP, RESTFUL SILENCE FILLED THE Elder Grove, broken only by the soft chirps of distant birds or trills of other creatures in the woods. Faeries draped here and there over branches, spires, and open ground. Some hung half out of windows, others dangled from vines or floated in the fountain. An unconscious faerie man slid off the top of her head and landed in the grass beside her, not even waking when he struck the ground.

"Oh, my…" She stretched.

Kes walked out from a tree by her side. "Good morning."

"It's morning?" She shivered with anticipation. *I've been gone* another *day?* "What happened to the faeries?"

"They danced and drank until they could no longer stand. Most are asleep where they fell when the drink got the better of them." He grinned.

Neema pushed a twig and leaf off her face, grunting. After yawning, she got up and walked over, dragging her limp wings along the ground like a frumpled bedsheet wrapped about her shoulders. She yawned again, stretched, and sneezed, her wings snapping out straight with a puff of glowing white dust.

"Morning good!" she chirped.

"Mafindwel," said Emma. "May I return home now?"

"Course of!" Neema yawned again. "Need waking up. Give moment."

She flew a little, landed into a stumble, took wing again, and crashed headfirst into the water within the crystal fountain. After a second of blowing bubbles, Neema sprang out into the air, squealing.

"Wake!" The dripping faerie flew over and grinned. "Being ready."

Emma stood. "Me too."

Neema glided into the woods. Emma followed, holding Kes's hand while Mawr trailed along behind them. Once the roperoot trees became too thick for her to get by without climbing, she perched once again upon the bear's back. He stepped over roots without breaking stride, making the journey out to the circle, what had taken Emma over an hour, in perhaps twenty minutes. Neema flew ahead and landed upon the ground by a circle of flowers.

Mawr stopped nearby, and Emma slid from his back for the last time.

It hit her at that moment that he couldn't go with her. Danithar had made him with the enchanted water. Emma spun, wrapped her arms around him, and cried.

"Thank you for all your help." She sniffled. "I'm going to miss you *so* much."

"I will always be here," said Mawr. "And always your friend."

She cried harder. "You're my friend. The best kind of friend."

He emitted a warm rumble from deep in his throat, and nuzzled her.

"Well, I suppose it's time for you to go home to your family." Kes smiled, though his expression held a hint of sorrow. "It was wonderful to know you, Emma. Maybe I'll pop in to visit."

Emma hugged him. "You must." She leaned back and wiped tears. "You're my friend too, and you simply must visit."

He brushed his fingers down her cheek. "I could not suffer the torment of a month without seeing your exquisite face."

She giggled. "Why do you talk like that?"

"Like what?" He raised an eyebrow.

"Always calling me pretty and talking like a storybook."

He shrugged. "I don't know... I just do. It's true you know. You are pretty."

Her face grew warm. "I'm not old enough to get flowers from satyrs."

"What?"

Emma squinted at him. "You don't know? Every year on the Feast of Zaravex, all the girls sixteen or older who haven't been married get flowers from boys dressed up like satyrs."

Kes scratched his head. "I've not a clue about that. Sounds strange."

"Hmm." She folded her arms. "Mama and Da won't explain it to me either."

"I'm sure they will someday." Kes removed his fang necklace and offered it to her. "To remember me. Take it."

"Oh, Kes, I couldn't." She stared at it.

"I insist." He reached out and draped it over her head. "I shall talk about you to the trees and the air, and you will be with me."

Emma ground her big toe into the spongy green. "I will talk of you as well."

He smiled.

"Promise you'll visit?" asked Emma.

Kes bowed with a sweep of his arm. "But of course."

"Ready?" asked Neema.

"I'm going to miss you." Emma hugged Mawr. "And you too." She hugged Kes.

"Ask Queen Nymira Mawr guard Elder Grove the will. Honorary sentinel." Neema clapped. "Remain us with will he. Magic doing the queen Mawr to let talk the faeries."

"That's wonderful." Emma sniffled. "Protect them well, Mawr."

"Be safe, Emma." Mawr rubbed his massive head against her, as gentle as can be, and took a step back. "Return to your family where you belong."

Emma sniffled, nodded, and faced the faerie circle.

Neema took her by one finger, radiated a puff of silver faerie dust, and tried to pull her forward.

Grinning at the futile effort, Emma walked into the ring, still looking back at Kes and Mawr standing beside each other. Soft petals brushed her ankles, and the next time she blinked, her friends had vanished. The forest changed in a flash, less vibrant green, filled with much, much smaller trees. She recognized the woods a mere two minutes' walk from home. Neema floated behind her, waving.

"Will you?"

Neema nodded. "Will we."

The faerie disappeared in a wink of light and a tone like the soft peal of a bell.

Emma put a hand over her heart, breathless from momentary sorrow at leaving Mawr and Kes. She took a deep breath, let it out, and ran across the meadow to home. The bucket remained by the water pump as she had left it. Workers continued putting up spars for the new rooms, no further along than she remembered. She stopped halfway between the pump and the porch, looking back and forth.

"Goodness, Emma," said Nan from inside. "What's taking so long with the water?"

"Coming, Nan," yelled Emma.

She pumped the handle a few more times to fill the bucket and hauled it into the house.

Kimber hovered close by Nan, watching her slice up vegetables for the stew. The cauldron, empty, hung on the hook by the fireplace. Mama and Tam had not yet returned from her rounds.

Emma blinked. *It's like I've only been gone a few minutes...* Tears welled in her eyes. Relief, guilt, and exhaustion filled her. A lump caught in her throat, but she lugged the water to the cauldron and poured it in.

"One more for now, Em. Pour two in and fill a third for later." Nan smiled.

"Yes, Nan."

She hurried out the door to the pump, and got to working the lever. *Did that really even happen?* She eyed the woods, looked at the house, and sighed. Reaching up, she found a line of animal fangs across her chest, hanging from Kes's necklace.

It did...

Grunting, Emma pumped the bucket full a second time and carried it inside. The sorrow of wishing her friends farewell crashed into the joy of being home and left her unsure how to feel.

A FEW MINUTES

*A*fter pouring the second bucketful of water into the cauldron, Emma ran out to fill it a third time and carted it back inside. She set the filled bucket on the ground by the fireplace and darted across the room, plowing into Kimber and Nan, gripping them both in a fierce hug.

"Gah!" yelled Nan. "Be mindful, Em. I'm holding a knife."

"Urgh," muttered Kimber. "Squeezin' tae much."

Emma let go, a sheepish smile on her face.

"What's gotten into you, child? Did something give you a scare?"

They would never know what I did if I didn't tell them. She gazed down at her toes, dreading how much trouble she'd get in so soon after promising not to run off on her own. Guilt filled her stomach, making the idea of eating even Nan's amazing stew feel unwelcome.

"Something in the woods, yes." Emma took her position at Nan's right, and cut the potatoes and turnips into chunks.

Nan stroked her hair. "You've had quite the scare as of late. No shame in it."

She cringed. If she said nothing, she wouldn't get in trouble. They'd never find out.

Soon, Nan left Emma to the task of cutting up the remaining vegetables, and taught Kimber the spices to use (and how much) for the stew. Her sister doled out the seasonings and put them in the cauldron before carrying over bowls of ingredients. Nan went outside for a minute, and returned with a large eggplant-shaped piece of meat, with white leaves at one end.

Emma blinked. "Nan?"

The old one chuckled. "You've been feeling sad at the idea of eating what you can talk to, so I just made this." She waved the meat at her. "'Tis a simple food spell. It is like beef, but never talked to anyone."

"Meatplants?" asked Kimber.

Emma smiled, though the guilt refused to let go of her insides. "Nan… I have to tell you something… when Mama is home."

"Now I know something isn't right." Nan looked over, one eye wider than the other. "The last time you used that tone, you'd dropped the chamber pot in the privy."

Emma bowed her head.

"Very well." Nan tossed the meat into the pot. "I suppose it can wait for Beth."

"You'as do bad?" asked Kimber.

Emma ground her toe into the floor. "I'm not sure. Feels like it."

Nan guided Kimber back to the table. "She will tell us in due time."

Ingredients went into the cauldron one by one. Nan sent Emma to get wood from the pile out back, and soon, the beginnings of wonderful stew simmered in the fireplace. Nan added a little water from the bucket, stirring, adding a little more, stirring, and nodding.

Eventually, Mama returned and hung her cloak on the peg by the door. Tam rushed across the room, heading for where he'd left Stick Knight and Shrub Dragon. Emma caught him into a hug, sniffling with joy. It felt as though she hadn't seen him in a month. He hugged her back for a few seconds before the squirming started. She released him to his toys and walked up to where Mama discussed Hadrath's old sow with Nan, wondering if anything could be done for an unusual malady that had affected the old pig. Evidently, the animal had taken to belching constantly, and its tongue had turned berry pink.

"Mama? Nan?" asked Emma in a timid voice.

"Yes?" Mama smiled at her.

Emma cried and hugged her mother.

"Oh dear." Nan clucked. "She believes she's done something. I can't imagine what. She's been underfoot all day."

"What's wrong, Emma?" Mama grasped her shoulders.

Emma leaned back. "I did something foolish."

"What this time?" muttered Nan. "More thieves?"

"No." Emma shook her head. "Remember the faerie lantern?"

Mama nodded.

Nan scratched at herself as if taken by a sudden coating of fleas. "Faeries…"

"When I went out to get the water for the stew, Neema flew up to me and asked for help. She said something was killing faeries and they needed me."

Nan raised an eyebrow. "You went through a circle."

"Yes." Emma looked down.

"Well that explains why she's been so emotional…" Nan puffed a lock of hair away from her eye. "Like she's been away for a long time."

Mama patted Emma's shoulder. "What? Why?"

"Because she *has* been away." Nan set her hands on her hips. "How long?"

"It felt like about two weeks." Emma clasped her hands in front, and stared at the floor while telling them everything that happened. She took care to refer to the wood dragon as a 'Child of Linganthas' and avoid the 'd word' to keep Tam calm.

Kimber couldn't seem to decide if she should be thrilled, worried, or jealous. She swished side to side, chewing on her knuckle.

Mama pulled Emma across the room, sat in one of the cushioned chairs, and drew her up into her lap, holding her tight.

"I'm sorry, Mama. I promised not to run off and be foolish. I wanted to tell Nan that the faeries needed help, but Neema looked so scared. She said she was an adult, so I wasn't alone, and I felt so sorry for her and—" She buried her face against her mother's shoulder and cried. "I'm sorry."

"Well, Beth." Nan clucked. "Faeries can be rather persuasive after all. Perhaps she isn't entirely at fault here. And… she was only gone for a few minutes."

"Mother…" Mama stared at her. "She should have run right inside and told you."

"Yes, Mama. I should have. I wanted to."

"And what would I have done? At my age? If I'd crossed, I'd be stuck there." Nan winked.

Mama smirked.

Emma looked between them, confused by Nan's sarcastic tone. "You wouldn't be trapped?"

"Hardly," said Mama, in a flat tone.

"Because we're druids, or because we have elf blood?" asked Emma.

"Elf blood?" Nan cackled. "Where did you hear that?"

"The faerie queen."

"You'as saw 'a faeries queen?" Kimber's voice rose to a shrill; her whole body shook with excitement. The girl stared at her, wide-eyed. "Wha's she look like?"

"Like a faerie... with a crown. She had fire-red hair longer than her legs. Her wings glowed red too."

"Well." Nan whistled. "I suppose that's close enough. There is some fey magic in our family, but a druid with Linganthas' respect can traverse the rings regardless of age. Now, that conjurer fellow... he's stuck."

Emma squeezed her mother. "I wanted to get Nan. I wanted to stay, but I just felt so worried about the faeries, I went with her."

Mama sighed. "Sounds like you were charmed."

"Neema wouldn't..."

Nan chuckled. "Faeries are tricky, Em. They'll often do anything to get what they want. I bet she gave you her best wide-eyed pleading stare. Though, the Silverbells are not malicious. She probably believed that the only chance they had of surviving was for you to go with them."

"I'm not angry with her for charming me." Emma looked down. It *did* seem strange how she had decided to follow Neema so easily. "I'm sorry for disobeying you, Mama."

Heavy tromping on the porch preceded Da walking in fast. He leaned over to kiss Mama, gave Emma a quick hug, and headed to the cabinet. "I've got to head out to the north for a time. With any luck, I'll be back in time to enjoy that wonderful stew with everyone." He took some bread and cured meat from the larder.

"What's the rush, Liam?" asked Nan.

He collected Kimber in a one-armed hug while taking a bite of his lunch. "Some addled farmers from Imbril came running into town, prattling on about an entire village appearing out of thin air in the forest to the west."

Emma gasped, shaking.

"Em?" Da took a step toward her, raising an eyebrow. "What's wrong?"

She clung to him and hurried through a retelling of going into a faerie circle, the queen, the conjurer, and the strange village that wanted her to stay forever. "I... think they called it Brynshire. Everyone there was half a ghost, and they all wanted to feed me. They thought I was an orphan, and it looked like they were going to fight each other to see who took me in. They chased me into the village circle, and I saw magic lines going from all the people into the well. I found a bad talisman at the bottom. When I broke it, the village disappeared."

Da gawked at her.

"That was not my doing." Nan shook her head. "I was but a young girl when the curse befell Brynshire."

"There's no such town as Brynshire," said Da. "Never has been, though... I swear one of those villagers said that exact name."

"It's been gone quite a long time. From the sound of it, they made something quite angry." Nan looked at Emma. "What did this talisman look like?"

"It was wood and grass, moldy. Shaped like a man in a skirt holding a staff. I think it had a face drawn on it, but it faded in the water. It felt dark. Scary. When I touched it, my hands burned. It didn't want me touching it. All the ghost villagers' energy lines went into it. When you made the talisman for the spider queen, you told her not to break it or the magic would stop... so I broke it."

Nan patted her on the head. "Could have been an orc shaman. Perhaps a dark druid."

"There haven't been orcs in this area for three hundred years," said Da. "Humans pushed them out to the east a long time ago."

"Yes. I remember." Nan winked.

Da laughed. "You're wizened, but you're not that old."

As he turned to kiss Mama, Nan shot an innocent look at the ceiling, and wandered over to check on the stew.

Emma gawked at her, mouth agape.

"I'll be back. Off to check on this phantom town." Da started for the door, but stopped when Nan cleared her throat.

"The village is likely real, Liam. Tread with caution. Those people will have no idea of how much time has passed."

He gave her that look he always did whenever he didn't want to believe. Rather than sigh and walk off as he often did when magic came up, he bowed his head. "Do you think they will be cursed? Dangerous?"

Wow. Emma blinked. *Da believed me!*

Nan scratched at her chin. "Without feeling that talisman for myself, I cannot say. Though, if the magic were *that* dark, it would've terrified Emma straight into running away from it. You should expect confused people, but they may believe you are the one who is addled." She dribbled spices into the stew pot from a bowl.

"Indeed." He patted Tam on the head, then Kimber, and stopped in front of Emma. "And what are we to do with you, then?"

"I went with the faerie and I shouldn't have. Whatever you decide, I will accept." Emma looked down.

"Well, according to her story, she prevented the slaughter of an entire cove of faeries, saved the life of a faun, broke a centuries-old curse on a hundred villagers, and restored the sanity of an old mage." Nan raised both hands and waved them down. "All before lunch."

"That faerie charmed her." Mama waved her over. "She didn't have much of a choice."

Emma scurried into a hug. "I was homesick every day."

"All right." Da shook his head. He scooped her up and held her for a moment. "My parents told me that having a daughter would be quite the handful… They had *no* idea."

Emma risked a smile.

He gave her a squeeze and a back pat before setting her on her feet. "As much as I would rather remain here, duty calls."

"Yes, yes, go soothe the addled farmers." Nan scooped up a spoonful of stew and sniffed it. Not quite satisfied, she dropped it back in the pot and reached for a different bowl of seasonings.

"Indeed." Da walked out, grumbling and taking another bite of his bread.

Mama tugged her closer. "I will not call this a punishment, but because of what happened…"

Her chest tightened with worry.

"I want you to stay in arms' reach of me for the rest of the day."

Emma grinned and climbed into her lap. "Yes, Mama."

OF DRAGONS AND TEA PARTIES

*E*mma spent the rest of the day and the next hovering at her mother's side. That night, the workers joined them for dinner, their house filled with smiles and laughter. She noticed all the little things her family did: the way Da always stacked a bit of cheese on an apple slice before eating them both, how Tam tried his hardest to never be without his wooden sword, and how Kimber constantly fidgeted with her hair whenever her hands didn't have anything else to do.

That her sister seemed to no longer tense up at every loud noise made Emma feel warm inside. Mama always smiled whenever she looked at the children, no matter how frustrated or angry she may have been at something else—and she had a different sort of smile for whenever Da caught her eye.

The homesickness Emma had carried for the two-some-odd weeks she'd been away had morphed into a deep desire to never experience that feeling again. Da had asked Nan to help with the people of Brynshire, who remained convinced a little black-haired girl had jumped down their well, and didn't believe that they'd been stuck in the Faerie Realm under a curse for a long, long time. Nan thought it somewhat hysterical, as if an orc shaman had indeed been responsible, the Faerie Realm would've been the last place they wanted to send a human village. More likely, they tried to do something worse and made a mistake. Tam suggested Princess Isabelle maybe shot him with an arrow so his spell went wrong.

Neither Nan nor Emma bothered mentioning Isabelle wouldn't have been around three hundred years ago. Emma stared a question into Nan's eyes. The old one offered a blasé one-shouldered shrug.

Emma busied herself with her usual chores, but kept an eye on the tiny window to the left of the back door, waiting to see an acorn hanging there. Finally, on her second day back, the acorn appeared soon after the evening meal, when the sun weakened in the sky and the workmen had left for the day. The new section of house had finished walls and a roof, and the men had been building up the inside walls most of the day.

"Kimber?" Emma scurried over to where her little sister sat with Mama in the big cushioned chair, learning to knit.

"Hmm?" She looked up, grinning.

Emma winked at Mama. "Would you like to have a faerie tea party?"

Nan hurried to the stove and set a teapot on it.

Kimber held up her needles and yarn. "I'as knittin' an' it almos' dark."

"You've a little while yet." Mama smiled. "It's all right if you'd like to."

Emerald eyes gleaming, Kimber set her knitting down to the side on the little table, and jumped up.

Kimber took her hand and walked out onto the back porch, glancing over her shoulder at Nan with a confused expression. The stones they had set up for their pretend tea party remained as they had left them. Emma felt a twinge of surprise that no one had cleared away the rocks, but it *had* only been two days for everyone else.

"Why'as Nan makin' tea?" asked Kimber.

Emma giggled. "How do you expect us to have a tea party without tea?"

Kimber flopped on the porch by the tiny seats and table, and tucked a lock of hair behind her ear. "Tea'as p'tend, like 'a faeries."

"Hmm." Emma rubbed her chin. "Something's missing from this faerie tea party."

Kimber looked up at her with a slight tilt of her head.

Pimlin, Fila, Imril, and Raa floated up past the edge of the porch (behind Kimber), carrying a crown of flowers. Neema poked her head up over the boards, and grinned.

"Wha's missin'?" Kimber pointed at the stone 'chairs.' "I see the faeries."

Emma sat and crossed her legs. "Me too."

Tam's gasp came from the door.

Kimber seemed to notice the colorful glow on the wall from the faerie's wings, but before she could turn to look behind her, the faeries set the flower crown upon her head.

"Merry greetings," chirped Pimlin, her bright pink wings spraying glowing sparkles in all directions.

"Merry meet!" cheered Imril. He bowed before flying in a spiral around her, dusting her with energy the color of snow.

"Hello!" Raa beamed and landed on Kimber's shoulder, her pastel blue wings pulsing bright.

Kimber squealed so loud Emma thought the girl about to faint.

Neema zipped over and landed on Emma's shoulder.

"Mama!" yelled Tam. "Mama, come look!"

Three more faeries, green, gold, and silver wings aglow, shot over from the meadow and raced around Kimber before all eight of them landed on her. Kimber held her arms up as if afraid to move, lest she hurt them. The pure joy radiating from her face made Emma shed a tear.

Mama appeared in the doorway and put her hands on Tam's shoulders. "Mind yourself, Tam. Be polite."

Kimber got over her squealing and giggling fit in a few minutes. When Nan appeared with teapot and tray, the faeries took up their seats around the little stone table. Emma helped Nan serve small cups to the faeries. Her grandmother had made mint tea and even some Faeberry cakes—though the children were not to touch those.

Over the moon with excitement, Kimber chattered away with them about the Faerie Court. Pimlin told her about the various social ranks within their society: the nobles, the guards, the mages, the scouts, the lorekeepers, common fey, and the exiles.

Neema stole away long enough to whisper in Emma's ear. "Regrets sends Queen Nymira. Visit to wanted, but bound to Faerie Realm. Cannot leave her magic. Invites to Elder Grove tea for."

"That is a lovely offer." Emma smiled. "I have to ask if we're allowed to visit her before I can accept."

Kimber stared in silence for a few seconds before clasping her hands together at her chin, pleading.

"I can't say it's okay." Emma held her arms up. "I'm only ten."

The pleading stare Kimber focused on Emma shifted to Mama.

"We'll discuss it," said Mama.

The girls sat until dark, and a little after, having tea with Silverbell Faeries. Far too soon for Kimber's liking, Mama poked her head out the door and gave Emma a meaningful look.

Emma nodded to her mother, and stepped in to the ongoing conversation at the first opportunity. "Thank you all so very much for visiting us. You've made Kimber very happy."

Kimber grinned and nodded with such fervor, her floral crown fell into her lap.

"It's late and we must go to bed." Emma curtseyed.

Neema downed the last of her tea and set the little wooden cup back on the flat stone table. "Having party is generous you of. Had we fun all."

One by one, the Faeries glided over to give Emma delicate hugs… before they all dove on Kimber at the same time.

Kimber fell over backward, peals of laughter echoing into the forest.

After a moment of tickling her breathless, the faeries raced across the meadow like tiny shooting stars, heading back to the faerie circle, and home.

Emma grasped Kimber's hand and pulled her up to sit. "Time for bed."

"You'as really did help 'a faeries." Kimber couldn't seem to stop grinning.

"Yes."

She scrambled to her feet. "You'as 'fink Mama'll let us visit 'a queen?"

Emma thought back to what Nan said about druids and faerie circles. "Maybe… but I think she's going to come with us."

After a second of grinning at each other, they burst into giggles at the same time.

"Em," said Da from inside. "Your mother's said it's time for bed."

Emma gasped, grabbed Kimber by the hand, and ran inside.

THE NEXT AFTERNOON, EMMA SWEPT THE FRONT PORCH, STILL GRINNING from ear to ear at Kimber's reaction to the faeries. Her sister hadn't stopped singing all day, except when she spoke to imaginary faeries. She about reached the halfway point of sweeping when a finger-sized root grew up and over the edge of the porch, and tapped her on the foot.

Emma squatted and offered a hand. The root curled around her arm. "Thank you. I'll tell Mama when she returns from her rounds in the village."

The root uncoiled and rewound the other way, holding her hand. A mild sense of impatience radiated from it.

"I'm sorry. We'll be as fast as we are able."

After releasing her hand, the root brushed her cheek and sank into the dirt.

"Oh… Mama, please be quick." Emma resumed sweeping, hurrying the task without her usual care for not missing any spots.

Before too long, her mother appeared at the bend in the road, walking back from Widowswood proper. She stopped to speak to Mrs. Harrow, who leaned out from her window. Emma ground the bristles into the porch. *Hurry up!* In a few minutes, Mama waved to the older woman and trotted up the road home.

Emma practically threw the broom at the wall by the door and scurried to stand at the top of the steps.

"What is it, Em?" Mama ran a hand over her head and pulled her close.

"He's here. I asked if he could visit Tam, and he really came!" Emma bounced on her toes. "Can we go see him?"

Mama blinked. "You managed to talk a wood—"

"Shh… I want to surprise him." Emma grinned. "Yes."

"You know, Em… even I haven't met one of them."

Emma pulled on her arm. "Come with us."

Mama gave her 'the look.' "You thought you were going to meet him without me along?"

"No…" She grinned. "I want you to."

"All right." Mama smiled.

Inside, Tam sprawled on the floor by the fireplace, playing with Stick Knight and Shrub Dragon. Emma ran to his side.

"I want to show you something."

He looked up. "What?"

"You have to promise not to be scared."

Tam dropped the toys and stood. "I'm not scared." He hesitated. "'Snot Rydh?"

"No. It's not Rydh. It's much better than Rydh."

"'Kay." He ran to grab his wooden sword from where it hung on the wall and stuck it through his rope belt.

Mama stepped up behind Emma. "Let us hope he doesn't wind up refusing to come out from under the bed."

"He won't." Emma smiled and walked a few steps toward the back hall. "Nan?"

"Yes, Emma?" asked Nan from her room.

"We're going for a walk in the forest. Will you come with us?"

Nan grunted along with the scuff of chair legs on wood. "One moment."

Kimber set her doll down on the floor where she sat. "Kin I go?"

Emma waved her over. "Promise me you won't be scared."

"Scared 'a what?" Kimber stood and crept closer.

"It's a surprise for Tam, but it's not anything to be frightened of no matter what it looks like." Emma took her hand.

"'Kay." Kimber stared at her, biting her lip.

Nan emerged from the back and donned her shawl. Mama draped shawls around the girls before dressing Tam in his green wool cloak. Barely able to contain her glee, Emma led the way out the back door, over the porch, across the meadow, and into the forest to the west of their home.

"Linganthas, please guide my step so that I may find your child," whispered Emma.

Within seconds, a subtle feeling came over her, pulling her a little to the right. Mama raised an impressed eyebrow. Nan flashed a proud smile at the trees, as if to say 'see what my granddaughter can do?'

A few minutes into the woods, Emma spotted the 'hill' of roots, much as she had seen in the Faerie Realm.

She stopped walking, took a knee, and put an arm around Tam's back. "Look there."

He leaned forward, squinting.

Nan spotted him right away, and bowed her head in reverence.

Mama glanced at Nan, who gestured at the 'hill' and nudged her with an elbow.

"I don't see nothin'," said Tam.

Emma squeezed him close. "Don't be scared."

"I'm not scared of woods." He blinked. "Goblins?"

"No, Tam. No goblins." Emma looked toward the Child of Linganthas, and raised her voice. "Thank you for the favor of your visit."

Tam opened his mouth, but before a sound could come out of him, the 'hill' moved, unfurling itself into the shape of a dragon made of thick roots and vines, the glow of dark green energy deep within its heart. A brighter shade of light gleamed from its eyes, which narrowed in a friendly smile. Ivy and vine whiskers swayed from his chin as he stretched up to stand.

"Great Linganthas," whispered Mama.

"It's not Linganthas," said Nan. "But a wood dragon. The plant spirit's presence in our world."

"Aaaah!" said Tam, waving his fists and shaking with excitement. "It's a mama Shrub Dragon!"

Emma laughed. "Maybe Shrub Dragon's Da."

He gasped. "Sorry!"

Kimber jumped on Emma, hiding behind her.

Emma led Tam by the hand up to the wood dragon. Kimber seemed more afraid of letting go of Emma than approaching the creature, so she followed. Mama and Nan walked a few steps after them, Nan calm and smiling, Mama wide-eyed with awe… like Tam.

Tam scrunched up his nose and looked at Emma.

"What?" asked Emma.

"Why's he made out of wood and not made out of dragon?"

Emma giggled and tickled him. "He's a wood dragon. Linganthas is the spirit of the forest, plants, and flowers. These are his children, guardians of the most sacred places deep within the woodlands."

Mama tilted her head. "Where did you learn that?"

"He told me." Emma nodded toward the dragon.

Tam walked closer, reaching up to touch the dragon's chin. "Wow…"

The dragon emitted a low rumble of contentment.

"Em?" whispered Kimber. "Stick Knight… is 'e a' baddie 'cause 'e keep tryin' ta kill Shrub Dragon, an' a' shrub dragon's nice?"

Tam gasped. "My dragon isn't like this. He's made out of dragon. *Bad* dragon, an' Stick Knight's gotta save the village." He traced his hand over the creature's jawline. "This dragon's a nice dragon."

Mama walked close, bowed to the dragon, and caressed the side of his head. She muttered at him in another language that sounded a bit to Emma like Faerie spoken much, much slower. The Child of Linganthas responded in the same language, tolerating Tam climbing up onto his back and cheering. When their conversation ended, Mama bowed again as if she'd agreed to do something.

The dragon stood up to his full height and flared his wings to either side. "I must return to my home."

"Tam, come down." Mama reached up for him.

Roots grew from the dragon's back, lifting the cheering boy and passing him from strand to strand until they deposited him in his mother's arms. He perched on her hip, fists in the air, whooping and hollering as the house-sized creature leapt into the air.

A great rush of wind pulled after him from behind, flinging Emma's hair forward. Nearby trees bowed inward at the gust as well. In under a minute, the dragon had gone too high up to see as much more than a bird-sized speck against the sky.

Emma took Kimber's hand and held out her left arm for Mama to hold as they started back toward home. A few paces out of the forest, the spritely notes of a quiet flute melody emanated from the trees behind them.

Emma gasped with delight, and looked back over her shoulder.

In the shadows among the trees, a pair of bright amber eyes appeared. Kes, flute to his lips, peeked out long enough to wink at her—and vanished. She stared after the spot in the woods for a few steps, before turning her broad smile to Tam, and singing:

"The daylight is fading, the wind turning cold.
　　A house, warm and waiting, the hearth burning gold.
　　Through forests and fields, how far you did roam.
　　Dear little brother, run far away home."

With a gleeful cheer, Tam held his wooden sword high, and charged across the meadow toward the house. Laughing at the little warrior racing off into the tall grass, Emma took Mama and Kimber's hands, and walked with them, following Nan home.

fin

The adventure continues in book 4 - Emma and the Elixir of Madness!

Emma tries to balance her newfound abilities as a druid with only being ten years old. Chores and having to go inside before dark leaves only a few hours a day to save the forest—or at least her home town.

Strange magic plagues the people of Widowswood Village. None of the adults take it seriously, as the effects are short-lived and whimsical. Emma suspects something darker is going on, having listened to Nan's tales of night pixies who aren't as nice as the Silverbells. Convinced someone or something wishes ill upon her home, she decides to do what the adults won't.

Amid the chaos, the daughter of a wealthy gem merchant goes missing. Emma's father and the entire Widowswood Watch spend all their time searching for the abducted girl. Worse, a bully blames Emma for the girl's disappearance, but after dealing with a banderwigh and the silk thieves, he doesn't scare her at all—until he turns violent.

Emma *knows* everything is connected, and isn't about to let a mean-spirited older boy stop her from protecting her home.

ACKNOWLEDGMENTS

Thank you for reading Emma and the Silverbell Faeries!

I'd also like to thank Kate Bystrova for editing, and Ricky Gunawan for the cover and interior art.

ABOUT THE AUTHOR

Originally from South Amboy NJ, Matthew has been creating science fiction and fantasy worlds for most of his reasoning life. Since 1996, he has developed the "Divergent Fates" world, in which *Division Zero, Virtual Immortality, The Awakened Series, The Harmony Paradox, and the Daughter of Mars series* take place. Along with being an editor at Curiosity Quills press, he has worked in IT and technical support.

Matthew is an avid gamer, a recovered WoW addict, Gamemaster for two custom RPG systems, and a fan of anime, British humour, and intellectual science fiction that questions the nature of reality, life, and what happens after it.

He is also fond of cats.

Visit me online at:
    Facebook: https://www.facebook.com/MatthewSCoxAuthor
    Pinterest: https://www.pinterest.com/matthewcox10420/
    Goodreads: https://www.goodreads.com/author/show/7712730.Matthew_S_Cox
    Email: mcox2112@gmail.com

OTHER BOOKS BY MATTHEW S. COX

Divergent Fates Universe Novels

Division Zero series

- Division Zero
- Lex De Mortuis
- Thrall
- Guardian
- Harbinger

The Awakened series

- Prophet of the Badlands
- Archon's Queen
- Grey Ronin
- Daughter of Ash
- Zero Rogue
- Angel Descended

Daughter of Mars series

- The Hand of Raziel
- Araphel
- Ghost Black

Virtual Immortality series

- Virtual Immortality
- The Harmony Paradox

Divergent Fates Anthology

(Fiction Novels - Adult)

The Roadhouse Chronicles Series

- One More Run
- The Redeemed
- Dead Man's Number

Faded Skies series

- Heir Ascendant
- Ascendant Unrest
- Ascendant Revolution

Temporal Armistice Series

- Nascent Shadow
- The Shadow Collector
- The Gate to Oblivion

Vampire Innocent series

- A Nighttime of Forever
- A Beginner's Guide to Fangs
- The Artist of Ruin
- The Last Family Road Trip
- The Phantom Oracle

Standalones

- Wayfarer: AV494
- Axillon99
- Chiaroscuro: The Mouse and the Candle
- The Spirits of Six Minstrel Run
- The Far Side of Promise anthology
- Operation: Chimera (with Tony Healey)
- The Dysfunctional Conspiracy (with Christopher Veltmann)

Winter Solstice series (with J.R. Rain)

- Convergence
- Containment

- Catalyst

Alexis Silver series (with J.R. Rain)

- Silver Light
- Deep Silver
- Silver Quarrel

Samantha Moon Origins series (with J.R. Rain)

- New Moon Rising
- Moon Mourning

Vampire For Hire series (with J.R. Rain)

- Moon Master
- Dead Moon

Maddy Wimsey series (with J.R. Rain)

- The Devil's Eye
- The Drifting Gloom

Samantha Moon Case Files series (with J.R. Rain)

- Blood Moon

Immortal Operative series (with J.R. Rain)

- Broken Ice

Young Adult Novels

The Eldritch Heart Series

- The Eldritch Heart
- The Cursed Crown

Evergreen Series

- Evergreen
- The World That Remains

Standalones

- Caller 107
- The Summer the World Ended
- Nine Candles of Deepest Black
- The Forest Beyond the Earth
- Out of Sight
- Evergreen

Middle Grade Novels

Tales of Widowswood series

- Emma and the Banderwigh
- Emma and the Silk Thieves
- Emma and the Silverbell Faeries
- Emma and the Elixir of Madness
- Emma and the Weeping Spirit

Standalones

- Citadel: The Concordant Sequence
- The Cursed Codex
- The Menagerie of Jenkins Bailey
- Sophie's Light